AN ARROGANT WITCH

WITCH KIN CHRONICLES, BOOK 2

E M GRAHAM

An Arrogant Witch

For Christine, who understood magic.

1

Old buildings are the worst for being portals into the Alt world, it has something to do with the stone walls not releasing the vibrations of past emotions that have collected, and the Craft Council's home was no exception. There were ghosts here, way up in the attics on the third floor, and there was also something nasty lurking in the far corners of the cellar behind the clay studio kilns.

Devon House, it was called, and this stone structure was one of those landmarks that predated even the big fire of 1892 which razed most of the town. Perched over the harbor, the picture windows at the back looked right out through the Narrows and over the water to Fort Amherst. As I waited in the second-floor gallery to be called for my interview, I looked out at the Southside Hills all gray in the November drizzle, and I shuddered. The fairy den was up there, right at the top of that wind-lashed rock. Perhaps they had Jane's baby, perhaps not.

'Dara Martin.'

Martin is my mother's family name. My father, John de Teilhard, is the head of the Witch Kin - I get my magic blood from him but not his name, which makes me a half-blood and a bastard if things like that matter, and they seem to matter to a surprising number of people.

The woman who called my name jerked her head toward a narrow dark corridor. My first ever job interview. I pulled my shoulders back and glanced into a mirror to check there were no smudges on my nose, checked my boots and jeans to see that all was in order, and moved towards the small ill-lit space.

If I'd been born legitimate, I'd be enjoying a full magical education with Spring breaks in the south of France, but as a mere half-blood witch, I wasn't allowed to train or develop my natural powers. After Mom disappeared, Dad stepped out of my life and returned to his wife and other children, sending just enough money for my upkeep and school to fulfill his obligations. The only stipulation was that I had to turn my back on my magic and pretend it didn't exist.

If I was one of his *real* kids, I would have my own credit card. I wouldn't need to look for a job in order to buy Christmas presents.

However I did need the money, so here I was. I took a deep breath and turned into the doorway, but before I could take another step, I found the hair on the back of my arms suddenly standing straight out and a chill was creeping into my gut.

Dad may have forbidden me to develop my powers, yet the magic remained in my blood and in my nature. Even if I didn't actively use my magic, it used me - it pierced the veil between the Normal and the Alt, and Dad could never stop that no matter how deep he buried his head in the sand.

There was something terribly wrong in the air, like that feeling during an earth tremor when the light is misplaced and time wavers from its axis, your body not where it was the moment before in relation to your surroundings. And like a tiny earthquake, it lasted but a fraction of a moment, but that was enough to warn me. The atmosphere was darkening, I could taste it, and I knew that something bad was waiting for me in the room beyond, something or someone was lurking, anticipating, like a spider waiting for a fly to enter a carefully spun web. Was it a malevolent spirit lurking in the house's bricks and mortar, or an emanation originating from the Alt of the building? I'd never felt it here before, not this strong.

This presence was more than an angry spirit unloosed from its body and time, much more. This was living and breathing... and hungry, voraciously so. I could almost smell the very need in it that made it so dark about the edges, lurking around the corners and searching for crevices in which to lodge itself.

I couldn't force myself to walk across the threshold, so I simply stood silently in dread, waiting for this feeling to pass. Directly ahead of me, a man stood with his back turned to me, speaking with my future boss. Could the darkness be coming from him, that evil intent washing off him like waves? My hackles were on full alert, the hairs on the back of my neck shivering with that cold touch and I wanted to growl at this being and unsheathe my claws and lash out and tell him to get the hell out of my town.

But that was no way to begin a job interview.

I took a deep breath and at the sound he turned around, his pupils widening just the slightest at the sight of me as if in recognition, as if he'd been searching and just then realized what he was looking for when he'd found it. He sized me up and down with a glint in those pale gray eyes like he knew me. Time wavered again, slowing down then speeding up and I knew he saw the witch blood pulsing through my veins.

I hesitated in that doorway as if on the edge of a chasm, caught between fright and flight, and in his steely gaze I saw the depths I could attain with my inborn power. It was as if he offered the world to me, and I could choose to leap into the abyss and fly freely along the winds of magic like I'd never known, like I'd never dreamt possible for a half-witch like myself, a terrible future he laid out for me like a banquet for the starving.

Or I could withdraw, whimpering, from those dizzying heights, clinging to the solid earth and never claim the rights of my blood, never live properly. Ever.

All that happened in a split second of time, the world offered up in his luminous eyes, silver gleaming in the dark and I couldn't help but draw closer to the magnetic lure. I stood before him naked but not in a physical manner. It wasn't my body he claimed. Power spoke to power, like to like - he wanted the still-raw magic in me that had been clamped down all my life, the part of me rejected by my father and his Kin. For the first time, I knew I was seen as the powerful witch I was, and I was desirable.

I truly believe he ripped a hole in my heart in that moment, opened up a crack to let the dark shine through, and I fought in my mind but it was too late, the damage was done, and this was my only excuse for all that happened later.

Tearing my eyes from his awful promises, I stared instead at his shoes, shiny polished black leather that could never survive the weather in these parts. He was not a witch, and I don't know how I knew that. Something about the cut of his coat, perhaps, or his lack of physical glamour.

I could feel him smile as that thought ran through my mind, like he could see right into my head.

And with that, the spell was broken as if it had never happened.

'Alright, then Willem, I'll see you later.' Unaware of what had just passed, the stocky woman behind the desk stood up and held out her hand, a look of simpering puzzlement still on her face. 'I apologize again, I was sure the booths had all sold out, but I'm so delighted that it turns out we can fit you in. Your work will be a great addition to the fair. Just the sort of thing we love here at the Craft Council.'

'What luck for me,' he said in a low voice, and his eyes met mine again. The menace was gone as if it had been merely a figment of my imagination all along, a momentary aberration brought on from lack of food and too much coffee, and before me stood a mild looking man of indeterminate age and sexuality. He was short of stature, non-descript to look at with his wispy blond hair and general colorlessness. There was no echo of what had just passed between us, nothing about him spoke of the terrible power of him. Had I imagined it?

I stood by to let him pass, and felt nothing more from him, just as if he was another laid back, ordinary crafts person.

'You're Dara then.' Kim interrupted my thoughts and held out a sheaf of papers at me. 'You're free for the week of the craft fair? Great. I need you to fill out your information and pass these in to the front desk. I have some other work I need doing before the fair opens, like postering downtown. We'll provide the tape.'

This was my job interview? I had the feeling the request to see me had just been a formality, as if the only requirement for the job was proof that I was a living breathing being.

Or as if there had been a supernatural hand in the selection, the way a booth had magically opened up for Willem, that dark figure. But I couldn't let my mind go there.

***

So that was it. I had the job and would have cash for Christmas presents, for Aunt Edna and Mark and my best friend Alice. Maybe even a little something for Dad, although I couldn't for the life of me think what I could get him that he didn't already have ten of, or that would be meaningful for him. Maybe I'd get him a fancy hand-made card from the craft fair, and one for Hugh too while I was at it.

After purchasing and eating a KitKat bar, I was able to shove the incident with Willem firmly to the back of my mind.

I headed back down Duckworth Street. Funny thing about this road, no matter which direction you go, east or west, if there's any kind of wind you're always walking into it. I had battled against it on the way up to Devon House, and now again it was in my face as I made my way back along the route. I shoved my hands into the pocket of my heavy winter hoody and marched on.

Right at the very far end of downtown in the ramshackle wooden buildings backing on to George Street there was activity happening and I had to stop and watch.

Zeta's *House of Magick* was undergoing a rebirth of sorts. The store had suffered arson in late September, back when the wave of prejudice against half-blood witches was at its height, and the building had sat empty since then, a plywood board blanking the window of the narrow shop. Zeta was only now getting back to sorting the place out.

She wasn't a real witch as far as I could tell. Although she claimed to come from a long line of witches, she had never heard of the Witch Kin. Her store was filled with herbs and spell books, but also with plastic crap and unicorns, posters of pretty fairies, all that sort of thing, with hardly anything magical in the place.

Except the coin. I'd felt it when I'd last been in her store before the fire, the magic calling to me from deep within a basket full of junk. In fact, I'd been rummaging around with my hand in that bin and actually felt the tingle of power in my fingers when she'd diverted my attention. I hadn't had a chance to revisit before her store got burned out.

It wasn't just the magic of the coin or talisman or whatever it was that had called me. The moment I'd touched the warm metal and felt the power, I knew it had something to do with my mother, and it was the first hint I'd ever found that confirmed my feeling that she might yet be alive.

I had to check out if the coin was still in Zeta's shop.

2

The new plate glass window still had the manufacturer's sticker on it, and the store only smelled a little of burnt wood and electrical wires. Zeta stood in the center of the room giving directions to two workmen in a loud, flustered voice.

I walked on in through the unlocked door, trying to sense that magic of that coin again, but she swooped down on me the moment she saw me.

'I'm sorry,' she said. 'We're not opened for business yet.' The tall blonde blowsy woman hadn't changed a bit, her hair still a mare's nest of frizzy curls. The floaty Indian cotton dress was now covered with a thick shapeless hand knit cardigan in keeping with the chilly November air.

'Glad to see you're rebuilding,' I said. 'That was a nasty bit of arson. Did they ever find out who did it?'

'No,' she replied in a distracted voice as she watched a workman replacing shelves on the far wall. 'Lower, please. I need room for five shelves there.'

Zeta turned to look at me again. 'The arson? I believe it was the center right, those blockheads who refuse to open their eyes to the possibilities around them. The unbelievers.'

'Mmhmm,' I said. I knew full well it had been the youth of the Witch Kin, the friends of my half-sister Sasha, but who was I to break the woman's bubble? 'I just dropped by to... to see if I can help you in any way.'

She looked at me closer. 'Oh, you were here right before the fire,' she said in recognition, a hopeful smile breaking over her face. 'You bought a spell, and were going to join the Thursday night classes. We'll be starting up again this week.'

I looked around at the disheveled space. 'You have a ton of work to do before then,' I pointed out. 'Do you need help with the organizing?'

'I can't afford to pay anyone,' she said, her voice guarded.

'Don't worry about it. Consider it my good deed for the week.' I looked casually about me as I spoke, as if I was sizing up what I could do to help. Most of the goods previously for sale were nowhere to be seen. Had everything been thrown out, too damaged by smoke to sell? If so, I would be wasting my time here. I couldn't sense that magic coin anywhere.

'It would help a lot,' she said slowly, as she considered the offer. 'Tell you what, come down to the cellar and help me sort stuff.'

We introduced ourselves as we made our way past the remnants of the beaded curtain and into the dark space at the top of a flight of steep wooden stairs. How can I describe the smell emanating from the pitch black that yawned before us? It was as if generations of mice (or worse) had lived and urinated and died among the cast-off detritus of centuries, and it also smelled strongly of damp, charred wood.

'Hang on a moment, I'll get the light.' Zeta melted into the depths of the cellar. I could hear her slowly creaking down the steps.

It felt like a long time, but could only have been a moment before I heard the click of the chain pulled and a dim light made its way up the stairwell. I could now make out the individual planks of the uneven stairs, so I cautiously started down.

Zeta stood under the single bare bulb which still swung on its cord, the low light serving to highlight the frazzle of her bleached hair but little else. Shadows danced and jumped, bouncing off the stone of the cellar walls and the boxes piled higgledy-piggledy in the long narrow space.

This place was even creepier than the basement of my own home. If it wasn't for the lure of that magical coin, I would not go down into this space where century-old spider webs blurred the dark corners and broken chairs lay abandoned any which way to the sides, while dangerous rusted iron hooks were affixed to the floor joists at regular intervals. I couldn't even guess at their original purpose in this cold cellar, or at least I could and it wasn't pleasant.

The light was too weak to reach all the way to the end of the room, the part that should extend towards Duckworth Street, but the whole dimensions of the room were wrong, at least what I could see of it. There should have been a further twenty feet of cellar to my right, towards George Street but instead there was only a stretch of crude stone wall behind the goods piled up, and the rock looked fresher than those of the walls to either side. And there was a door in it too, but it was nailed shut.

'Why is it so short here? This room feels all wrong. What's going on?' I must have spoken aloud although I didn't realize it.

'Oh, there's another property behind me. You know the Grog Shop on George Street?'

That clicked. It claimed to be the smallest bar on the island, although it had room for a bandstand besides the single toilet stall and a few tables and chairs over by the rough counter. It was also rumoured to be the oldest drinking establishment on the street.

George Street was a full 12 feet below the neighboring Duckworth, and the two roads connected at this point by a set of stairs set into the hill. Now that she mentioned it, I could feel a faint thump of bass coming through the stone from the bar next door.

Yet, if a full third of her floor space in the cellar was taken up by the bar next door, why did the rest of her cellar seem to stretch so far in the other direction? I peered into the gloom.

'All this stuff here?' Zeta was pointing to the closest pile of boxes and baskets against the Grog Shop wall. 'I really need this sorted. After the fire, I just sort of threw everything together without checking to see what was still good or how much smoke damage there was, so if you wouldn't mind...'

I stood there with my mouth open for a moment as I surveyed her piles of creosoted crap. Guess I hadn't realized the scope of the job when I offered my services for free, and if it wasn't for my hopes of finding the magic of that metal disc I would have turned and gone right back up those rickety stairs. Still, I could quit as soon as I found it, and that prize would be payment enough for my time.

'I'll bring you a cup of tea in a bit,' she said, a little sheepishly, as she too realized the extent of the job she was asking me to do. 'And if you don't get it all finished today, you can come back any time.'

Zeta didn't see the dirty look I sent her as she hastened back up the stairs.

I tied my hair back in a ponytail and set to work. To save myself some effort and time, I first put my magic senses to work, trying to find a hint of the coin over the pile of things lying against the shared wall. I squinted and sniffed and felt about with my fingertips in the air, but was coming back with nothing except the barest whiff of magical power.

It was tantalizing, that whisper; it could have been the coin or it might have been something else altogether but that's all it was, a hint of it on the air. I couldn't find the source here in this dimension.

The easiest way to go about finding the coin would be to go into Alt, I knew, for then the magic would jump out at me. But there was no chance in hell I would do that in this cellar. You see, the thing about Alt was, you had to know what you were getting into before you switched. Alt and real time were fairly close geographically, but Alt didn't necessarily keep up with the modern geography.

For example, last September on the day I met Hugh, I had been hanging out at the harbour down by the iron fence which lined the apron and feeling all angsty and mad at Dad. In real time, the harbour had been reclaimed and filled with rubble to enable enough space for a parking lot, the new road and the concrete harbour apron where I'd been standing.

But because of my mental state, I'd let my guard down and before I knew it, I had flipped full on into Alt. The iron fence was gone, and so was the apron along with Harbour Drive, even the parking lots. Instead in Alt, the original beach with the long finger piers still existed, the rickety wooden wharves running directly into the harbour from the back loading doors of the merchant shops. So when I accidently flipped, I was teetering on the edge of an old timber pier and about to fall into the murky waters of the harbour full of sewage and dead rats. It was only by quick thinking I could bring myself back into real time and the safety of the concrete harbour apron.

As I said, there was no way I was going into Alt in this ancient cellar because God alone knew where I would end up. Alt was a dangerous place. So I had to sort and sift through all of Zeta's tacky, ash-smelling junk by hand. After a half hour, I accepted that the coin wasn't here.

There was a flashlight at the bottom of one of the boxes though, and I idly flicked the switch to see if the battery was still good. It was. I aimed the light further into the long narrow space, to the parts where the overhead light couldn't penetrate, and caught a gleam of eyes which quickly scurried away out of sight. Gross, rats. And where there were rats, there was rat poo and the bugs who ate it. Zeta should have given me a mask to filter the air while down here.

The rest of the cellar was littered with older debris and cast-off furniture, some of it from the Victorian era from what I could see under the dust. But way, way in the back, at the farthest end, a gleam of tarnished metal caught my eye, so I focused the beam on the center of the wall. But it wasn't a wall, not all of it anyway. Through the layers of cob webs strung all around, I could barely make out that the stone foundation was interrupted by an ancient door, a rough arch made of planks with two iron hinges, a handle, and a rusted padlock.

It looked a long ways away, that door, longer than the floor of the store above. I thought perhaps it was just a trick of the bad light down here, so I ran the beam slowly over the wooden floor boards above as I counted a rough estimate of the length of this underground room. Halfway down the space, the beams were replaced by a stone roof, arched like a medieval monastic cellar. Yeah, this room was definitely longer than the corresponding space upstairs by a good ten feet.

It must extend underneath Duckworth Street, one of the oldest streets in the North America. Naturally, I had to explore it, I couldn't leave this although I should have known better. I picked my careful way over everything, trying to touch as little as possible, till I reached the door. I could vaguely feel the rumble of traffic rolling over the ancient cobblestones far above my head, long since tarmacked over. The lock held true despite the rust and grime of years.

Which left the burning question – where did that ancient door lead to? The whiff of magic was much stronger here, but the door was solidly built.

And was it padlocked to protect something in the room, or to keep something outside from getting in?

'Dara?'

I heard Zeta's voice as she clumped down the stairs, and quickly made my way back into the light.

'Hey, Z,' I greeted her as I nonchalantly walked out of the gloom.

'God, I could hear you but couldn't see you! What were you doing back there? Are you sure it's safe?'

I wondered if she'd ever looked towards the back of this long room, if she even knew about the existence of the door under the street. I don't know why, but I held back from mentioning it.

'Nothing there, just the rest of the cellar,' I said. 'Well, look at the time, I better get going.'

'You don't look like you got much done here.' She sounded disappointed. 'All the stuff is just spread around, and you didn't clean anything by the looks of it.'

What, did she think the free labour extended to scrubbing the smoke off her cheap plastic shit? *Get real, lady*, I thought to myself.

'Maybe I can come back again in a few days,' I said aloud. 'Do a bit more, help you out.'

And find out what that door is hiding.

'Oh, would you? That would be such a relief, I've got the workmen up here all the time and I have to keep such a close eye on them, I don't know when I'll find the time to get to all this stuff down here.'

'No problem,' I told her as I followed her long cotton skirts up the stairs, ducking at the right spot so as not to hit my head on the beam.

3

That night in my room, I set the volume dial of Aunt Edna's old 'Eighties boom box on bust with some of her Leonard Cohen CDs as I attempted to work on the Folklore paper which was due the following week. I'd chosen to write about the Lord of Misrule, that ancient tradition of electing a fool to rule for a short period of time around the Christmas season. Also known as the Abbot of Unreason, this lucky citizen presided over all the courts and games for the time period, wreaking as much havoc as he could.

In the pre-Christian era, the mock lord would be sacrificed at the end to ensure the return of summer.

But by medieval times, the period of unrule was a great opportunity for everyone to pay back old grudges. Our local modern-day mummers' tradition was a direct descendant, with folk dressing up in old clothes, disguising themselves any which way with pillowcases or brin bags over their faces to make their rounds of the neighbors, demanding food and drink. It's become very popular and sanitized and politically correct these days of course.

But historically, mummering had been outlawed here in Newfoundland back in the 1880's, due to the murders in Bay Roberts by persons unknown who'd disguised themselves as mummers. Authorities had thought it was part of the on-going religious wars between Protestant and Catholic at the time, and they were probably right. Still, it's a pretty creepy thing if you think of it, people disguising themselves and hammering on doors and demanding entrance in the middle of the night. You might not know who was behind those brin bags, or what their true intent was.

This was all very interesting but of course my mind wandered back to that door set in the ancient cellar wall, the hinges thick with spider webs. It probably hadn't been opened in fifty, no, seventy-five years, maybe more. Say if a person found another ancient big iron key, like the ones hanging in the pantry of my home, and tried it in the lock, how much wiggling around would it take to work open that padlock? If, just say *if*, a person could get it opened, what would they find?

With the road works and modern sewer systems in St. John's in the past century, the door would probably just open on to rubble and landfill. If this had been London or another truly ancient city, the door might lead onto forgotten sewage and waste water bricked tunnels, but I was pretty sure early St. John's had never had anything that elaborate in its infrastructure.

I'd heard rumours through the years of an ancient tunnel system linking the cellars of some very old buildings down town. These had come in handy for smuggling and other nefarious activities, but I'd never really believed that story -

it was right up there in the local urban myths like the caves below Signal Hill. Of course, in Alt these things could be real.

In a break between songs, I'd become aware of a steady moan through the walls, intermixed with irregular thumping and crying sounds, and it had probably been going on for a while before the caterwauling broke through my reverie.

One of the things with living in the old homestead is that we inherited the ghost of Maundy along with it and she couldn't be exorcised because she was family. I was the only one who could see her, so I guess she was just my problem.

'What?' I screamed out over the music only to hear the sobbing start up again. Maundy, my fourth, or was it fifth cousin, the ghost I shared a wall with. She was an emo kid from way back before emo kids were a thing, who died at the age of thirteen sometime before the end of Queen Victoria's reign and had been miserable ever since.

Of course, I'd known Maundy all my life. Edna had thought she was an imaginary playmate until the whole witch-blood thing came out into the open after Mom's disappearance and my aunt had to open her eyes to what and who Dad really was. And that I had inherited his magic ability.

The sobbing only increased in volume the longer I waited, so I just sighed and turned down the violins and angel choruses. Maundy was a weird ghost in that she hated rock music or anything modern. Country suited her fine, especially Hank Williams, and some nights we could even compromise on rockabilly or blues. But sometimes she just complained to get on my nerves, those days when nothing would satisfy her.

'Happy now?' I called out, but received no answer. My neighbor, having gotten her own way, was peaceful again.

Hal the cat wandered into my room now the music was lowered, and found the nesting point behind my knees where he settled in for a snooze. This paper wasn't getting done tonight, so I gave up even pretending to work on it and got lost in thought instead.

Of course my mind was on the coin that was no longer among the junk in Zeta's. I could curse myself for not grabbing it when it had literally been at my fingertips last September, but I'd had other things on my mind at the time, things like fairies and Nan Hoskins's haunting, and I hadn't been expecting to find something of real magical worth in the shop.

That whiff of magic I'd sensed in Zeta's cellar just that afternoon – was it the coin? Yet it hadn't been in real time; the metal had to have been in Alt, I was positive, and someone must have placed it there in that other dimension. Not Zeta, surely – she wouldn't know Alt if it bit her in the face. So who?

Hal's purrs slowly morphed to snores, and the rhythm lulled me into an unexpected nap. I drifted off and found myself in Zeta's cellar, barely lit with that single bulb swinging from the joists yet the old wooden door at the end of the room was eerily illuminated as if from within. I could hear soft music and laughter coming from behind the oak and could feel the warmth emanating from that hidden space. It called to me and I was helpless to resist.

As I drew closer the longing to be on the other side of that door grew ever more; it filled my head and heart, and I could see the padlock had gone. There was nothing stopping me, all I had to do was open the door and all my dreams would be fulfilled, dreams I didn't even know I longed for.

Yet the moment my fingertips touched the cold iron handle I was seized by dread and foreboding and knew this was wrong. That door must not be opened, yet my mind could no longer control my body and I watched in horror as my hand insistently grasped the latch and began to pull. The wooden door creaked on its hinges as I tried to tell myself to stop, but to no avail.

Suddenly all went dark. The open door was filled with the pitch black of a moonless night and even the swaying bulb so far away snapped out and I was left alone, bereft, and unable to see yet feeling the evil all around I had unleased by my action.

I woke up – at least my eyes snapped open but everything about me was still dark and I could not move a muscle. I was back lying on my bed and paralysed, sensing motion above my head yet unable to wrench myself away from the threat.

4

'Dara, wake up.' I heard a soft voice. 'You're having the old hag again.'

And Edna broke the spell. I opened my eyes for real and could see her caring blue gaze in the soft light from the bedside lamp, her familiar presence reaching to me. Hal still snored by my side undisturbed by my nightmare.

My aunt gave me a quick hug and told me to go to bed properly and not to go sleeping on my back, then left me to it.

I lay there, my chest still heaving quickly as I waited for the rush of adrenaline to pass. The hag and I were old acquaintances, yet every time she visited it was like the first. Never sleep on your back, for that's when you open yourself to her.

As a student of folklore, you'd think I would have conquered her by now. I had studied the phenomenon extensively ever since my mid-teens when it had started to haunt my sleep, and found that almost every culture in the world had a name for her. She was commonly seen as an incubus who sat on a person's chest, causing the paralysis, the panic and inability to breathe – almost the same symptoms everywhere in the world that people live. The old hag is actually such an ancient idea, she is the original 'nightmare', the 'mare' being the old Proto-Germanic word for demon. Well anyway, the point is it's a common physical phenomenon, not a proper haunting, although when she's got you in her grips logic doesn't come into it.

Yet... That cellar door. Physical reaction or not, I couldn't help but feel the dream was warning me against further exploration of Zeta's basement, which was a shame because my curiosity had been sparked and I was too nosy to let things lie.

·····•·•·····

Stepping out of the shower the next morning, I heard a car pull up the driveway and the sound of our back door opening and closing. Edna had gone out, so she'd probably forgotten to lock the door again. Her boyfriend Mark was a cop and he was always getting on her case about that, but as she pointed out, there really wasn't anything worth stealing in the house, for all the valuable stuff had been sold years ago when we'd needed a new roof. When I wrapped a towel around me and rubbed a circle of steam off the glass, to my delight I saw the Batmobile down below me.

No, it wasn't really the superhero's car, just a black low-slung sports car of European origin and far out of the price reach of most people, but I knew who drove it.

Hugh! What was he doing in town again so soon?

I couldn't wipe the grin off my face as I hastily scrubbed myself dry and combed my damp hair. Hugh was one of my most favorite people in the world.

Like I said, we'd met two months ago in September. He'd recognized my magic blood straight away and told me he too was a half-blood witch, as if it wasn't anything to be ashamed of despite the prejudices still rampant in the ranks of the Witch Kin. Hugh was the one who convinced Dad to send me away to Scotland next year to amend my badly needed education in witch craft.

Hugh believed in me, and was the first to recognize that I was a powerful witch despite having a Normal for a mother, one with no supernatural blood in her at all. Yeah, I sort of had a crush on the handsome Scotsman. Who wouldn't, under the circumstances?

So he was just a few years older than me, but I knew he was way out of my league. He was confident and powerful, and internationally respected among the Witch Kin despite the circumstances of his birth. Where he came from, nobody cared about that sort of thing, and besides, the northern Scottish islands were the first seat of organized Witch Kin and no one would ever dare argue with them, no matter their prejudices. Another thing, although no one had really come out and said it, I had the feeling Hugh was being groomed to marry my half-sister Sasha, Dad's legitimate daughter.

The Witch Kin of Newfoundland were still an old-fashioned, traditional group. Strongly patriarchal, they clung to the old ways which included arranged marriages in order to further political alliances and keep the blood lines pure. Despite his half-blood status, even Cate would accept Hugh into her family for with his heritage it would be a coup for her Kin.

So he was totally off-limits for the likes of me, out of my league. But I could still count him as a friend and as I ran down the back staircase pulling my sweater over my head, I yelled out to him.

He caught me as I jumped down the last three steps and whirled me around, surprised at the vehemence of my greeting.

'What are you doing in town, Hugh?'

He'd already helped himself to Edna's coffee, so I poured myself a mug and sat across from him at the kitchen table. He hadn't changed at all. Still wearing the black leather jacket and jeans, his tousled dark hair naturally falling away from his face like a rugged James Dean, the gold flecks in his green eyes shone when he looked at me.

'Business,' he replied, then laughed. 'I was at a loose end with work and thought I'd come back to give you a bit of a crash course in the basics of magic. The foundations, so to speak. It's bad enough that you'll be starting with the young ones, I don't want you to have to sit in the kindergarten class with the babies.'

He was teasing me, I knew, but I didn't mind, I was just so frigging happy to see him. And the fact that he'd said he'd come across the water specifically to see me, well, that made me puff up a bit.

'I have a new job,' I said, eager to pass on my news. He was aware I was no longer baby-sitting, and why. 'Just for a week. I'll be a roustabout with the Craft Council craft fair, the big one they have every year. But I'll make enough in that week to do me till I go away.'

His brows drew together, those lovely thick dark brows of his. 'What about university?'

I shrugged uncomfortably. Bugger. Why did he have to act like an older brother? It wasn't his place. 'It's only for a week,' I said. 'I'll make up for the time. It's going to be fun, sort of like being a carny, but for crafts people.'

'Really wish you wouldn't,' he said after a pause. 'You have to concentrate on your studies. You already got behind once this semester. And I have a lot of work planned for you.'

'I'll manage it all.'

'You'd better, Dara, or you won't be able to go to Scotland after Christmas.'

'Never mind, you know I will,' I said, brushing away his worries. 'I'd rather learn the basics of magic. Let's get started!'

'Right here.' He slid a pile of thick hard-cover books across the table to me. 'They're in the order that I need you to read them.'

My face must have shown the dismay I felt, because he laughed. 'You thought we were going to go out in Alt, did you? Well, I'm sorry to tell you that there'll be none of that. I said you need the foundations, and that's what I'm giving you.'

'But...' I fingered the books. Some were leather bound and ancient looking, others appeared to be from the middle of the last century. I flicked through the top one. Not a single illustration, just all words. Three hundred pages of words. 'This is going to take me ages,' I complained. 'I don't have time for this before I leave.'

'Correction,' he said. 'You don't have time to work for a solid week with the craft fair. If I were you, I'd let them know you can't do it. The sooner the better, to give them time to find someone else who can spare the time.'

'But I've already read lots of books about magic,' I insisted. 'All of the Harry Potter books, and Aleister Crowley – you name it, I've gone through everything I could find. I think I probably have enough foundation, just try me!'

'The first thing you need to do is wipe all of that nonsense from your head. In order to harness the power of your magic, you need to understand the rules of the medium you're working in. Math, physics, biology... even Latin, everything you've tried to avoid so far. You have a ton of work ahead of you before you can even begin to sit in basic witchcraft classes.'

'But I've flown, remember that? And I can switch into Alt on a dime, you even said I did it perfectly like a... a gymnast! And that was with no training from you at all,' I replied.

'You didn't fly, you sent your mind out of your body. Not the same thing at all. And the Alt thing... you have to know what you're doing before you make any more moves like that. Dara – you need to understand that you know nothing, and ignorant use of powers is perhaps the most dangerous thing of all.'

His Scottish accent came out strong when he came over severe and grown-up like that, but he wasn't going to change my plans. 'I can do it,' I insisted. I could feel my lower lip pouting out and made a conscious effort to pull it back in.

'We'll see about that,' he replied. 'Now come on, let me give you a ride to the university.'

I got my book bag and coat together reluctantly, my plans to skip class and return to Zeta's cellar that morning disappearing like a puff of smoke. I consoled myself with the thought that the secret door wasn't going anywhere and no one else had approached it for many years, hidden deep under Duckworth Street as it was. I had the ring of ancient keys in my knapsack and would find a chance to jimmy that lock soon enough.

5

Kim called me later that morning and told me the posters were ready for plastering around downtown. Classes were finished for the day, so I didn't even have to skip one in order to begin my job. I wished I could have the satisfaction of pointing this out to Hugh.

As I headed downtown in the cool November sunlight, my mind of course went back to Hugh. He had said he'd returned to teach me the fundamentals of magic, but all he did was shove those old books in my face. Seemed a little farfetched if you asked me, to come all that way just to deliver a few thousand pages. Why not just mail them to me?

Maybe he had an ulterior motive in coming here in person. Maybe what Dad's wife Cate had hinted was true, he was going to marry Sasha. Perhaps he'd omitted to tell me the truth and was actually here to work out the arrangements. I kicked a rock out into the gutter and stamped through the damp pile of leaves at my feet.

Stupid Sasha.

We'd been pretty close once, me and Sassy, back when we were kids. She was a year older than me, and part of Dad's legitimate family. Back when Mom was still alive, I mean when Mom was still here, Dad used to bring her around when he came over. We knew we were both his daughters from different mothers, and back then it didn't bother us a bit because no one told us it wasn't normal.

Sasha and me used to amuse ourselves playing in the gardens of Richmond Cottage, and she had taught me how to use my early powers. Despite her formal training and my complete lack of it, I'd been pretty much able to hold my own with her. Of course, they were just stupid kid games, like directing the spray from the old copper fish fountain which still worked back then, and moving things using mind power alone. Not real magic as such, at least not what I thought real magic must be.

Just as I inherited my looks from Mom with my straight brown hair, blue eyes and five foot six frame, so Sasha was the spitting image of her mother Cate. In other words, she was tall with raven black hair, a flawless complexion and drop dead gorgeous. Having access to Dad's money probably helped no end with beauty treatments and designer clothes.

And she'd turned out to be a bitch, too, just like Cate. Her mother must have poisoned her mind against me, because the next time I saw Sasha back when I was fifteen and entering high school, she snubbed me something rotten. And not just that, she also got her Witch Kin friends to play horrible pranks on me. School became a lonely place for me because no one wanted to be associated with me in case the witch kids targeted them, too. I only had Alice and the nerds who didn't notice social niceties like that.

We had almost made up our differences last September, but as you can imagine, there's not a lot of love lost between us, which made the idea of her and Hugh together even more hurtful, because for sure he wouldn't be allowed to hang out with me if he married my half-sister. Well, we would be family I guess in a way, but it's not like I'd be invited round to the birthday celebrations or anything.

I picked up the posters, tape and staple gun from Devon House and set off on my route.

Looked like I'd be getting plenty of exercise in this job, good thing it was such a great day for walking. So close to the harbour, the wind was usually icy cold and biting but today there was nary a breath of wind at all, giving the sun a chance to be almost warm on my face. The sidewalks were busy with all the office workers finding any excuse to be outside enjoying the last hurrah of fall. With weather like this, a person could pretend the coming winter wouldn't be so bad after all. It actually made the reality of winter all the crueler.

I'd done the circle of the two main downtown streets and was headed up the back of George Street, my postering done for the day. Then I found myself outside the door to Zeta's store.

I hesitated before I went in. All of a sudden I didn't have a good feeling about this place as if there was something in there I didn't want to meet, or something in the air that was going to poison me. But I shook that foolishness off me, it was probably just a hangover from yesterday's cellar nightmare.

She looked about ready to re-open the store already, with the shelves up and piled with things to buy. I didn't see any of the tat she'd asked me to clean up yesterday, so she must have purchased all new stuff to sell. Zeta also had company.

First I saw Carrie, an old acquaintance, her sheepskin coat shrugged off to reveal a loose sweatshirt, the kind that is designed to fall off one shoulder in a provocative way. She had her hand on the arm of a slightly built person in a long black coat whose back was turned to me, and was leaning in as if to speak softly in their ear. I'd seen that trick of hers lots of times, especially in bars when she was looking to have another drink bought for her.

Zeta was standing close by them, speaking over whatever the younger woman was whispering, trying hard to get the attention focused on her. If I didn't know better, I'd say they were in competition. But for what?

Their companion turned his head towards me as the door shut behind me, just a glance before he looked away again.

Willem. That odd little man I'd met in Kim's office the other day. With his short blond hair and not a spare ounce of muscle or fat on him, he looked like a non-descript David Bowie except that his chin was too weak and his eyes set just too closely together to be called handsome. Right at this moment, he had the appearance of being a harmless non-entity.

So why was Carrie salivating over him like he was the hottest thing around? I'd seen that girl in action around men, and believe me, he wasn't her usual type.

I looked closer, trying to see the attraction, but nothing was apparent to me. He was slightly built and looked washed out; I couldn't even get a hint of the evilness I'd felt the first time I met him.

'Oh, Willem, this is Dara.' Zeta was still anxious to get his attention. 'She wants to be a witch too, she'll be attending our little get-togethers on Thursday evenings.'

He gave me the once over with his pales eyes, and once caught there I couldn't look away, I was stuck in his gaze. There was nothing of the hunger and greed which I had sensed before in his presence, this was a warm feeling, like the burbling of a gentle stream filling my head as the rest of the room fell away. The touch of his mind was soothing and persuasive as if he'd sent out slight tendrils right inside me, assessing me, trying to look into my soul.

Mesmerizing me like a fly in a spider's web of the softest silk, he promised so much as he tried to creep around my natural barriers, the way a wisp of gentle mist pervades even a stone wall.

My eyes widened when I realized what he was doing, and I automatically blocked his access against my thoughts as I had learned to do under Hugh's tutelage.

He smiled, a humble small lifting of the corners of his lips. 'I sense you are a witch already, Dara,' he said, caressing my name in his odd European accent. His voice was clipped yet sing-song in its cadences. 'I look forward to seeing what heights we can reach.... together.'

I didn't like to admit it, but now I could see how he had caught my friend's attention. Carrie's eyes sparked like daggers at me as she hugged him closer to her, and Zeta moved uncomfortably, realizing she had unwittingly introduced another competitor to the mix. I physically stepped back to give them room and broke the eye contact.

'I'm pretty busy these days,' I mumbled, looking at the floor. 'Got the craft fair and university courses, you know, I don't think I'll be able to make it to the sessions.'

'Yes, the craft fair,' he said and I could hear the gentle smile in his voice. 'I too will be there, and I look forward to our time together.'

'Willem is a warlock and a craftsman,' Zeta proudly pushed her way back into the conversation.

'Sorcerer,' he said, cutting her off, a touch of menace suddenly in his voice. 'I'm a sorcerer.'

'Witch, warlock, sorcerer,' Zeta tittered in embarrassment. 'We're all in the same boat, aren't we? Living on the sidelines, doing our work behind the notice of society...'

'I think Dara understands the difference,' he said, trying to grab my eye again. 'Dara knows the nuances of this life.'

A sweat was breaking out over the back of my neck, prickling the hairs. I didn't actually know the differences between the three, but Hugh would. All I did know was that there was something incredibly unsettling about this guy, that the physical form which he presented to the world was a lie for there was no weakness or gentleness deep within his mind. He was hungry for something, and I had an uncomfortable feeling that it might be me.

'And I know what you're looking for,' he said in a softer voice, right next to my ear so that only I could hear. I hadn't seen him sidle up so close to me. He wanted me to look him in the eye again, I could feel it. 'But it's not a coin.'

How could he have known? I stood my ground for a moment longer, hating the feeling of his breath on my neck, but then I made my excuses and turned and raced back out the door without even saying good bye and onto the sun warmed street outside and didn't stop till I was down past City Hall.

There was no way I could have gone back down in Zeta's cellar to check out the secret door that day, not with that guy hanging around. It would have to wait for another time.

6

I needed to tell Hugh about this new guy in town and what had just happened, to get his take on it, but he wasn't answering his phone. Damn. Why couldn't he be available when I needed him? I tapped the phone with my fingernails as I thought.

Yeah, Hugh had advised me to concentrate on my studies ... but Willem knew about the coin, or medallion or whatever it was and somehow this so-called sorcerer was also aware that I wanted it. It stood to reason, then, that Willem knew where to find it. I had no choice – I had to get my hands on it, and I was pretty sure Hugh wouldn't be willing to help me with this. Perhaps I should get in deeper with Willem and go to his meeting as he suggested. Yuck. I'd sooner stick needles in my eyes than hang out with a bunch of delusional pretend witches.

Was he really a sorcerer as he claimed? One thing was certain - whether wizard, warlock or sorcerer, he was one weird dude. His words and appearance were meek and gentle, yet when he got into my head I had felt the strength of him, his desire for what I was hiding from him, deep below the feathery touches from his mind. I remembered the dark presence I'd felt in Devon House. It had to have been him giving off those vibes, but he could hide his power well when he chose.

Just what was the difference between a warlock and a sorcerer anyway? I tried to remember the few times I'd played Dungeons and Dragons with my geek friends in high school, but the game had never much caught my interest. The guys were intent on creating long-winded and intricate battle scenes, with frequent arguments about each character's specific rules for what they could or couldn't do, and my attention span could never keep up with their convoluted meanderings. Besides, I was just there for the weed.

Hugh had said to disregard all the stuff I'd read or heard for it all bore no relationship to the actual magic I'd be learning in the Outer Hebrides. All of the Tolkien, and CS Lewis, even the Harry Potter series, all that was just fiction, he said, and would have no bearing on my education. Hugh's magic was going to be all about learning algebra and chemistry and physics. Gawd, if I'd wanted to do that I could just stay here in town, and not bother going to his sunless northern island.

I had to face it - his magic did not sound very sexy or fun, nothing like the stories I'd read. In fact, if the books he gave me were any indication, it all promised to be hard work and drudgery and I found it difficult to justify. Yes, I wanted to develop my natural power, but to spend the next however-many years studying all that stuff...

What was the point of having magic if you couldn't be magic with it?

I was down on the west end of Water Street before it hit me, and I stopped outside one of the antique stores which huddled together on that road. Willem had known what I was searching for in Zeta's shop, for he'd told me it wasn't a coin that I sought. So yes, he must be a sorcerer as he claimed or something like it.

Yet, he was also entered in to the craft fair. Sure, this was one of the biggest and best fairs in Atlantic Canada, but seriously, what kind of sorcerer would demean himself by working with his hands and selling his wares at a craft fair? Sorcerers considered themselves to be the cream of the crop, the elite amongst the magic lines, didn't they? More than mere magicians or wizards, a sorcerer was the most powerful of the lot, so it was strange that one of them would have to support himself by the tedious process of hand making creations to sell in a public market.

He must not be a very good sorcerer, I decided. Which would make my job in getting the medallion from him pretty easy.

7

E dna wasn't too happy to find out I would be taking a week off my studies to work with the craft fair, either. She shut the microwave door with a bang and set two plates on the table.

'You're kidding me?' Her face foretold all the reasons she thought it was a bad idea.

'Calm down, it's not so bad,' I said. 'I'm already caught up with most of my work, and we have more than a month left to the semester. I just about have my big paper for Folklore finished.' Well, it was *almost* just about finished. All my research was done, I just had to organize my thoughts on paper.

'And math? You're keeping on top of that? Cause that's the one that you have to work at steadily, every week. I know you can write a paper off the top of your head, but math is actual work.'

Fortunately for me, I'd found an almost foolproof way of passing math exams with my rediscovered magical powers. It involved sitting close to someone smart and getting inside their mind during the exam, but I wasn't going to share that with Edna.

'Trust me, my schoolwork will be fine,' I told her. I was more of a last minute scholar, anyway, and there would be loads of time after the fair was finished.

'Because if you're serious about wanting to go away after Christmas...'

'Yeah, yeah, I already got the lecture from Hugh.' I swallowed back a further retort and changed my tactics, for Edna was going to be at that fair selling her books and would be keeping a close eye on me. I had to get back on her good side or she might just get Dad to forbid it. 'Look on the bright side, I might be able to booth sit for you, let you take a lunch break.'

The fair would be five days long, each day opened from ten in the morning to ten at night. I often came up to relieve her when she did these things, if my schedule allowed.

'And you won't even need to be giving me rides.' I pointed out another benefit to further sell the idea. 'The other guy, Jack, he'll come pick me up and drop me off every day. My hours are going to be a lot longer than yours.'

The role of nagging parent had never come easily to Edna, so in the face of my logic she gladly relinquished the fight with a doubtful murmur to mark her stance, then set about eating.

'Hey, did you know? Hugh's back in town,' I told her.

'Why so early?'

'He said he wanted to give me some books for foundation,' I said. 'That pile of books over there on the counter.' Although Edna was well aware of the magic and the half-blood and Dad being a witch, we tried not to say the words out loud. This made it easier to have conversations when other people like Mark were around.

She looked up from her dinner and glanced over to the thick stack over her reading glasses. 'Really?'

'Yeah,' I said, a little hurt at her tone. 'Why not?'

'Why would a man like Hugh come all the way from, where is he, Scotland, to deliver some books to you?'

'Because he likes me?'

'Dara...'

I hated when her voice took that note.

She sighed.

'Just say it, why don't you?' I could feel my face growing red.

'Okay I will,' she replied and looked directly at me when she spoke. 'He's part of the Kin. Need I say more?'

'He's a half-blood, like me.'

'Doesn't seem to matter, does it? He's one of *them*, and you can't get away from that.'

I refused to answer, but that didn't stop her from pressing her point home to make sure I understood.

'I don't know what he does, but he's tight in that circle,' she said. 'I mean, he stays at your Dad's house and I wouldn't be surprised if...'

Our eyes met over the table, in the light cast by the glass pendant fixture above our heads. I dared her to bring up Sasha and the fact that maybe Hugh was supposed to marry my sister.

'Just don't want you to get hurt, is all,' she said in a small voice as she stood and began to clear the dishes away.

I didn't see Hugh over the next couple of days, and I was starting to suspect that Edna was right. It did make far more sense that he was in town for Kin business rather than just to hand me some mouldy old books, and I was beginning to feel like a dumb little kid hanging around hoping that the bigger kids would invite me to play. He was probably spending his spare time with Sasha doing, I don't know, interesting things to do with magic and power. She was a fully educated witch, after all. Like him.

One of my questions about Willem was answered soon, after we'd done the hard work of preparing for the craft fair. We had two days of set up before the fair actually opened its doors to the public, and I found out what a huge amount of work it took to organize an event like this.

The first time I walked into the old stadium space where the fair was to be held, all full of anticipation and memories of fairs gone by, my heart sank. The harsh blue-white overhead lights were on full force, illuminating every hole and splinter of the ratty old plywood which covered the ice. This huge empty space was freezing, and I didn't see how Kim was going to be able to transform it into the magical wonderland of booths and alleys that I remembered from fairs past.

'Okay,' Kim said as she bustled in, setting right to work. 'Here's the floor plan and a measuring tape and a box of chalk. Jack-o, get down here! Dara, that's Jack. He's your co-worker for the week. He's done this before so he'll tell you what needs doing. Get moving you guys – this has to be done this morning.'

She walked down the bleacher steps to the stadium floor and began setting up a table for herself. Without even turning around to see what was happening, she yelled out again. 'Jack, did you hear me?'

The guy called Jack unfolded himself from the bleachers, his long legs taking the stairs one at a time.

'Hey,' he said as he passed me while totally ignoring me otherwise. His baseball cap with a beer logo on it sat low over his face, and his jeans were faded and torn, while his lumberjack shirt hung off his rangy shoulders unbuttoned and with tails flapping.

He waited down on the ice for me to catch up, then we began the long walk to the far end of the stadium rink. Despite the slowness of his gait, his legs were super long and I found myself skipping now and then to keep pace.

Two guys from the stadium had already begun laying down black rubber flooring over the plywood, to better protect the ice underneath.

Jack directed me to take one end of the measuring tape and mark off the increments he yelled out across the width of the ice rink. We slowly made our way up to the half way line on the floor. It was hard work, pacing out the steps, then crouching down to mark off the booths with the chalk; we must have gone through ten large sticks before he called it quits. My hands were crusty with the dust – I should have worn gloves.

'Alright, let's take a break,' he said. Stepping back to look at the overhead clock, he gave a slow whistle. 'We're making pretty good time.'

He headed through the open door leading to the corridors under the bleachers. When I didn't follow him, he came back and hurried me along.

'We have coffee set up in the change room,' he said. 'You want one?'

Oh, yeah, I was never one to turn down a bit of caffeine. We went out into the fresh air so he could have a cigarette with his brew.

I was surprised he encouraged me to come along with him for our break as he'd been so unfriendly and truculent this morning, but he loosened up once his coffee was half into him.

'So what's your story?' he asked, pointing his cigarette at me. He wore his cap the old-fashioned way, with the brim to the front, and it shaded his eyes from the weak sun.

'Me? Depends which story you want to hear.'

I lightly kicked the cement block wall of the stadium.

"I think... how about, the story of how Kim finally found someone who knows the meaning of work to be my partner,' he replied with a dead-pan face.

I barked with laughter, couldn't help it, he caught me so off guard.

He turned a tentative smile towards me, his eyes still half hidden by his brim. 'What's so funny?' He almost sounded menacing as he asked.

I explained to him, and then it was his turn to snicker aloud. In fact, he became quite animated then.

'You're kidding, right?' he said. 'Every year, Mom gets me some crazy rich girl artist to work with me, and you know what? It's easier just to do it all myself, just let them sit in the booth and pretend they know how to operate the credit card machine.' He leaned against the wall and adjusted his hat so he could look up at the weak November sun.

'Wait a minute! Kim is your mother?'

'Yeah.' His voice held a mixture of pride and defiance. 'And yes, I get the job because of her. A classic case of nepotism in the high flying world of craft.'

He made me laugh again. I liked this guy, we were going to be a good team.

'So I take it hiring the rich artsy girls as assistants is also a form of nepotism?'

'Oh you better believe it,' he said. 'All the kids of the patrons and board members come through my hands, and I am totally sick of it.'

'I'll warn you upfront, I'm a nobody,' I replied. 'Kim only hired me because she was really stuck and it was at the last minute.'

He lit up another cigarette. 'S'alright by me.'

Jack's voice was growing deeper as he relaxed, and I could see he was kind of cute with his freckles and curly auburn hair shoved under the dumb baseball cap he wore. He looked to be about my age, but carried himself with the confidence of an older guy. Perhaps this came from years of responsibility working under his mother, from knowing exactly what each large event needed behind the scenes, from being a master at this craft of his.

We returned back to attack the floorplan with a renewed vigor, and it only took us a couple of hours to finish marking out the floor. After a quick sandwich lunch and more coffee, we returned to the rink to find it invaded with electricians and people setting up rods and curtains to mark off the booths according to the chalk marks we had laid down. I watched in awe as electrical outlets were lowered down from the rafters one by one on their thick cords.

Then it was time to unload the rental truck filled with what seemed like hundreds of boxes. I was glad Jack knew what he was doing, because I found it all really overwhelming.

'It's all organized,' he told me. 'Just put all the boxes with the same letters in piles together. The A boxes over there, the B cartons here, and so forth. You'll catch on.'

It was a crazy scene with people all over the place, but Jack was right – everything was super organized. Everyone concentrated on the job they were there to do, but with lots of laughter and carrying on as if they knew each other well. I guess they'd all worked together for years doing this, coming together for any events at venues all over the city.

The camaraderie was comfortable. As the fair took shape before my very eyes, it had a feeling of a carnival atmosphere as if people weren't really working, they were just hanging out together with old friends and creating something fun. There was a specialness happening here, a bond forged amongst the behind-the-scene folk, those people who all played their part in creating the illusion; they understood it wasn't magical but was a lot of hard work and discipline and a bunch of people coming together to work as a team, yet they knew their work was well done. The magic would be in the finished product.

We stayed till ten o'clock that night under the bright fluorescent overheads, sorting strings of Christmas lights and different kinds of boughs and putting together the trees.

'Why don't we do all this tomorrow?" I asked him. 'We've still got another day before the fair opens.'

'Oh, no,' Jack said. 'We have to get this all done today while we have the mental space. The crafts people will be here tomorrow, and believe me, you don't want to still be organizing things when the artists come on board. It's a crazy scene.'

And he was right yet again. We arrived at the stadium at eight o'clock the next morning and people were already milling around the entrances, unloading their boxes and claiming dibs on the available trolleys. I was issued a walkie-talkie to clip on my belt and a t-shirt which

44

proclaimed me as staff, and felt quite important as I bustled around doing errands and handing out the information packages and helping set up road signs and lamp posts. I was beginning to understand how the illusion of the magical Christmas wonderland was created.

The day passed quickly, and after supper there was a fresh wave of booth holders coming in, those who worked at their crafts part-time throughout the year while holding down full-time jobs. Soon, only one booth lay dark and uninhabited, a small space tucked into a dark corner.

'Did we miss something?' I asked Jack anxiously, pointing to the blank space.

He looked down at the clipboard in his hands and flicked through some pages. 'That's the last minute entry,' he said. 'Wonder if he realizes he's supposed to set up today? I'll let Mom know.'

Jack had no sooner gone up the center aisle than I felt a cool breeze brush through my hair and down my neck. I looked up and there, silhouetted by the streetlight outside the opened loading door beyond the bleachers, stood a familiar slight figure, his long black coat almost sweeping the floor and a humble smile on his face.

Willem. His arms were empty, but as he strode into the rink he lifted one hand to direct those who followed him, burdened down with clumsy large cartons.

I was about to slip away into the avenue of booths but he looked up and speared me with his glance.

'Dara...'

He looked like he was about to float over to embrace and kiss me in the European manner, so I quickly ducked out of reach.

'Willem, I believe that's your booth over there, in the corner.'

'Yes, that would be right,' he said. 'Carrie, Zeta, lay the boxes over there. I'll also need you to get the shelving and other equipment, if you would be so kind.'

My eyes almost bugged out of my head to see my well-to-do friend performing physical labour and what was stranger, even doing as he bade her without arguing or questioning or resentment. There were two other women with them, and between the four they had the booth set up in no time.

Of course I had to stick around to see what he would unpack from the cartons, so I busied myself making unnecessary adjustments to the closest Christmas tree.

Willem dismissed his followers. I could feel his gaze on me as if he was willing me to approach, but I clamped down my mind and refused to let his suggestions in.

When I eventually turned around again however, to check on his progress, I found nothing but a black curtain covering the entrance to his booth. Damn! I was going to have to wait till the next day to see what hand-made creations the self-proclaimed sorcerer would be selling at the fair.

The only hint he gave of his wares was in the form of a wooden sign hung above, the hand painted lettering only three words long, silver paint on black.

LORD OF MISRULE

8

The next morning Jack picked me up at seven, three hours before the fair officially opened. He said the extra-early morning was necessary in order to deal with any last minute problems and to set up the coffee urns for the crafts people. As juried members of the lofty Craft Council, they all expected basic catering. We stopped at Tim Horton's on the way, filling up with extra-large dark roasts to tide us over.

Just before ten, everything was in place, all the crafts people making last minute adjustments to their booths and both large urns of coffee half gone.

'This is my favourite part,' Jack said from our vantage up in the bleachers. He had a soft smile on his face and his long legs rested on the seat ahead of us. He pointed to the stadium below. 'There she goes.'

We watched Kim stride down the avenue of booths, calling out to the stadium security guards, who nodded and headed back behind the scenes.

'Five, four, three, two...' Jack chanted, then the overhead lights went off, those harsh fluorescents that had bathed the rink in cold blue for the past two days, leaving the space in sudden darkness.

As our eyes adjusted, the huge magical fair of my memory slowly emerged, first the old-fashioned lamp-posts on every corner lit the corners of the aisles, and then in every booth appeared strategically placed spotlights and Christmas twinklers, even an electric fireplace or two dotted around the space. It was an indoor wonderland of lights.

We sat for a moment in awe of the illusion we had helped create, then Jack jumped up. 'Come on, we gotta run,' he said. 'You're on the credit card stall first. Make sure your walkie-talkie's turned on.'

People were already streaming through the doors when we reached the front of the rink. I took my place behind the desk and plastered a smile on my face, but my services wouldn't be needed just yet. The early customers needed a chance to explore and find their favourite artists, and see what all was new this year.

While waiting for the first purchasers to come, my thoughts wandered back to the puzzle of Willem. Who was this man who claimed to be a sorcerer? He certainly had Carrie and Zeta in his thrall, but I really couldn't see the attraction. Physically he was unprepossessing, a slight man with a weak chin and narrow eyes and no eyelashes, yet I'd felt the air of his power when he directed it to me. He had to be as he claimed, else how would he know what I was looking for?

I'd called Hugh last night before going to bed, asking him if he knew Willem's story. It took a moment for him to reply.

'Willem...' There was a pause while he consulted with someone he was with. Maybe it was my Dad. 'You don't mean Willem de Vriejz, the Dutch guy?'

'I might,' I replied. Dutch, yes, that could be his accent. 'I only know him as Willem. He says he's a sorcerer.'

Hugh's tone was disparaging. '*Wanted* to be a sorcerer, I'm afraid he failed out of PEAWS exams. That's the Pan European Academy of Wizardry and Sorcery.' A funny thing about Hugh was that he loved acronyms. 'He tried to worm his way in with your Dad's Kin, but of course they're having nothing to do with him.'

Of course. The Witch Kin everywhere were terrible snobs. They ruled much of the Normal world, having placed themselves in advantage points of power and wealth throughout the centuries. They were the old aristocracy of Britain and Europe, the early settlers coming over on the Mayflower, the Brahmin caste of India. You get the picture. The only place the Witch Kin didn't have a strong presence was in Australia, but that wasn't through lack of trying. Their mistake had been in sending the rejects of their own society over there first, the thieves, and the outlaws and the half-blood witches. This new crowd had developed their own stratified society, leaving no room at the top for the Kin.

'Not much to him, I'd say.' Hugh dismissed the man out of hand. 'Why do you ask?

I hesitated. I knew nothing about that bit of metal my fingers had merely brushed on in Zeta's shop, only that it called to me with a faint whisper of my mother's voice. It might have been my imagination, for my mother hadn't been a witch and had no magic that I knew of.

And yet Willem knew I was looking for it, and his voice had been triumphant as if he himself possessed the object of my desire.

'Oh, nothing,' I mumbled. 'He's got a booth at the fair, and I met him in Zeta's store. He seems an odd sort.'

Hugh laughed. 'I suppose he's using his power to enthrall the ladies,' he said. 'Willem de Vriejz, he is simply a poor user of magic. He still resents being flunked out, but he was caught cheating so there you have it. Not allowed to practice professionally, certainly not allowed to develop the dark arts.'

He paused, then continued in lecture mode. 'You see, sorcery is a different ball game altogether from witch craft. Only the cream of the crop are allowed to graduate. Anyone else who is not found up to snuff is forced to drop out and give up the trade.'

'So what do they do with their training?' I asked.

'They find other ways to weave their spells. Some become authors, some politicians. An education is never wasted.'

That was all Hugh would give me.

I got my chance to check out Willem's booth in the post-lunch afternoon lull. I didn't want to meet up with the man again, so when I passed by and saw the booth unoccupied, I took my chance.

I was flabbergasted. He had two different kinds of offerings on display.

In the center back of his booth, a tall shallow case held rows and rows of small stoppered glass bottles filled with a rainbow of coloured liquids. A sign proclaimed 'All Your Dreams Come True'.

He was selling spells. In public, for any Normal to come and peruse and choose and buy and change their lives. Was the man mad? The Witch Kin would be down on him in a flash.

I could smell a waft of magic in the booth, just faintly, like a day old fart in an airless room. It was almost visible at the corner of my eye, but the magic wasn't coming from the spells so colourfully displayed against the black backdrop. Those glass vials were pretty but worthless.

It was coming off the other merchandise in the booth, lined up against the side walls on black shelving. I had figured him for a metal worker, or a stone sculptor as he struck me as a cold sort of man, yet his other works were fanciful and brightly coloured figures a couple of feet tall. They all appeared to be made of fabric and paper, the child's art of papier mache with touches of wool like the felted mittens Edna would make me every year for Christmas.

Apart from the center light shining on the display of spells, the booth was lit only by tiny individual spotlights bathing each of his figures in brightness against the blackly draped walls of the space. It was like entering into a wax museum of miniatures, for each small mannequin which stood about two or two and a half feet tall had a look of life in their still figures, as if they were holding their breaths and just waiting for me to turn my back. When no one was looking they might leap off the glass boxes and scheme amongst themselves.

They were horrifying in their aspects, and terrible in visage.

I had to get closer to examine them. The first one in the circle, the closest to me, was a demon with long horns curling away from his head, his eyes rimmed with red and mouth drawn back in a snarl to reveal uneven, pointed fangs. Yet the white fur surrounding his face was soft and combed and silky. His yellow goat eyes stared right at me - I could have sworn I saw his chest move with breath.

'His name is Krampus.'

I looked up to see that Willem had silently appeared, and was watching for my reaction to his creations. Dressed in a long, unadorned black robe, he stood with his hands clasped as if in reverence, and he proceeded to guide me through the exhibit.

'Krampus, sometimes called the evil twin of Santa,' Willem said, his eye lingering fondly on the horrific creature. 'He visits little Austrian children who have misbehaved. Of course, Krampus is a much older being than the Christian St. Nicholas. He was born in a time of strife, before the world knew benevolence. Note the basket strapped to his back and the birch stick in his hand. He beats the naughty, sometimes packs them away to eat later.'

Willem gave a light laugh.

'It's... very life-like,' I said, still staring at the creature.

'Is he not magnificent?'

I nodded, and swallowed. Magnificent was one word for it. Maleficent might be a better one.

He moved me on to the next terrible figure, a hag the color of bread mold with a hooked nose and bright eyes staring out at me.

'Dear Frau Perchta! Did you know that she visits during the twelve days of Christmas, and good boys and girls may receive a silver coin from her. Bad children, however, will have their bellies slit by her great claws so the intestines fall out, and she replaces them with garbage!' He gave a delighted laugh.

All twenty of the grotesque figures had their own story and their own life.

'These are incredibly horrible, Willem.' I had to be honest. 'Do you really think people will buy these?' I shuddered to think that anyone would want the creatures in their homes. They would give me nightmares.

'You'd be surprised,' he replied and leaned down to speak only in my ear, for the aisles were filling with customers again and two people had entered the booth, entranced with his work. 'People collect Santa figures, do they not?'

I nodded glumly. Yes, even Edna had a collection of Santas she brought out every Christmas: jolly ones in red and white, vintage in long gowns and capes, knitted, brass, all dressed in varying interpretations of the traditional St. Nicholas. I'd never quite seen the appeal of them, truth be told, it felt like overkill on the Christmas theme.

'In this very weary consumer world we live in, people quickly tire of novelty,' he said, his pale gray eyes boring into mine and his Dutch accent becoming increasingly staccato as the passion filled his voice. 'They are saturated with the need to buy more and more to reward their loved ones at this time of the year, and Saint Nicholas, or Santa, if you prefer, has become the modern patron saint of consumerism. I offer the irony of the anti-Santa, the punisher of bad deeds and thoughts. It is appealing to many, in an ironic kind of way.'

If they weren't all so awful and scary, I might think of getting one for Edna's collection, just to make a point.

'How much are they?' My eyes had settled on one of the smaller Icelandic trolls.

He whispered a sum into my ear.

'What?' I looked back at him in amazement. At that price, did he really expect to sell any? I couldn't believe people would pay so dearly for a bit of irony, no matter how well crafted.

Well, I had planned on getting Edna a new scarf anyway which was just as well for an anti-Santa was far out of my reach. Besides, I would have hated having the creepy critter anywhere near me.

'They are unique, and one of a kind,' he said snootily, drawing himself up to his full height, which wasn't much more than my own. 'Only a certain well-heeled segment of society will appreciate them.'

'I wish you the best of luck,' I told him with sincerity, then I looked toward the back of the booth. 'Those are spells?'

'Interested in a little magic, are you?'

'No!' I said quickly, for I had plenty of magic of my own, I had no need for his. Then my curiosity got the better of me. 'I don't think they're real.'

I started to wander over to them, the better to examine them. He slipped in front of me, blocking my way and getting right in my personal space.

'They are as real as a person wants them to be,' he said in a low voice. The garlic from his lunch engulfed me and I turned my head away, yet still his pale eyes bored into mine. 'What is real magic? What can help change the life of one who is not blessed with the abilities that you and I have?'

He went on to answer his own question. 'Belief. Nothing can change in a life if one does not believe,' he said. 'And these potions offer hope that dreams can come true.'

'So there's no real magic in them, that's what you're saying?'

'Who can define magic for another person?'

Flim-flam and snake oil, that's all he was selling to the unsuspecting public of Normals. I stepped away from him in disgust. A failed sorcerer, Hugh had said. And yet...

Before I left, I had to ask him about the not-coin. Aware that people were waiting to speak with him, I spoke to him quickly.

'In Zeta's the other day, you said it wasn't a coin I was looking for...'

He nodded, his face blank.

'What did you mean by that?'

'What did you think I meant?' he parried.

The walkie-talkie on my belt sputtered. Kim was looking for me, I needed to get back to my station. I sighed.

'Do you have it?' I asked him urgently. 'Did you find it at Zeta's, that coin or whatever it is?'

'Maybe I did, maybe I didn't,' he said, taking his time. 'Why don't we talk about it after the fair? I really must get back to my customers.'

As I turned to go, he called me back.

'Perhaps you can do a little job or two for me,' he said. 'In exchange for what you seek. Call me next week.'

He handed me a simple black business card which gave only the name he was going under, *Lord of Misrule*, and a phone number written in silver.

I hated the thought of him touching the medallion, fondling it, tarnishing her memory. Creepy little dude.

My skin crawled as I left, feeling the eyes of his creatures on me as I walked away.

9

I spent most of my supper breaks during the run of the fair giving Edna a chance to go stretch her legs and get some fresh air. One evening, I was joined by Mark, her boyfriend who was a cop with the Royal Canadian Mounted Police, the RCMP. He was a nice guy and I liked him, loved him even for Edna's sake.

'I found the perfect gift for Edna!' Mark was speaking in a very low voice although I knew for a fact that she was gone to the canteen. He was really excited. 'You know that guy in the corner, the one who pretends he's a wizard?'

'Sorcerer,' I said, not having a good feeling about this.

'Whatever,' Mark said, brushing aside the semantics. His brown eyes shone and he had the hugest grin on his face. 'I'm buying one of his anti-Santa's for her. Get it? For her Santa collection. The ultimate in irony!'

'That's... funny, and ironic,' I said, my heart sinking. 'But Mark, wouldn't she rather have something like a really gorgeous hand knit sweater? Or, if you're shelling out that much money, maybe buy her a new fridge, the kind with the freezer on the bottom that makes its own ice cubes?'

'She'd kill me if I bought her a *fridge* for Christmas,' he said. He looked at me as though I'd lost my marbles. 'This is the perfect thing for her. It's decorative and hand-made. A little scary, like the books she writes.'

'I hate to ask this, Mark, but can you really afford that?'

He smiled. 'I told him who it was for, and he's giving me a discount.'

And this was even more unsettling. Edna being Edna had told all her old friends here at the fair that I was her niece and word would have reached Willem. Was I being paranoid? Perhaps, but those chills running down my spine were real.

The creatures were horrible, and looked as if they were alive and would knife you the minute you turned your back on them; Willem had ensured there would be one coming into my home by offering that discount to Mark. Dear unsuspecting Mark.

But before Mark could make his purchase, Willem's booth was shut down by the Witch Kin. Oh, they didn't do it directly, they used the forces of the government under their control, but it was obvious enough to me whose hand was behind it. And to Willem.

The second day of the fair, I spotted my Dad, Jon de Teilhard and his wife (the rotten witch) Cate strolling through the aisles of the fair. We all preferred to ignore each other, so I slipped into another aisle to avoid being forced to greet them.

I snuck around behind their backs though. I hated them both but that didn't stop me from being curious. He was my father, after all, and he used to love me.

Besides, they were nearing Willem's booth, and I had to stick around to watch the action. I almost held my breath in anticipation.

Cate, her long black hair done in a sleek bun at the nape of her neck, prowled around the aisles like a panther on the hunt, narrowing in on her prey. Tall boots encased her legs and a military-style wool coat wrapped her slim body. Her dark eyes sparkled bright as she smelled the magic coming from the sorcerer's booth.

She stopped dead center of his booth, and I could almost see her tail quivering as she honed in on the vials of potion. A quick glance was exchanged between Jon and her, and that was all it took.

Willem stood to the side, ostensibly talking with a customer, but his eyes were narrowed on the pair the whole time. His shoulders were tense.

Cate's tinkling laugh rang out as she sized up the rainbow of coloured glass before her. Her blood red nails ran down the crystal display. 'How amusing, Jon,' she tossed over her shoulder. 'Just think - magic in a bottle!'

He stood close behind her, not saying a word, as she further mocked the contents of those vials.

And her words were true – there was not a drop of power to be had in the display, for all it was enticingly laid out and promising the moon. And despite her mockery of the fake potions, they were not even the object of Cate's true attention. She didn't look to either side of her at the papier mache trolls and evil ones, but I knew – I was very aware that her senses were turned fully on and she saw the magic in them.

The whole scene took less than two minutes to enact before she walked out again, apparently intent on examining the knit wares in the booth next door.

Willem stood stock still, staring at the departing backs of the de Teilhards. None of the nuances of what had just happened had been lost to him, and there was murder in the Dutchman's eyes.

So it didn't come as a surprise to me, or Willem himself I guess, the next day when the Department of Health officials came to the fair and headed straight for the Lord of Misrule. They confiscated his vials of 'magic potion' and listed off the myriad laws he had broken by selling for consumption without having the necessary paperwork stamped.

Willem didn't bother with the fair much after that. He packed up the papier mache creatures, the ones still unsold, and the corner booth quickly faded to black again as if he'd never been there.

....

The full week of my work at the fair passed pretty quickly. I put plenty of hours in over that time with the very early mornings and late nights, and I was looking forward to getting that paycheck. I was also looking forward to not getting up so early in the morning again.

Jack and I sat in the bleachers, our own work done, for the take down of the event went much faster than the initial set-up. We were just waiting for the company that owned the curtains and rods to be finished, and the last of the potters who had to pack the leftover goods very carefully.

My companion hauled out his cigarette pack.

'You're not going to light that up here inside the stadium, are you?'

He looked at me with his funny little crooked grin. 'Dara, every single door in the place is open, there's more fresh air in here than out there. You really think anyone'll notice or care?'

One of the things I'd come to appreciate about Jack was his way of pointing out the ridiculousness of many situations, but in a nice kind of way so everyone laughed and no one felt hurt. He sure was easy to be with.

'So, what do you do now the fair is over?' he asked, idly blowing smoke rings into the chill air.

'Back to university,' I said, pulling a face and leaning back against the riser behind me. I squinted at him through the smoke. 'I have to get through this semester whether I like it or not. How about you?'

He shrugged. 'I work here, and there,' he said. 'Maybe I'll get the band together for some rehearsals. We have a gig coming up next week at the Grog Shop. Do you know the place?'

That was the bar which abutted Zeta's cellar.

'Yeah, been there once or twice,' I said.

'Maybe you want to drop in, if you don't have anything else to do?' He ground the cigarette under the heel of his steel-toed boot and fidgeted. 'We could, maybe, I don't know, hang or something afterwards.'

I sat up straighter. Was Jack asking me on a date? I looked over at him, where he was studiously avoiding my eye. His face was quite pink in color, and it wasn't just the cold November air in the stadium. I nudged his foot with mine.

'Dude. You asking me out?'

'No,' he said quickly, then his eyes slid towards me and he shrugged. 'Maybe.'

I found myself grinning at him. Jack was cute, and fun. He might not be used to women, but he was sincere and straightforward.

'Give me a break,' he said, looking at me from under the brim of his cap. 'I don't do this much. Don't laugh at me.'

'I'm not laughing at you,' I said. 'I'm considering.'

We'd worked closely over the past week, but I realized Jack knew nothing about me, not about the magic and Alt and me being related to the most powerful witch in the province. 'I should tell you though, I'm going away to school in January. To another country. I don't know when, or if, I'll be back.'

I felt his body relax next to me.

'That's cool,' he said. 'Sort of takes the pressure off, doesn't it? You're not here long enough for us to get involved or whatever. We can just hang out, enjoy each other's company. You can come hear me play bass in the band, and be my first groupie.'

'Gee, when you put it like that, how can a girl refuse?'

We shared a shy smile.

The crush I had on Hugh? Well, that's surely all it was. Like I said before, that witch was out of my league, while this guy from the bay in his beat up jeans and baseball cap and his off-center smile was more my style.

10

Edna placed the coffee before me on the kitchen table. Our north-facing kitchen was dark in the late November morning, even though it was already nine o'clock, and it looked like the weather had turned overnight. I could hardly make out the bare branches of the trees through the drizzle on the window.

'So you had a good time working at the fair?'

I nodded and slurped the coffee.

'That guy, Jack,' she continued as she pretended to bury herself in the newspaper. 'Seems like a nice boy.'

'He's okay, yeah,' I said.

'Handsome,' she pointed out. 'Respectful. Nicer than most of the fellows you've hung out with before.'

'I never went out with Benjy Hoskins,' I told her flatly. Alice's brother Benjy had been my first crush, but that was years ago. He'd been tough, and cool, and had an edge to him, and he had never dismissed me for being merely his kid sister's friend. When you're thirteen, that means a lot.

But me and Benjy? No way, it had never happened. Thank God.

'You should invite Jack up some time over the holidays,' she said, now looking up at me. 'Before you go away.'

'Maybe,' I said, not committing to anything. 'It was fun working there. I see why you keep going back every year. How were your sales?'

'Best year yet,' she said. 'People are really buying up the books, asking me already when the next one is coming out. The grislier they are, the more they like them.'

'So we can get the oil tank filled this weekend?'

'Even better....' She had something to say to me, but she was nervous, I could tell by the way she kept brushing her curly brown hair off her face. She had the same blue eyes as me and Mom, but our hair hadn't received the curl genes she had been graced with.

'Well?'

Edna took a deep breath. 'Okay. You know how Mark has been spending more time here?'

It was true. We'd seen a lot of her boyfriend here in the evenings in the past couple of months, and I didn't have a problem with that at all, and not just because he insisted we eat real food regularly. Left to herself, Edna would eat sandwiches for every meal, except for the odd time when she would be stricken with guilt at not providing a normal home life for me. Her attempts to cook were sort of hit or miss, and fortunately the mood didn't come often. Over the years I had learned to put together pasta dishes with very few ingredients but I didn't love cooking either so we went through a lot of bread in our house. So yeah, I'd noticed and welcomed Mark's presence around the house.

'Are you trying to tell me he's moving in officially?'

'Maybe,' she said. 'We'd been sort of talking about the winter, after you go, but his house has sold already and the buyers want to move in before Christmas. Thought I'd broach the subject with you first.'

'I have no problem with it,' I replied. 'Mark's a great guy. But I'm surprised. I know you like your space.'

And by 'space' I meant breathing room, days of no communication with the outside world while she got lost in the stories she wrote, along with the not showering or washing her hair that this life style sometimes entailed.

Edna nodded, her face very serious. 'Yeah, I know. It's sort of scary. But I like having him around.'

'He's a good fit for you,' I said.

'And also...'

I sipped my coffee and waited.

'He's pretty handy, you know? He's itching to help fix the house up. If he could mend the windows, put in insulation and God only knows what else he wants to do, then there would be lots of space, usable space, in the house again.'

She had a point. The house had slowly been closing in on us through the years, with first one room, then another being unfit to use, till we were basically confined to the back part of it. All the glorious drawing rooms downstairs and the main staircase, it had been five years since we'd opened those doors, and the beautiful long French windows which graced the front of the house had been nailed shut for ages.

'And he would be busy doing this in his free time, making it easier for you to ignore him?'

'I would be able to get lost in my creative endeavours, yes.' She shot me a pretend dirty look.

'Okay, sounds good. He wants to move in for Christmas?'

'You okay with it?' she asked. 'He could always rent a hotel room...

She looked up to gauge my reaction to this *fait accompli*. I smiled at her.

'As long as he keeps up the gourmet dinners and take out, I'm okay with it all,' I said. 'Maybe he could even put in a dishwasher?'

'I'm sure he'll figure it out after he's been here a week or two,' she replied with a perfectly straight face. She went back to her newspaper, but caught me before I left the room.

'It's the mummer's parade next week!'

I looked over at her happy face. Edna just loved everything Christmas, including that dumb parade where everyone dressed up as mummers and paraded around the downtown in the cold and slush underfoot. The mummers were an old tradition, brought over from England and Ireland, but the parade was a relatively new thing.

Why did people want to do this? I wasn't sure. Perhaps they hadn't had enough of Hallowe'en.

My research told me that mummering had been a bloodthirsty, scary tradition, and the modern equivalent just seemed so pretend-fake-happy like a sugar coating on a rotten apple. Yet I would have to go with her yet again this year, because no one else would. I bet Mark would conveniently find work that had to be done that night, so I would be left holding the bag.

'Oh, and this year?' Edna continued. 'I want us to dress up and be a part of the parade.'

She grinned at me. 'Won't that be fun?'

11

I caught up on my university course work pretty quickly, except for that stupid Folklore paper on the Lord of Misrule. It was a case of knowing what I wanted to say, but being reluctant to actually write it in case it turned out to be a pile of crap.

Willem had called his booth *Lord of Misrule*. What was on the go with that? I hated when unexplained coincidences happened in my life. The two weren't connected at all, but my brain had to worry the issue, trying to find a pattern where none existed. If I could just get the stupid term paper out of the way, I'd be able to let it go.

I shifted uncomfortably on my bed. A hollow wind whistled through the grate in my bedroom. The fireplace had been blocked up years ago, yet tonight a rogue breeze had found its way down the chimney and through the cracks. There was something wrong with the house, it had been feeling weird lately as if there was an unquiet spirit abroad, and I didn't know what could be causing it. As if a bit of Alt had slipped in under the crack of the door, yet the only thing that had changed was the presence of Mark, and I knew he could have nothing at all to do with this feeling of something wrongfully placed.

Maundy might know what was going on. My resident ghost next door never left the house, so she could have a better understanding of what had changed, if anything. The weird thing was, she'd been strangely quiet lately. I knocked on her door before I entered.

'Maundy?'

She was lying prostrate on the bed, the old patchwork quilt visible through her long grimy dress.

'You okay?'

She emitted a low moan, just being her usual dramatic self. I prepared myself to act my part in her pre-written scene.

'What's going on?'

Maundy lifted her head. 'Make him leave.'

'What? Who? Mark, no way, what's he done to you?'

She sighed and turned her face away from me.

Honestly, I didn't have the patience for this, so I cut to the chase. 'Look Maundy, have you noticed something in the house which shouldn't be here?'

'It's him. I told you.'

'No, it's not Mark!' Edna's boyfriend was one of the most solid comfortable people I'd ever met with not a whiff of the supernatural about him. I couldn't even tell him about my half-blood, for fear he'd think I was crazy. 'He's been coming here for years, and you're only just now noticing him?'

'He brought the demon in, with all his banging and hammering. Make him stop, Dara, make him leave my house. He's ruining it all.'

'You're upset because he's doing renovations to the house? But we need these done, the place is falling down around our ears.'

She groaned again.

'Listen up, Maundy,' I told her, determined to nip her objections to Edna's boyfriend in the bud. If she decided she didn't like him, she could make life here hell, for me at least; it probably wouldn't affect Mark and Edna because they didn't believe in her.

'Mark is making this place like it used to be, in your time. Remember? All the teas you used to have on the lawns outside, the ladies in their long white dresses, the elegant tea services...'

She sat up. 'You mean you'll start dressing like a lady again and not a street urchin?'

Her leaps of logic astounded me sometimes. This spirit made an art form of not making sense.

'No!' I said. 'What I'm trying to tell you is that I feel like there's something wrong in the house, but I know for a fact it's not Mark. Unless....'

She perked up, ready to hear me condemn him.

'Unless he's stirred something up, something that shouldn't have been messed with? Maybe he unwittingly loosed some kind of spell. Do you get that feeling at all?' Though for the life of me I couldn't figure out what that might be, I'd spent lots of time in the rooms downstairs when I was young, and had no memory of anything magical or supernatural there.

Maundy flopped back down on her bed again and emitted a ghostly whining noise.

'You're not listening to me! He *is* responsible, I told you. Get rid of him, and the evil will leave!'

'Y'know what? You are the most unhelpful ghost I've ever met.' I turned and left her room, banging the door because I knew how much she hated loud noises.

I had to get out of the house, I was really starting to get creeped out by whatever was in there, lurking at the edge of my sensors.

12

J ack and his band were playing at the Grog Shop that
   evening, so this was the perfect opportunity to get out
and clear my head. I'd questioned why the early start time
of eight o'clock, as most grunge bands didn't bother starting their sets until eleven at least, when the drinking crowd
were just getting on the go for the night. He laughed at my
ignorance when we spoke on the phone.

'We're the warm-up for the opening band,' he said. 'Don't
you know how popular this place is? We're lucky to get a foot
in the door, nobody knows us yet.'

He was proud and ambitious and dedicated to his craft,
willing to work the crap hours until the band had gained a
following. I liked that about him. He was solid.

So I got there in the middle of their first set. Even so early
in the evening, I had to squeeze in and find a space for myself
against the back wall, the one abutting Zeta's cellar. The
modern fake brick wall covering was cold on my back, and

I could feel the vibration of Jack's bass thudding through the old slate floor.

They weren't half bad, and I liked watching Jack up there on the small platform at the front of the room. From this vantage, he looked long and lean and moody, all dressed in black for this special occasion, even his baseball cap was black with a white Anarchy symbol on the front. Our eyes met over the crowd, and he flashed a smile just for me.

I was sipping my draft beer when I first felt the stirrings of something changing, the room and the loud music coming and going like a bad radio signal and static filled the spaces in between. What the hell? It felt like...

Alt. I had done nothing to move into this realm, yet there I was suddenly, sitting in the original Grog Shop before it even had a sign over its door, back when it was just a hole-in-the-wall shanty on the arse end of George Street.

I can usually control my entry to Alt, especially if I'm aware of the process and doing it on purpose. It's like a balancing act in the mind, I try to keep one eye in real time while the other explores Alt Town. It's never a good thing to go fully into Alt, you need to have a quick escape route left open.

But not this time. It was as if I'd been sucked in by a force beyond my own, and with no warning, I couldn't stop the process. I spit out the rum I'd just imbibed from the filthy clay mug in my hand and looked around me.

The Alt Grog Shop was filled with sailors and prostitutes and other dregs of society, all bent on getting enough rum and gin into themselves to dull the pain of their existences. All were filthy and half-way to their destinations already.

A man on the bench to the left of me stirred as I appeared, his four day beard evidence of when he'd reached the port of Alt Town in his wooden sailing vessel, and his teeth were all broken and stained. He put his arm around me and latched on fast. The smell of his unwashed body was overwhelming and I nearly retched.

I broke away, wrenching my body away from his grip and stood up only to be faced with his cohorts. I heard a buzz in several languages go through those of the crowd who were still able to be coherent.

'Who's a pretty boy, then?' A prostitute in a tattered once-red dress screeched. Her breasts threatened to come out of the filthy corset and shift which contained them as her claw-like hand raked through my hair, threatening to pull me towards her while her drinking companion looked at me lustfully, his hand already creeping down inside his pants.

I whirled around, looking for an escape, and then I saw him. Willem, standing in a low arched door, one I swear hadn't been there in real time. He held out his hand and grasped mine, pulling me through the crowd and ducking, through the old doorway. The heavy oaken door slammed behind me.

'Willem? What the frig is going on here?' I frantically combed my hair with my fingers where the woman had touched me. I had no desire to pick up Alt cooties.

We were in Zeta's cellar next door to the bar, the stone chamber barely lit by a single tallow candle attached in an iron holder against a wooden beam. The screechings of the crowd barely came through the solid wall.

It was freezing cold down here. Great sides of beef and hams were hung from the iron hooks on the joists above our heads.

'Imagine meeting you here,' he murmured. 'What's a nice girl like you doing in a place like that?' The smile on his face was so calm, so pleasant, that I almost thought for a moment it *was* a coincidence. But then I saw behind his facade the smirk of triumph and that made me really mad.

'You kidding me? You brought me over to Alt, asshole, and I want to know why.' I felt like a kitten desperately spitting at a looming Doberman, despite the fact he was no taller than me. How did he force me over into Alt like that? I had seriously underestimated the man's power. And so had Hugh.

'I haven't heard from you,' he said, the hint of a pout in his voice. 'I was expecting a call.'

'Why would I contact you, you freak?'

'Here I was, thinking I had something you wanted,' he said, his hand reaching into the folds of his black gown. He withdrew it, and I could see the faint sparkle of gold in the candle light.

More than that, I could feel the magic of the object he held. Over here in Alt its force was magnified, and I heard the siren whisperings of my mother's voice so much clearer than when I had grazed the object with my fingers, back in September in real time.

I reached out and touched it but he quickly snatched his hand out of my reach, laughing as he did. Yet that quick glancing touch had been enough to sear an impression on my body and in my brain. That coin, or talisman, or medallion, whatever he wanted to call it, it had been held by my mother, and not casually. This had meant something to her, and I could still feel the vibrations of strong emotions. Joy. Fear. Anger, then... despair. But not death.

His eyes grew speculative as he watched my face.

'And what so interests you about this medallion?'

There was no way I would confide in him, so I withdrew my hand and shut my mouth tight. I crossed my arms and clamped my mind shut against him for good measure.

'No matter,' he said, his eyes still watchful on me. 'It's not my business. It is enough for me to know you want it.'

Willem gave a small laugh and continued. 'I can give you this object.' He casually tossed it from hand to hand.

'In exchange for what?' I kept my voice hard. I was no innocent, I knew a man like him would want a price paid.

'Something that won't cost you anything at all,' he replied, his voice growing silky soft. The shadows from the candle jumped in an unfelt draught and I heard a far off drip, drip, drip deep within the cavern. 'Something that may actually give you … pleasure, if you will open your mind to it.'

He leaned closer, seeing the disbelief on my face.

'You do not even know, do you?' he asked. 'You don't yet know the meaning of true power. You are like a rough diamond, unshaped. Work with me, I can show you the path, the road to everything you've ever dreamed of. Never mind the Witch Kin and their rules, Dara. You will never be accepted as one of them, but that's alright, because you have no need of them.

'You can ride with me, Dara, just think of it. Ride with me to the heights of power.'

I laughed, unable to hide my scorn. I would be attending the North Scotland Academy of Magic, or as Hugh put it, NSAM. And I would be a star student. 'You? I have enough power of my own. What use would I have for a failed sorcerer to tow behind me?'

He winced visibly, then his brow darkened.

I felt the unease of Alt growing on me, the sweat along the nape of my neck and the cold setting into my very bones. I had to draw this visit to an end and get out of Alt before I fell ill or worse. My eyes flicked towards the medallion still clutched in his hand. If he would only drop it, or relax his grip for a moment, I would be able to grab it.

As if reading my mind, Willem shoved the medallion deep back into the pocket of his robe. 'As you wish, my dear,' he sighed. 'Perhaps we will not be partners after all. And yet... I still hold this object you desire. We are at a crossroads, you and I. You can choose to come with me on my path, and I will give you the medallion. Or we can part ways here and now and you will never gain the secrets it holds within.'

The clamminess was creeping up the back of my skull by now and I could hardly think straight. I knew I had to get out of Alt soon. I also knew that the object in his pocket was important, beyond price, because it held a clue to my mother's disappearance. I could not chance losing it forever.

I nodded. 'I might work with you, up to a point,' I said.

'And that is all I require,' he said, breaking out into his toothy smile. 'Now, make sure you call me this time, okay my sweet? Why not come to our Thursday night meeting?'

With that, he touched my face, then sent me spinning back into the craven grog pit behind me. The smell washed over me as I shut my eyes tight and threw myself out of Alt and back into the bar, where Jack and his friends were just finishing a tune.

Our eyes met, and his open face was clouded with worry.

'What happened to you?' He looked down at me as I leaned against the fake brick, out of breath and still with the uncomfortable clammy feel of Alt on my skin. The stereo played grunge rock, loudly, at a level that hurt even my ears. We had to yell at each other to be heard. 'One minute you were there, and then poof! You were gone. What the hell was that about?'

'I had to go to the bathroom,' I told him weakly. There was no way I could have begun to tell him what had just happened to me.

'You must have moved pretty damn fast then, because the toilet's clear on the other side of the room, and I didn't see you in the crowd.'

I stared up at his clear hazel eyes, and understood that it was only concern for me that was making him sound so pissed off.

'I'm not feeling so well, Jack,' I told him truthfully. 'I'm sorry, I better go home.'

'Do you need a ride?' Now he looked worried again.

'No, I'll be okay once I get out in the fresh air,' I said. 'Might be coming down with something, I don't know. Besides, you need to finish your set.'

He glanced toward the platform where his bandmates were looking over at him, impatience on their faces and in their movements.

'At least let me call a taxi for you,' he said as he reached into his pocket for his phone.

'It's all right,' I said as I placed my hand over his. 'Seriously, I just need to walk. I'm sorry to have to leave.'

'Okay then,' he said reluctantly. He drew his arms around me and we stayed in that soft hug for a moment. We'd never touched before, and he felt good and solid and strong, despite the lean lankiness of his limbs.

'And Jack?'

'Yeah?' I could feel the rumble of his voice though the thin fabric of his t-shirt, my cheek on his chest.

'You're good. Your band I mean. You guys are really going to go somewhere.'

He gave me a squeeze. 'Thanks for that.'

Jack moved his body back just a bit while still holding me in his arms, the better to look down at me. His eyes held concern, and something more, a shyness. I lifted my face up to his in answer to his unspoken question and our lips met, softly at first.

It was my first real kiss. I kid you not. Yeah, I'd kissed guys and been kissed before - hell, I wasn't even a virgin – but that was just from curiosity. This moment with Jack was like nothing I'd ever shared before. I mean, the earth didn't move and angel choirs didn't burst into song, nothing like the romance books lead you to expect, but it was real.

His lips were soft yet hard, and he tasted of the beer he'd drunk and the triumph of his night. His kiss was warm and crossed the barriers of our self-consciousness, touching me deep inside, and I just wanted to stay in that strong embrace forever and a day.

Maybe it doesn't sound romantic, but it was. Two people who genuinely liked each other's company, and liked what they thought they knew of the other. As if you took your best friend in the world and upped the intimacy level by ten and no one was worrying about stupid things like breath or body shape or a pimple marring the perfection because all that wasn't important. It was a kiss without expectations.

The chords of the new song rang through the room and already I could feel him pull away, torn between leaving me and joining the music he loved. I let him go.

'I'll text you, okay?' He gave me one last light squeeze.

'Yep.' I watched as he leapt back through the crowd and on to the platform.

The fresh air did help clear my head a bit. The night was cloudless and the wind sharp, shooting needles in through the seams of my winter hoody, the one lined with fake fleece.

It was a warm coat but no match for this wintry wind. I headed straight into the ice of that breeze, down towards the west end of Water Street and home.

My feet didn't want to go this path, but I forced myself into a brisk pace. Water Street was a funny kind of road. The middle bit of it, the downtown section with all the old stone business buildings and the traffic lights and the crowds, well, that was historical and so had a bit of magic infused everywhere you looked.

But on the west end of Water Street where I was headed, it was way worse. Not many streetlights lit the way, and the inhabited buildings were few and far between. You rarely passed other pedestrians along here at night, and if you did they were the sort you'd rather not see, and that was in real time.

The veil between real and Alt was thin on this road at this hour of the night, and I was already weak from my experience with Willem. I was a moving target for any unscrupulous supernaturals who might be lurking.

So I was more than happy to see Mark's white SUV pull silently up by me to give me ride home. I didn't complain when he gave me a scolding for walking alone along here at night, just relaxed into the solid passenger seat of his vehicle and smiled as he squawked about my foolhardiness.

If he only knew the half of it.

13

Just that slightest touch of the metal coin in Alt had been enough to tell me that my mother was still alive. Somewhere. Maybe not in real time, maybe not even in Alt, but it filled me with hope that I would find her. She was not dead.

I also knew her disappearance had something to do with magic, so I strongly suspected my father's wife Cate. That witch was a cold-hearted bitch who had never shown any love for me. The one and only time she'd ever crossed our threshold had been shortly before Mom's disappearance all those years ago. I could still recall the terrible screaming match between the two women, muffled as it was behind the heavy doors leading to the parlour.

Oh yeah, if anyone had anything to do with my mother's disappearance, it was Cate.

I gave Mark a quick hug before I turned to go upstairs

'Thanks, Mark,' I said. 'You came along at the exact right time.'

He held me away from him. 'Why didn't you just call me? You know I'd come and get you. I hate the thought of you walking alone at night in that neck of the woods. There's all sorts of weirdos out and about.'

I merely smiled at him fondly.

'I don't mean to nag,' he added. 'I'm not your father, but I still worry.'

No, Mark certainly wasn't my Dad, but he'd been more of a father to me in the five years he'd known Edna than my own father had been my whole life.

How could Maundy object to Mark's presence in the house? He was the antithesis of evil, that guy with not a bad bone in his body, and not a magical one, either. He was as solidly Normal as a person could be.

Maundy was a crackpot ghost who just hated change. If she had her way, we'd all be pretending to live just like the family did in 1900 or whenever it was she died, not changing a thing about the house even as it rotted away beneath our feet.

Tired and ill as I was feeling after my time in Alt, I knew I wouldn't be able to sleep. My nerves were jangling from the experience and my new certainty about Mom, so I decided to go up to the attic where all her stuff was stored. Yes, Edna and I had gone through everything with a fine tooth comb just after she disappeared, looking for a clue or a hint as to where she'd gone to but we'd found nothing at the time. A couple of years later Edna had lovingly packed everything away in to those cartons and lugged them up into the attic, but she'd said nothing as things of Mom's started reappearing on me, like her jean jacket and her favorite blue scarf. My aunt understood.

Despite the single bulb which barely broke into the dark of the top story, this wasn't a scary place for me as I knew it like the back of my hand. A narrow set of stairs wound around up to the attic door which never quite latched and had to be tied in place to prevent the draughts from reaching the second floor below. Inside that door, the dormered attic stretched off in two directions, and the light bulb sat at the junction of the wings. The two tiny windows were dark with just a faint glow from the city lights beyond.

The trunks and boxes which held Mom's stuff were over to the right, further on from the Christmas decorations. I could barely pick out the individual items in her boxes, but that was okay, I knew them all by heart. Besides, I was looking for something magical that might have been overlooked, and for that I could use my fingertips.

The wind was still galing at a pretty steady clip outside, and the noise of it almost masked the soft rustling from within, to my right, from the darkest corner of the attic. I stilled my hands in order to hear the noise better.

Great, I thought to myself, a squirrel or some other small mammal making its winter nest up here. Just what we needed. But when I sniffed I couldn't find any animal smells in the close air of the attic. And then out of the corner of my eye, I saw a slight movement. It could have been caused by a swaying bulb, except that this single light was firmly fixed into place.

I moved slightly to allow the light from the bulb to shine without shadows on the spot, but instead of a nest or a furry body all I saw was a large cream coloured paper bag, the kind with the stiff cardboard handles. This was brand new, and it looked just like the kind of bag I had sold by the hundreds to craftspeople, last week at the fair.

The rattle sounded again and I stared in horror as I watched the bag shake as if something was bound within but trying to free itself.

Yes, there could have been a squirrel inside that bag, but seriously? I knew the difference, I could feel the magic coming from it. That was no cute furry vermin.

I'd now found the reason I'd been feeling dread in this house. Maundy was partly right, in that Mark had brought this into our home.

14

M ark was still in the kitchen downstairs, fixing himself
a second supper from leftovers.

'Hey, I thought you'd gone to bed already,' he said. 'Want
a hot turkey sandwich?

I shook my head and plunged in.

'Mark, did you get Edna a Christmas present?'

He looked up, surprised and proud. 'Yes, I did.'

'And was it...was it from that guy Willem's booth?'

He grinned as he poured the gravy from the pot over his
open face turkey sandwich. 'Oh yeah, I couldn't resist it. The
troll I told you I was looking at? And the guy gave me an even
better discount, a really big markdown and all on account
of you, after his booth got closed down for his other stuff. I
almost had to buy it, it would be criminal not to at that price.'

Yeah, that would be the way Willem worked. How was I
to tell Mark he had to get rid of the thing? If I told him the
truth, I'd have to tell him that he'd brought an enchanted
troll into our house. And then I'd have to tell him everything,

all about Willem and Alt, and a million other things which would just blow that all too solid mind of his. How much could he handle?

I bit my lip as I stared at him, then I tried.

'Maybe it's not a good idea to have it in the house,' I began.

'It's safe enough, she won't see it. Edna has her head in the clouds most of the time, you know that.'

'Yes but... Christmas is coming! She'll want to get the decorations down from the attic. She likes to start early, you know.'

Mark chewed his first bite as he thought, then nodded. 'You are so right,' he agreed, pointing his fork at me. 'It's a good thing you thought of that, or the surprise would have been totally ruined.'

'There has to be a more secure hiding place,' I said, pretending to think hard.

'How about one of the front rooms?'

I shook my head.

'Well, the basement then? She never goes down there,' he suggested.

'I don't know...' I needed the creature out of my house or I'd never be able to sleep. 'Maybe you could take it to your office?'

I held my breath as he thought about it, then my whole body relaxed with relief as he nodded.

'That's a good idea,' he said. 'Then I can get it gift-wrapped while I'm at it.'

'Great,' I said. 'That is just such a ... a great idea.'

'Okay, I'll retrieve it from the attic next week.'

'No, do it tonight. Please Mark, it's got to be tonight.'

'Jesus, Dara, what's with you? It's just a stuffed toy,' he said, looking at me closely with his cop senses on alert. 'Isn't it?'

I shrugged, and turned to fiddle with Hugh's books which had by now migrated to the side counter along with the take-out coupons and dead batteries and bills and other stuff no one wanted to deal with.

'What aren't you telling me?'

This was it. This was my chance. I took a deep breath. 'It's creepy. Everything about Willem is creepy. I don't want anything from him in this house.'

Mark was silent for a moment, and I could feel his stare boring into me.

'Has Willem done anything to you?' His words came slowly, and he spoke in a soft, non-threatening manner just like the school counsellor would do when she asked me why I'd been cutting classes in high school.

Besides hauling me into Alt against my will and asking me to be a part of his weird schemes? Besides taunting me with the only hope I had of finding my mother and making me dance to his tune? I couldn't begin to explain all this to Mark.

'I know he seems like a nice guy on the surface, but anyone can be nice,' Mark continued. 'Has he given you reason to be uncomfortable around him?' He led me to the nearest chair and made me sit. As he placed himself across the table, he stared at me with concern under the light from the pendant lamp.

I hesitated.

'Has he come on to you, Dara?' Mark continued in that slow voice.

'No, nothing like that, but...'

'But what?' He waited two long moments for me to speak, then continued. 'The guy is plenty weird, like you say, a grown man pretending to be a sorcerer and playing dress-up. He's a narcissistic wanker, if you ask me.'

I smiled weakly at him, and nodded. 'Yeah, he is that.'

Mark thumped his fists on the old oak table top in frustration. 'That's it! I'm bringing the stupid thing back. I will not support a creep like him.'

'No! Don't do that,' I said, quickly. 'At least not yet.'

He meant well, but that would not be the best action. If the troll was returned, I'd never get my hands on the medallion that whispered of my mother. Willem was a failed sorcerer, kicked out of sorcerer's college, Hugh said. He had some power, sure, enough to get me when my guard was down, and enough to put enchantment in the needle felted creatures he created. But I had power too, even though I'd barely begun to learn how to use it, and I would be careful. I would get that medallion, but returning the troll would only be telling the sorcerer that I knew what he was at.

'Why? Why not yet?'

'Mark, I need something from him,' I confessed. 'I can't tell you what it is, okay, please don't ask. I can't stand the man, but I don't want to alienate him just yet.'

He leaned back in his chair and crossed his arms as he stared back at me for a long moment, weighing something in his mind. 'Don't play games, Dara. He may be crazy enough not to be totally harmless. Don't get caught up with him.'

'I'll be okay,' I said, pretending to be more certain than I felt. I straightened my shoulders and lifted my head to meet him in the eye.

Mark slowly shook his head. 'I don't know about this, Dara. But tell you what - I'll run a report of him when I get back to work, maybe get the RNC to pay him a little visit. Never hurts to let creeps know they're being watched, even if he is harmless.'

'I'd just be happy to have the troll out of the house right now,' I said. 'I just... hate the thought of it in here!'

He nodded slowly. 'Okay, I'll remove it from the house tonight if you feel so strongly,' he said. 'But I get the feeling that you're not telling me the whole story. I don't want to push, but if you ever think you're in danger from this guy, or if you just want to talk, well you know where to find me.'

....

Jack texted me. It was short and to the point.

OK?

I texted him back. *OK.* I added a smiley face then just as quickly removed it, because Jack wasn't really an emoticon kind of person. Neither was I.

There was a smile on my face though, as I remembered that kiss and the solidity of his arms.

But later, laying on my bed still fully dressed and with my bedside light on, I couldn't stop thinking about the medallion, or coin, or whatever it was. My mother had touched it, I knew this, it had whispered her name to me. I closed my eyes the better to remember what had flashed through me when I touched it for that brief moment before Willem snatched it away again.

The second my finger had touched the cold metal, I'd been surrounded by the feeling of Mom, but not the cozy loving mother feeling of my childhood memories, the Marian in the photos of the daisy fields with me at her side. The Mom who gave me hot chocolate on cold winter nights and snuggled in front of the TV with me.

This Mom was angry and dark, someone I didn't want to admit I knew, yet I did. It reminded me of the last days before she left. Memories came through that I had long buried in the mists of time; the quarrels behind closed doors when Dad came to visit, no more Sasha in tow. His pleading voice, hers harsh and unyielding.

Could that be possible? Jonathan de Teilhard, that arrogant full-blood witch who had the world at his feet, pleading with my mother? Over what?

I waited quietly, but nothing else came to me, just that flash, the feeling which lingered and saddened my heart.

Mom had held this medallion shortly before her disappearance, and it had been a black time for her, the leftover emotions still vibrating through the medallion told me that.

I had to get it from Willem.

And he had promised to give it to me if I went along with him - God alone knew what he wanted with me, but it probably wouldn't be pretty.

Willem as a sexual being? Nah. Despite the way Carrie was hanging off him and Zeta devoured him with her eyes, I just couldn't summon up any idea of him as being sexual. He was too cold, too reptilian.

He wanted more than my body, but I also had a strong foreboding that the sorcerer might never give me what I wanted, that it would be a continual carrot on a stick, forever just out of my reach.

Willem was not to be trusted, yet I was going to have to pretend to go along with him in order to be close enough to steal the medallion from him. It would be a delicate dance along a razor's edge, yes, but I was confident.

For I had natural power, even Willem had seen that. I had flown, well, something like it. Hugh had been by my side the first time, but the second time I'd done it all by myself, and in Alt! I'd learned to block my mind from a powerful witch like Hugh without even being told how to do it. And Sasha and I had played magic games when we were little, all those years ago. It had been effortless.

I was the daughter of Jonathon de Teilhard, and I had his magic blood running in my veins. Hugh had insisted I was a powerful witch, hadn't he? I already had the power, Hugh only wanted to teach me the rules.

Look at all those books he left for me, I'd flicked through them and none of them were about magic. Psychology and Algebra, Philosophy and Latin. I would learn his rules, just not right now.

This failed sorcerer would be no match for me. I would enter the lion's den, alone if necessary.

15

So the next evening I went along to the meeting of his ramshackle coven at Zeta's store.

He looked up at me, up from the shadows of the hood pulled over his head and his eyes glittered in the candle light as his small hand beckoned me on.

Carrie and Zeta and the other women looked over too, frowns on their faces as they watched me approach. All the women wore long flowing skirts in brilliant colours like the plumage of birds. I stuck out like a sore thumb in my sweatshirt and jeans, but I didn't care. I had more power in my little finger than the lot of them put together.

'The circle is now complete,' Willem said without introducing me. 'Places everyone, we will begin our evening's work.'

He bade us all to hold hands in order to unite the circle and then started on a low chant, nonsense words or perhaps Latin, I couldn't tell. All the others stood with their eyes closed, the anticipation of ecstasy written on their faces in the wavering light from the candles.

It was hypnotic, sort of, and I admired his style and ability to transform the room in to a space infused with power. I found myself closing my eyes too, and swaying with the women in time to his rhythm as I went along with the ride. As his voice rose and fell, so did my attention as if I was being focused against my will, but without my protest.

And then I could feel it! Willem was there in my mind, reaching out from across the circle, and I felt his presence and his power. The women to either side of us, even though there was no magic between them, their focus also helped and I could feel them too as we all united into this glorious blaze of power, all of us equal, yet not.

Everyone must have felt it, this unification, for we opened our eyes all at the same time in wonder. As Willem let go of the hands he held and brought his own up into the air, so we all broke contact yet the circle remained. We watched as a blue light formed between his raised hands.

He caught my eye and nodded slightly, and I too raised my hands about six inches apart like he did. Without him telling me, I knew what to do, and I stared at my palms and willed the light to appear there.

It did, just a faint blue buzzing at first, but it grew in strength the more I opened myself to the circle and the more I poured myself into it, till finally the ball of energy sat between my hands as if I held a globe of the world in my grasp.

I laughed with delight and that caused my companions to look at me too, and I felt triumph in the jealousy on their faces even as I pulled the power from them. Foolish Normals! Wanna-be witches who would never know the thrill of creating magic like this, but yet they hungered after it and hated me for doing what they knew, deep down inside themselves, that they could not do. I instinctively understood that Willem had whipped them into a frenzy of desire for the sole purpose of unleashing their frustrated emotional energy which they flung around heedlessly; it was this I was drawing from the air with the help of Willem. This blue energy they longed for was their own.

The sorcerer met my eyes over the circle and there was triumph on his face too.

I played with the ball of energy between my hands, exploring the nature of it, fascinated by this outward manifestation of my power and loving how the more jealous the women grew, the more they hungered after this phenomena for themselves, the stronger this ball of light itself grew.

But what could I do with this? I shot a question to Willem with my eyes and saw that he held a flask in his hands. He left the circle to approach me and nodded to the glass beaker in his hand.

I played with the magic a moment longer – it felt like quicksilver, so light and electric in my palms, then reluctantly poured it into the flask. Little bubbles of blue escaped into the air as if it knew it was to be locked away and lose its newfound freedom.

He quickly stuffed a cork in the top while whispering another incantation, and shoved it into the deep pockets of his robe.

After that, it was a bit of a letdown. I was still buzzing with this new magic, but he broke up the circle and started explaining to the women what had happened, or at least his version of the events.

'You see what can happen if you apply yourselves,' he said to the group. 'Dara, although just starting out, she has the necessary purity of heart and desire to please the gods. And through this single-minded devotion, she is graced with the magic.'

'But how can I... we do this?' One of the women broke in and asked him.

'You must continue to study hard,' he said sternly, then turned to snuff out the candles and bring the overhead lights up softly. He continued over his shoulder, 'A new course will be starting next week, and I don't believe you've all signed up for it yet. There are limited spaces available, you understand.'

'But the expense,' one of the women murmured. 'Christmas is coming up, and I don't know if I can spare the money.'

Willem rounded on her coldly. 'If you are not wholly dedicated to the craft, then the craft is not for you. This opportunity will not be offered again, not at this cheap price. You might as well leave now if you're not going to carry through on it with all your heart. I require nothing less than total devotion.'

Like a clutch of hens, they crowded around him, waving their credit cards and elbowing each other in the race to sign up. He pushed them away.

'I told you - I accept only gold, silver if you must, jewels if that is all you have,' he said, brushing aside their plastic cards. 'I have no use for currency which is imaginary. Come back tomorrow morning, leave me now.'

I slipped my jacket on as I laughed silently to myself. They had no idea of the con he was playing on them. I might have felt sorry for them all, but I was too busy gloating in this new found magic of my own.

I pushed through the throng as I approached him and took him by the elbow. 'Do you have something for me?'

He looked up and a small smile began to form on his face. 'Your payment, you mean? Afraid not, dearie, not yet. We've only begun to work together. You haven't earned anything yet.'

My face burned as he openly sneered at me, and I flung away his arm as if scalded. He was playing me for a fool, dangling the medallion on a string just out of my reach. But two could play this game.

One thing I had gotten from the evening was that Willem was right, I didn't need all of those stupid thick books Hugh had asked me to read. And there was no doubt in my mind I could grab that medallion from Willem. I was merely softening him up for the kill, and would pounce when he was least expecting it.

My anger quickly swallowed, I nodded. 'Okay, no problem,' I said as I looked him in the eye. 'I rather enjoyed tonight, and look forward to more.'

I was playing Willem at his own game, and it felt good.

······

Jack and I had agreed to meet for a coffee at the Rocket that same evening. A date, I guess, but a low-key one in this funky little place. The storefront had started life as a hardware store, and it still had the fancy wood cabinets along the walls. It was an old building, with lots of history and magic contained within its three floors.

I looked around the room as I sat. If I wanted, I could cause havoc in this room without lifting a finger, I could blow the minds of all these unsuspecting diners. The energy was still buzzing around inside me despite having poured most of it into the flask, and I was on top of the world.

All these Normals, living their sad pathetic normal lives, they couldn't dream of the other realm all around them. Couldn't even see the ghosts and other supernaturals who hovered in the room – old Mr. McNeil, the owner of the original shop, still in his leather apron as he waited to count out nails to customers who never approached him. The goblin with his smutty face, lurking in the corner as he waited for coins and pastry crumbs to be dropped. Even the woman in Edwardian garb who stood rooted right at the entrance to this room – people passed through her and merely shivered at the sudden draught.

And there was Jack himself, his eyes lit up at the sight of me as he stood in the doorway. He didn't shiver, didn't even look around as he passed through the ghost.

'Hey,' he said as he placed his coffee and change on the table.

'Hey yourself,' I replied. He looked damn good and I couldn't help smiling at him. So solid and... Normal.

Oh dear God. Suddenly I found myself tottering between the horns of the worst dilemma ever. Here I was, still buzzing with magical power, ready to step out into the world and become a real witch, and the guy who made me smile, this great kisser, he was a Normal without even a smidgeon of magical sensibility in his genes. How could this be?

I must be mistaken – perhaps he was hiding something.

'You didn't find it... cold, when you walked in here?' I asked.

Jack looked around in surprise. 'Cold? No, not at all,' he replied. 'You want to go somewhere warmer?'

'No,' I said. 'I'm fine. Just wondered...' I paused as the goblin sidled up to us, his hungry eyes on the coins by Jack's mug. I pretended not to look as he reached through the veil of Alt and tried to grasp the two-dollar coin in his dirty paws, but out of the corner of my eye I saw the toonie inch toward the edge of the table.

I looked at Jack. He wasn't noticing a thing. 'Your money …'

He looked at me uncomprehendingly, then glanced down at his change in time to see the coin teeter off the table edge.

'Wow, my money's running away from me,' he laughed as he scooped it out of the air, right out of the grasp of the frustrated goblin. 'This table must be wobbly.'

Shit. He couldn't even *smell* that filthy green creature who was now cursing him soundly and stamping his unshod foot on the wooden floor.

I was conflicted, and not a little pissed at the unfairness of life. Now, if it had been Hugh sitting with me, he would have side-stepped the ghost at the door, maybe even sent the goblin packing with a scowl from his finely sculptured face.

But Hugh wasn't the one who wanted to kiss me so tenderly. I kicked out with my foot, almost connecting with the creature and it scuttled away back to its corner, screeching.

'Dara, what's up? You seem… different tonight,' Jack said, looking at me closely from across the table. The soft yellow lights of the cafe burnished the auburn highlights in his curls, like a halo of fall colours. His eyes narrowed. 'You high or something? Not that I care, but you might want to share whatever you have.'

There was a tinge of bitterness in my laugh. I was still buzzing so much I was hardly able to sit still in the wooden chair, and I glanced around the room at the people sitting over their steaming drinks and stuffing their faces with pastry. High? I guess I was, at that. Willem had shown me how to unleash the power inside me that night, it was so simple

I was surprised I had never stumbled on it myself. It would have happened sooner or later, for sure.

And Jack was solidly normal.

He was waiting for an answer.

'No,' I told him. 'Haven't smoked anything. I just... oh, I had such an experience tonight.'

Damn – I was itching to share this with someone, but as I met his clear gaze I knew it couldn't be him. Could never be him. Shame, really, for Edna was right, he was a nice guy.

I couldn't even share this with Hugh, for although he would understand about the magic he would deeply disapprove. Those luscious brows of his would draw together in a frown and he would turn all boring with his 'I know better than you' attitude.

'Nothing to do with that guy Willem, was it?' Jack asked this casually as he stirred his coffee.

'What makes you say that?'

He shrugged. 'I followed you in here,' he said. 'You came out of that flakey shop up on Duckworth Street, what is it? House of Magick or some weird thing?'

'What if I did?' I asked, drawing myself up stiffly. 'What's it got to do with you?'

'That guy's got a screw loose, I think,' he continued, then paused before he spoke again. 'You know, Dara, I like you, and I thought we could have something going here. Early stages, I know, maybe I shouldn't be so presumptuous. But if... if you're messing around with the likes of him, well, why don't you just admit it?'

I stared at him, the hostility gathering in my voice. 'What, like you think I'm screwing him or something?'

He stilled his hand, his gaze meeting me full on and something gave a little twinge inside me. 'Are you?'

'No,' I said, half turning away in my seat. Oh I would be fucking with that sorcerer all right, but not in the way Jack meant. Willem was messing with me, dangling the goddamn medallion over my head like he was trifling with a cat, but he needed to be careful, for this cat had claws and I intended to use them.

But I couldn't tell Jack that.

'Listen,' I said, turning back to him as I fixed a smile on my face. 'Sorry for jumping down your throat like that. But I promise you, I am not thinking of sleeping with that guy. Gross! How could you even think that?'

Finally he relaxed and smiled back at me, and gave a one-shoulder shrug. 'I've been burned before, you know,' he said. 'And I never want that to happen again.'

I let the smile linger on my face, and nodded, brushing aside the nagging of guilt I felt deep inside. No matter. I would get what I wanted from Willem, and then Jack and I could figure out a relationship. No problem.

I knew I could take on Willem in a battle of wits to get my hands on that medallion, but it came to me that there was another, easier way.

There was always Alice, I could get my friend on my side. Two powers were always better than one.

Alice Hoskins, my best friend from grade school, Alice had elf-blood in her. It had been diluted over the years, but somehow her great-grandmother's genes had produced it in her. She was fast, super-smart, tall and skinny with long hair that was colorlessly blonde. She even had the pointy ears that screamed 'elf', for God's sake, as if further proof was needed.

But Alice was in complete denial over her gifts, wasn't interested in finding out what her powers might be. She'd immersed herself into the world of science as if looking for proof that all this supernatural stuff was just a lie, and she still blamed me for last September, never mind that I'd only been trying to save her brother from the Southside Hills fairies in the beginning, and things had ballooned from there.

She refused to believe in the supernatural, but I knew how to get her on board.

16

My phone buzzed in the middle of Folklore class, and it was a welcome distraction. I'd been listening to the prof with only half an ear, the rest of my attention worrying between the stupid paper I had yet to write and the larger, more compelling problem of Willem.

Hugh. He wanted to see me, offering to pick me up after class. I glanced outside to the early afternoon dreariness where it was pissing out rain again, so I welcomed the relief of getting a ride instead of having to wait for the bus in the cold and wet. I texted him the details of where and when to pick me up. If I played my cards right he might even buy me a bite to eat.

Squashed into the crowded steamy entrance of the Arts Building with all the other soggy undergrads who were waiting for their parents to pick them up, I couldn't help but feel superior to them all. Normals, all of them, not a magic drop in their veins, nothing to lift them out of the rat race they had been consigned to by their unfortunate births.

Study hard, work harder, and they might sometime be awarded with a mortgage for an overpriced home in a suburb of sameness where they could have their 2.5 children and slave until their underfunded pensions gave them an illusion of freedom. They were here waiting for their parents' mini-vans or Corollas; they could only dream about the glamour of being picked up in the Batmobile. Like me.

I wished it was brighter outside so they could see the full glory of the exotic beast driven by Hugh, the blackest of black low slung European sports car. They would know that Dara (de Teilhard) Martin was an important person.

The phone buzzed again. Hugh.

I'm here.

I don't see you?

Honda Civic. Red one.

WHERE'S THE BATMOBILE???

There was a pause before he replied.

Just come out would you?

'Where'd you get this boring old car?' I slammed the car door behind me as I slumped onto the cloth seat.

'The Batmobile, as you call it, belongs to your father,' he said. 'He put it in storage for the winter. This is my rental, what's wrong with it?'

I shrugged into the seat belt. It was too tight so I tugged it hard and heard the snap as it latched into place.

'How're your readings going?' he asked.

'Oh, you know...'

'You haven't touched them, have you? I bet they're still on your kitchen counter.' He pulled out of the parking lane, the wipers at full speed.

'I have looked at them! They're all words though, no pictures or diagrams. Not even any spells in them,' I said, turning to look out at the rain drizzling down the glass. 'Jeez, it's just been so busy lately.'

He waited, indicator light flashing to indicate his left turn onto the busy road.

'I have to go to Paris,' he said.

'Have to? What a drag that must be. I'd hate to have your life.'

He smiled without looking at me. 'Work calls.'

'What do you do, anyway?'

'I told you before,' he said. 'I work with the EUROs, sort of an Interpol, an international policing for the Witch Kin. Any more than that, I can't explain.'

'Can't or won't?'

'Legally prohibited,' he said. 'I've signed a non-disclosure agreement.'

I thought for a moment. 'I'd like to do something like that, after I graduate all this, and after I finish up in Scotland. I'd love to travel and be right in the heart of things like that.'

'It's not that easy,' he said. 'You'd have to apply yourself a lot harder than you're doing presently.'

'You said I have natural ability,' I reminded him.

He gave a cynical laugh as he shot out into a break in traffic. 'Ability doesn't count for much unless you know how to apply it,' he retorted. 'And you seem to be having difficulty with the old nose to the grindstone part.'

'So,' I said, just a little annoyed. 'You wanted to speak with me?'

'Mmm,' he said.

'Maybe over a little late lunch?'

'We can do that,' he agreed. 'Have any place in mind?'

'Smitty's,' I said decisively. 'A late, late breakfast is actually what I need for today.' Breakfast at two in the afternoon was a rare treat. As the car splashed down the hill and through a puddle, the idea of greasy sausages and hash browns and toast with red jam was now firmly in my mind and my stomach didn't want to let it go. Raspberry, preferably, but strawberry jam would do.

The pots of tea were strong with endless refills, and we were in my favorite booth overlooking the Square. I hung my wet coat on the hook at the side and settled back with a smile. Hugh did the same with his leather jacket, then rolled back the sleeves of his white shirt, showing wrists which were wiry but strong, like a pianist's, and his fingers were long and sensitive.

I liked that everyone in the Square could look in and see me with him.

'So what did you want to speak to me about?' I asked, drawing in the warmth from the mug with both hands. The overhanging light between us cast a dome of intimacy, the soft yellow light contrasting with the gloomy greyness outside.

'Just thought I'd touch base with you,' he replied. He leaned forward, with one hand on his chin and his thoughtful gaze on me. The white of his shirt brought out the touch of gold in those eyes which saw everything. I mentally tucked away anything I didn't want him to know, for this witch could read my mind effortlessly, hear every thought I broadcast through my head if I wasn't careful. 'How're things?'

'Y'know,' I shrugged, sliding my eyes away from his. 'I still have that paper to write, exams coming up.'

'And your math course – you keeping up on that?'

'Yes, Hugh.' I caught my eyes beginning to roll, and brought them to attention to match the smile I pasted on my face.

'There's something bothering you though,' he said, cutting through all my facial contortions. 'What is it?'

There was no way I was going to tell him about the medallion that whispered my mother's name. I don't know why, but I had the feeling he would immediately ban me from further exploration of this without telling me why. I hated how he treated me like a kid sister sometimes; we'd only known each other a couple of months, and he really had no right to do that.

And there was no way I was going to tell him what I had experienced the other night. No frigging way at all.

'Willem,' I said, having made a decision. 'That guy is creepy.'

He raised an eyebrow as he sipped his tea. 'You're finished with the craft fair, are you not?'

I nodded.

'Then why is he bothering you? Surely you're not still in contact with him?'

'It's not just him,' I told Hugh. 'Mark, Edna's boyfriend, he went and bought one of his trolls to give her for Christmas.'

Hugh didn't move a muscle but I could feel his interest sharpen. 'I heard about those creatures. And?'

I told him about my feelings of discomfort and dread which had culminated in my trip to the attic and the discovery of the parcel by the Christmas decorations. About how it rattled and moved as if trying to free itself, and how I could feel it trying to draw me in.

'So there's something weird going on with that guy,' I finished. 'And he gave Mark a big discount when he found out his connection to me. Practically gave it to him, after his booth was closed down.'

'It's out of the house now?'

'Yeah, Mark took it out that same night.'

'Good,' Hugh said. 'Trust your senses. And stay away from Willem, don't have anything to do with him.'

'Mmm,' I said, nodding to show that I was on board with him.

He sat up straight in the booth, his height towering over me even when we sat. The lamp glowed around his dark hair like a halo and his eyes were shaded.

'Dara! I mean it,' he said, the soft Scottish accent hardening with force of his feeling. 'Will you not listen to my advice for once? I'm not trying to control you, this is for your own benefit. You have not got the skills to be messing around with Willem. And what are you looking to get out of it?'

I could tell him about the medallion now, I could pass it all on to him and he would take care of it, I knew, but that's not what I wanted. He would just forbid me to get involved. I sat tall in the booth too, as tall as I could and drew my shoulders back. This was my journey, my business, my mother. Not his. Hugh would never understand. He could stick his arrogant ways up where the sun didn't shine.

'Don't be so bossy all the time. Stop telling me what to do!' My words didn't nearly convey my feelings and I hated how I sounded like an undignified toddler, stamping her foot on the floor and refusing to eat her vegetables. I hated how Hugh had this effect on me.

'I will tell you what to do,' he shot back. 'Because you're obviously bent on doing the absolute wrong thing. How are we going to work together if you won't listen? Why are we bothering, if you're just going to embarrass me every step of the way? I refuse to waste my time if you're not one hundred percent dedicated to this venture.'

His fist slammed on the table just as the waiter came up to us with our food. The young guy bravely looked at Hugh, then me.

'Everything okay here, miss?'

I sat back, stunned, then collected myself enough to nod at him. 'We're good,' I said in a small voice.

When the food was steaming in front of us, I reached for the ketchup and started to shake it over my potatoes. Hugh's outburst and physical display didn't bother me. It was the meaning behind the words which had floored me.

'We'll be working together?' I asked him, trying to get my head around it. 'What? How?'

He sat back with a deep sigh. 'That's really what I wanted to discuss with you today,' he said. 'I'm to be your tutor when you go north in the New Year.'

Those fine lips turned down at the corners as he gazed at the darkening skies outside the window, as if he was not relishing the prospect.

My heart, however, let out a little bubble of delight. Yes, Hugh was bossy, but he was familiar. I'd never been anywhere but my home at the edge of the ocean, never even been off this island before. Never been anywhere where I wasn't known as Dara Martin, bastard child of Jonathan de Teilhard.

The one thing I hadn't been looking forward to with leaving the country was the fear of the unknown – going to a strange land with unknown faces, where nobody knew me. It actually terrified me, but I'd been squashing that fear deep down inside me and telling myself I'd be okay.

'Wow,' I said, trying to sort out all the questions which were jumping into my head. 'But... but what about your job?'

'I'll still be working,' he replied with a sigh. 'But closer to home, to keep an eye on your studies.'

'That's great news,' I said. And I really meant it.

He looked at me with narrowed eyes. 'Is it?'

Then he took his focus away from me and used his fork to pick at the food on his plate without eating anything.

'Yeah, for me it is,' I said. 'Sorry if it doesn't thrill you.'

He sighed again, and let the fork fall with a clatter against the plate.

'Look,' he said. 'The only way it's going to work is if you really want to be there. And by that I mean you have to be prepared to work hard and apply some discipline. I have no desire to fight with you in order to force you to learn. If I see that you're not focused, I'll advise for you to be failed out and sent back home. You're an adult, and I'm going to treat you as one. I'm not going to stand for your tantrums.'

I was left with my hand in midair and my mouth wide open. I quickly shut it and looked down at my plate.

'Got it,' I said shortly, my face burning with embarrassment by now. I let my hair fall around to hide it. My late, late breakfast was quickly congealing on the plate and the milky tea left a ring around the mug. I really wasn't hungry anymore. 'Loud and clear.'

The silence between us was growing awkward, as it does when someone unexpectedly gets something off their chest, holding up a mirror and forcing the other to see herself through his eyes. It hurt, like the sharp clarity of fresh air on exposed nerves.

So it wasn't just me who hated when I whined like a child.

'Why were you asking about Willem?'

'This girl I know, Carrie,' I said quickly. There was no way I'd tell him about the medallion now, for sure. And I silently made the promise I wouldn't hold anything else back from Hugh, never, after I got my hands on that medallion. 'I'm worried about her.'

'That the silly rich girl who fancies herself a Rastafarian?'

'Yeah,' I said. 'The thing is, she's glommed on to Willem like nobody's business, and it's not natural. She's all over him like some kind of groupie.'

'Stay out of it.'

'But really, he's not her type. She goes for the flashy guys, the musicians and the artists...'

'It's none of your business.'

'But...'

'Why don't you consider that I am already your tutor?' Hugh's voice was dangerously patient, his eyes daring me to disagree. 'As of this moment forward, that is how we will act. Two adults. One respected teacher, and one student striving to show her maturity and to prove she is an appropriate choice for the opportunity she has been given.'

I bit my lip to stop the outburst which had already formed on my tongue.

'This will give me an opportunity to see how much you really want this education,' he continued. 'Before we go to the expense of shipping you out to Scotland. If it doesn't work out, well then, we will have saved everyone some bother, don't you agree?'

His stare was burning into the top of my head and I nodded, still hidden behind my veil of hair. This was all so grossly unfair.

'Good.' He hailed the waiter. 'I think we're done here.'

'But Hugh...'

'Yes?'

I wanted to plead with him for reassurance. I really wasn't so awful, was I? I was trying to do good, I wasn't evil or creepy like Willem. I just wished Hugh didn't see me as an arrogant little snot.

And he might not, if I told him everything.

'Forget it,' I said. I stood up and shrugged on my jacket.

17

The minute Hugh's boring red car left our driveway, I got on my bike to head down to Alice's house on Southside Road. I knew she would be home at this hour because this was the one day of the week she didn't have classes or labs, and she would be spending the whole day in her pj's doing catch-up chores like laundry and lab reports.

I needed to get Alice on board since Hugh wasn't going to be of any help to me, and while I was coasting down the hill, my mind worked fast.

How could Alice help me?

She could pretend she wanted to join the coven; Willem would eat that up. All she had to do was open those big grey eyes of hers and act as if she was latching on to every word he spoke. He would be a goner, for no man could resist her. It was strange how my friend had no idea of the effect she had on the opposite sex or how frigging gorgeous she was - Alice firmly believed she was unattractive and that this was the reason she didn't have a boyfriend. The reality of the matter was that her beauty and strong intelligence intimidated any guy who dared approach and they were too tongue-tied to say anything halfway intriguing enough to catch her interest. Alice saw only what she wanted to see in her personal life, which was a weird characteristic for a scientist.

I threw my bike down in her driveway and banged on the back door before bursting through it. Like most homes, the front entrance was reserved for strangers to the home, ones who acknowledged they needed formal permission to approach. For a long-time friend like myself, it would be considered rude not to just walk right in the back, as if I thought myself above them all and on a different social level.

The whole family was seated round the kitchen table when I opened the mud room door. Mr. Hoskins with a beer in hand, priming himself for an evening at his local bar; Mrs. H still in her drugstore uniform, the shadows under her eyes showing the burden of being the breadwinner of the home; Sal, Alice's younger sister; Benjy her skeety older brother, and Alice herself, dressed in her fuzzy pj's as I had predicted. No one said a word to me, but that was just their way. I didn't greet any of them either.

'Alice I need to talk with you,' I said. But I couldn't do it here in the kitchen, not with the whole clan listening in, and I still hated to go in the parlor which was the domain of her dead great-grandmother's ghost.

'What?' She was pouring canned milk into a mug of tea.

'Can you come outside?'

'It's raining out there,' she told me with dismay. 'You're all wet.'

Her persnickety fear of getting mussed and uncomfortable in the elements was just another evidence in favour of her elf blood, but she would never admit it.

'We'll just go across the road,' I said. 'Come on!'

She sighed and threw her winter parka over herself like a hooded cloak, then shoved the nearest pair of rubber boots on her feet. I could hear her shuffling behind me and slurping her tea as we made our way across the road to stand under the overpass. Cars whizzed overhead, their tires splashing in the rain, but we were so used to the sound over the years that we no longer heard it.

Once she was firmly ensconced with her back against the concrete pillar, Alice looked at me warily as she continued to drink her tea.

'What is it this time?'

'I need your help,' I said.

'Right,' she replied. 'The last time you asked for help your sister almost killed me.'

'That's not really fair,' I said, stung. I faced her with my hands on my hips. 'It was her boyfriend who abducted you. And if you remember, I was trying to get Benjy away from the fairies? And Nan Hoskins was terrorizing your family?'

Alice shrugged off any mention of the supernatural as her personal force field only allowed in scientifically proven facts and anything outside of her narrow ken bounced off that bubble as if it didn't exist. She was funny like that, even if she did acknowledge her dead great-grandmother's ghost.

'Speaking of which,' I continued less vehemently. 'How is Nan Hoskins?'

'Quieter these days,' she said. 'Except we all have to watch Coronation Street or she kicks up a ruckus.'

'I thought she hated the TV,' I said.

'Go figure.'

We had a moment of silence in respect for the unaccountable ways of the family's matriarch, dead though she was.

'So...,' I began.

'Before you start, I'm letting you know that I'm not getting involved in any of your weirdness again, okay?'

'Nothing supernatural, I promise you,' I said, holding my hands up as if to show I was unarmed. At least, she wouldn't have to get involved in magic, I would handle all that side of things. 'It's just, this guy has something I have to have. He's not going to give it to me, so I have to pretend to go along. And I want you to come and distract him while I take it from him.'

'Steal from him?'

'Not really,' I said. 'What he has, it sort of belongs to me. It... I think it used to be my mother's.'

'What is it?'

'A medallion, or coin or something.'

'How do you know it was your Mom's?'

'It's magically charged. I can hear her voice when I touch it.'

'For frig's sake, Dara!' She dashed the dregs of her tea to the ground and turned to go back home.

'I'm not asking you to get involved with the magic part of it,' I said in a rush as I grabbed the sleeve of her parka to stop her from leaving.

'Who is this guy then?'

'He's a sorcerer, but don't let that bother you,' I said. 'He's not very powerful, he just thinks he is. He flunked sorcerer's college! I know you can do this, all you have to do is pretend to be fascinated by him, he'll be candy in your hand. And that'll give me time to get the medallion from him.'

'No magic or shit?'

'Nah, there'll be nothing,' I said, hoping it was true. 'Just a bunch of people pretending they're witches. Pathetic weirdos, really.'

I waited a moment to let her think this through.

'You have to help me, Alice,' I urged. 'I don't have anyone else.'

'When?'

'Tomorrow evening, just over on the west end of Duckworth Street,' I said, relaxing now. 'We can ride our bikes over.'

I hugged her through the thickness of her parka and she slipped away from my clutch like a scalded cat. Alice really was the best friend ever.

18

The kitchen windows were all steamy from the boiling pasta, and the smell of Mark's Bolognese sauce hit me like a solid wall when I let myself into the house. I was ravenous.

'You got garlic toast coming with that?' I shrugged my jacket off and slipped it over the back of the chair and sat down.

'Maybe even with cheese grilled over it,' Mark said as he looked up from the stove, then he shook the wooden spoon at me. 'But only if you hang that coat up where it belongs.'

I groaned but stood up again, retracing my steps to the back porch with its hooks overflowing with a rainbow of raincoats, scarves and other outerwear. All the mess belonged to me and Edna. Mark's coats were neatly hung up in the hall closet on hangers, even his cardigans were there.

Having Mark move in with us permanently was a good move, it really was, especially at meal times on cold wet nights like this. But the price of eating so well was having to put up with his little quirks. He insisted on tidiness and order, it was worse than being in the army, and sometimes I missed the comfortable dishevelment that me and my aunt had lived in for the past ten years.

'You wallowed in that mess,' Mark had pointed out when I said that to him once. 'Like pigs in a sty.' And give him his due, he gritted his teeth and let us have our untidy corners like the end counter. It was a compromise eased by his skills in the kitchen.

Over the radio news, I heard the sound of heavy boxes being shoved around in the hallway. I jerked my head towards the source. 'What's she at now?'

'Christmas,' he said. 'Early decorating. Good thing you warned me about that, otherwise she would have found the troll.'

He raised his voice so Edna would hear. 'Leave that, I'll move all the boxes, Ed. Supper's almost ready.'

Mark opened the oven door and withdrew the garlic bread with the cheese perfectly browned and bubbly and crisply, just the way he knew I loved it. While he drained the pasta, I wandered over and tasted the sauce from the spoon.

'Oh my God,' I said, after it had filled my mouth with its spice and tomatoey goodness. 'Edna! Come eat! I'm not waiting for you.'

She appeared in the doorway, her eyes alight and a smudge of attic dust on her cheek. 'This is going to be the best Christmas ever,' she said. 'You'll never guess what I found, Dara! The old stockings, the ones we haven't seen for years.'

'Not... the velvet patchwork ones?'

'Yes! They were tucked away in a box with your old baby clothes,' she said. 'God knows how they got there.' She shrugged and moved to the cutlery drawer, counting out spoons and forks and a knife for me because I preferred to cut my long spaghetti strands into manageable pieces.

These Christmas stockings were very special. They held more than the memory of candies, chocolate oranges and joke presents over the years – they held the essence of Mom and our lives before she disappeared, and I'd thought them lost forever. She had made the four stockings from scraps of velvet taken from old clothes and drapes, silks and satins and embroidery thread, hand-pieced together with love.

'I have to see them!'

'In the box right there around the corner,' Edna said as she took her seat. 'Don't get tomato sauce on them.'

The spaghetti was totally forgotten by now as I brought the carton back into the kitchen with me. Four brightly hued stockings lay inside, each with a name picked out in gold thread along the top. Dara. Edna. Marian.

And Jon. The one stocking that was still pristine, never having hung by the old fireplace in the parlour, the loved one who had never joined our Christmas Day celebrations. I left that one behind in the box.

'Oh my God, they're just like I remembered them,' I whispered, laying them reverently on the only available clean counter space. I stroked Mom's with especial love and care, and my fingers tingled as if with magic as they touched the velvet and silk. The stockings were full of Christmases past, the warmth of those celebrations like echoes in the cloth. 'Thanks, Edna.'

'Come eat now,' Mark said softly and he laid my plate down in my setting.

I didn't take my eyes off them all during supper, the rainbow glows filling my eyes so I could see little else.

It would be a good Christmas, Edna was right.

19

I loaded up the new dishwasher, the one Edna had predicted would show up soon enough. It hadn't taken Mark long to get one installed, he even did the plumbing himself. Edna and I cleaned up after the meal, except for the stove top which Mark looked after because somehow we always forgot about that bit. And when we'd all finished, the kitchen sparkled, most of it. It wasn't what we were used to, but I realized I liked it - tidiness and order were becoming our new norm.

I poured the hot water into the teapot and the radio news took up the space in the lull of conversation as we waited for the tea to steep. The announcer spoke of a rash of home invasions in the city, not much taken except money and Christmas presents.

'How absolutely mean is that?' Edna said as she brought out a multi-pack of assorted squares, the little cake bars made by every traditional bakery and sweet shop. She laid them on the table and opened the plastic top. I quickly grabbed a Nanaimo bar, my favourite.

'Yeah, what grinches – imagine stealing gifts from under the trees,' I agreed, then bit into the chocolate and cream. Edna took a date square and a carrot cake, one for each hand.

'There's a lot of badness out there,' Mark said as he belatedly handed out three small side plates to catch our crumbs. 'This time of the year, some people get to feeling like they don't have enough compared to others, and they take it upon themselves to redistribute the wealth. You've got the organized thieves like this, and then there's the ones who grab the Salvation Army buckets and run. Sometimes it seems like everyone's out to steal from everyone else.'

My mind wandered back to Willem and his coven of women. They were giving him their money, pressing it on him even, but he was still a trickster who played on deception and their deep desires. No better than the lowlifes Mark dealt with every day in his job as a cop.

What did that make me? I brushed the thought aside. I was only going along with Willem in order to get back what was mine, not really playing a part in his con game. I wasn't gaining money from his work.

My guilty thoughts were interrupted by a cold draft behind me as the inner back door creaked open. We all looked up.

Hugh. He stood framed in the light from the kitchen, his black leather jacket glistening with damp and a long Dr. Who style scarf about his neck. His dark hair was tousled from the wind and from never being brushed, and he had a strange expression on his face.

'Sorry for barging on in,' he said as he hesitated at the doorway. 'I did ring the bell.'

'The doorbell doesn't work when it's wet out,' Edna said with a smile. 'Been like that for years. Come on in and have a cup of tea.'

Our eyes met briefly. He gave a quick smile. I could have sworn there was a note of apology there on his handsome face, but maybe it was a trick of the light.

'Doesn't work when it's raining?' Mark said, looking appalled. 'Edna, did it never strike you that might be dangerous? It means there's water getting into the electrical system.'

'Yeah, you might want to check into that, Mark,' I said with a grin, light-hearted again because I hated when Hugh and I quarrelled. I moved my chair so he could pull up a spare to the table. He took off his jacket and slung it over the back. Mark didn't say a thing, just rolled his eyes at us all.

'So we're starting the decorating tonight,' Edna said.

Hugh's eyebrows rose a notch. 'This early? It's hardly...'
'Edna likes Christmas,' I interrupted him. 'It's important.'

'First of all, I want to hang those stockings,' she said. 'Just like we used to do over the fireplace. Mark – we're going to need another one for you.'

'Not in the parlour?' Mark had a look of alarm on his face. 'I need to plaster in there. It's not fit for habitation yet.'

'Is that really necessary?' Edna screwed up her mouth and she set the stockings back down on the counter. 'Why not just throw a bit of paint on the walls if you feel so strongly about fixing up the room?'

'Because that's not how it's done,' Mark said, standing up. 'It doesn't make sense to do half a job. I have to fill in the holes and cracks in the walls before I paint, otherwise...' He followed her out to the hallway, the two of them complaining about the other in a companionable way.

Hugh and I smiled at each other.

'They're lovely,' he said, nodding his head at the patch-work creations.

'My Mom made them,' I said, reaching over to take them in my hands. 'They've just resurfaced after years of being lost.'

'Your mother...' he said softly. Hugh was aware I was Jon de Teilhard's bastard daughter, knew about my half blood. Being a cohort of my Dad's, he stayed with Jon and Cate when he was in town in their huge mansion on New Cove Road, so he probably also knew how Cate felt about me and my Mom too, I guess. And about how Mom just disappeared so suddenly one day.

There was a look of sympathy in his eyes which I couldn't bear, not right then, not with Edna and Mark cheerful-ly squabbling in the next room and my belly full in the warmth of the kitchen. Not with the sudden appearance of the beloved stockings from a time when we were all happy.

'She's not dead, you know,' I blurted out, unshed tears making my voice rough. 'Everyone acts as though she is, but she can't be.'

He said nothing.

'She just went away,' I continued. 'She'll come back.'

'Do you remember then, around the time she left?'

I was quiet for a moment. 'Yeah, I do, a bit. It was in the late summer. Mom and Jon had been arguing a lot, every time he came over.'

Hugh was totally silent.

'It was chilly and damp that August,' I said. 'Everything was still green. I was up in my room one evening, trying to get away from the yelling. Edna wasn't home.'

I pictured it again in my head, huddled under my old quilts while my parents fought. The house had been cold, of course, despite it being summer. Sometimes the old radiators couldn't quite bring the hot water all the way upstairs. My parents had been below me in the parlour with the French doors that led out to the walled private garden. We still regularly used that part of the house back then.

His raised voice had rung through the floorboards, despite the solidity of the house's construction.

'You cannot mess with this stuff,' he roared. 'You know nothing of it. You'll put yourself in danger!'

There had been more back and forth between them, then the sound of his boots stomping out the front door. That may have been the last time he'd seen her and the last time that front door had been used. I'd had no idea of the events that would pass, and even if I had foreknowledge, how could I at ten years old have stopped them?

Those stockings hadn't hung by the fireplace ever again. Edna and I hadn't celebrated Christmas that year as we waited for Mom to return.

I gathered myself together and turned away so he wouldn't see me wipe the tear from my cheek. 'Sorry,' I said to him. 'Got lost there for a moment.'

He shook his head as if to say no worries.

'So, you came back here?' I reminded him.

He gave a start. 'Yes,' he replied slowly, leaning back in his wooden chair with his long legs stretched before him. 'I had to come back. I felt … I felt we parted on the wrong note this afternoon, and for that, I want to apologize.'

'Yeah,' I said. 'Well, thanks, I guess.'

Hugh stood up and took my hand. 'Let's go for a drive,' he said. 'I'm not finished yet, and it's hard to think here.'

The bickering between my aunt and her boyfriend had quickly turned to loud laughter and they'd started up the old record player, the one from the sixties. It was attached to an ancient cabinet that held a black and white TV that would still work except that technology had left it behind long ago and there were no longer any signals for it to pick up from the stratosphere. But the turntable gave off its true sound still, and the Beatles had joined Edna and Mark.

'Oh God, yes,' I said, letting his warm hand haul me up. 'They're going to break out the Glenfiddich soon and start dancing. Let's get out of here.'

20

We didn't go to a coffee shop or a bar. Instead, Hugh drove through the wet downtown streets and headed up to the top of Signal Hill, to the stone tower that overlooked and defined the city. He had taught me to fly there last September, or at least how to project my mind through space so I was like a bird flying overhead, able to look down upon the streets.

There was not much to see from this vantage point today and ours was the only car in the lot. He parked so that we faced the city, our backs to the big invisible ocean going on for thousands of kilometers with nothing but water between us and Ireland. The fog pressed in on the city from every direction as if this was all there was to the world, no east end or west end, even the university was shrouded so that all we could see was just this small island of humanity far below us, the vehicles bustling down the puddled roads, the streetlights weakly glimmering.

Hugh still said nothing, just stared straight ahead in that pensive manner of his. The wind was wickedly forceful up here, rocking the car and whistling through the vents. I waited for him to speak. He never did anything without a reason, and I was pretty sure he hadn't driven up here just to look at the fog.

But the tension got to me at last, and I couldn't hold back.

'So what?' I asked him. 'What is it? You want to say something, just say it.' I sat back in my seat and folded my arms.

'I'm going to Paris tomorrow, as I told you,' he said. 'But I feel it's important to give you some advice before I leave.'

I huddled into my jacket and brought Mom's blue scarf closer around my neck, for he'd turned off the engine and the car was quickly growing cold.

'First of all, I want to remind you that I require complete honesty from you, if we're to embark on your education,' he said slowly. 'It won't be an easy thing.'

'No problem,' I said, crossing only two fingers. 'I promise you, when we're over there, I won't... lie to you about anything, if that's what you mean.' I didn't really see what he was getting at.

'And also,' he continued as if I hadn't spoken. 'The first thing you need to know about witch craft, true power, is that a witch should have no ego when practicing magic.' He stopped and turned his head to look directly into my eyes.

'Ego,' I said. 'Lose the ego. Got it.'

He let out a deep sigh. 'I don't think you do get it, not really. This is why I left you the Psychology text book, so that you can read it and garner an understanding of things we'll be exploring up in Scotland. In fact, I gave you *all* those books for a very good reason. You need to have at least read them before you go, even if you don't understand them.'

'It's a pretty thick book,' I objected. 'They're *all* really big, no illustrations or pictures or anything. Hugh, I just want to learn how to do magic, I don't need all that other stuff.'

He shook his head. 'I do have serious doubts as to the viability of this plan.'

'It was your idea to begin with,' I retorted. 'Dad just wanted me to leave the city and get out of his hair. It was you who suggested Scotland, for me to learn how to develop my power.'

'Yes, your power.'

'And you said yourself, I have strong magic,' I continued in a rush, seeing my dreams about to go down the drain. He couldn't take this away from me, not now that I knew the magic school was out there and available for a half-witch like myself, that I could be trained to use the power I'd always known I had, even if I'd been taught to shove it away deep inside of me for many years. He couldn't do this to me.

'I may be behind all the students there, but I'll more than make up for the lost time. Remember how quickly I've picked up on everything you've taught?'

He nodded. 'I don't disagree with you, but that is precisely what bothers me,' he said slowly.

'I'm good, I'm powerful! I want to work with you, Hugh, please don't do this to me.'

'Yes, it is best for you to be trained,' he said. 'The alternative would be... awful, I'm afraid. Now that your power has reawakened.' He wasn't looking at me while he spoke now. Instead, he gazed at the blurry city lights below.

A cold chill went up my spine. 'What alternative? Hugh, what the frig are you talking about?'

'One of the elders... has concerns,' he said.

'Elders? In Scotland, you mean?' I asked. 'What concerns? They don't even know me.'

He nodded slowly, then turned his head toward me.

'They know enough. They all agree that you need the training, that really, it has to be done,' he said. 'However, there is some question as to your attitude. It is felt, by this particular elder, that you are too arrogant, that you have not developed the necessary respect for your craft.'

It was my turn to be silent. Was I being judged before they had even met me?

'News of the fairy incident has reached the wrong ears,' he said, then gave an uncharacteristic shrug. 'And the dwarves.'

'Enough, Hugh!' I found myself shouting. 'Stop throwing out all these hints, and just give it to me straight. I've screwed up, yes, but that's why I'm going away - to learn how to do magic properly, with all the basic foundational work and everything, so I won't make the sort of stupid mistakes which, I might add, only came about because I hadn't been taught properly.'

'Come outside,' he muttered and opened his door. I had no choice but to follow him.

The wind had blown away all the cloud cover up there on the high ground, yet the fog remained like a blanket in the shelter of the harbour and downtown at our feet. It was like we were on an island, a single tiny continent consisting of me, Hugh and the tower. We hunched against the wind and walked towards it, our path lit only by a single light pole at its base.

When we had reached the other side of the stone building, he paused and took my shoulders in his hands. He took a breath to speak but the foghorn sounded below, across the harbour at Fort Amherst, its loud mournful cry like a dirge.

'I'm only going to say this once, then we walk back to the car,' he said when it had finished, in a voice only loud enough for me to hear. 'The alternative I spoke about, if you don't get up to speed, is that your magic will be bound. Irrevocably. It is an unpleasant process for both the binder and the bound. The closest thing I can liken it to is a lobotomy of your magical soul. Don't ask me questions about this, and let's pretend I have not spoken these words. Got it?'

Although my front remained warm, protected as it was by Hugh's body, the wind was slicing through the back of my jacket like a butcher's cleaver through butter. I could scarcely believe what he said.

They had a process for this? It sounded like the worst kind of punishment, and I told him so.

'No, Dara,' he said as he looked at me, puzzled. 'Not punishment, not at all. This is a safety measure for the good of all, including the person whose magic is to be bound. If they're considered to be not able to handle their power, then their power has to be deactivated. That's all.'

He turned to go, but spoke again. 'I really don't want to see that happen to you.'

We drove down the hill in silence, Hugh's words still looming between us. I was speechless. Magic binding - how could such a thing be done? To even speak of removing my magical powers, so cold and merciless like... like shooting a pet dog who had bitten once, on the off chance that it might bite again.

When he finally drove up to the back door of my house, I turned to him before getting out, waiting for him to tell me it wouldn't happen, that this could never happen to me.

'So, this is it? You're going tomorrow?'

Hugh nodded.

'Okay,' I said. I opened the passenger door.

'Just...' he said.

I turned back to him quickly, hungry for reassurance.

'The arrogance, Dara,' he whispered. 'Lose the arrogance. You'll be fine.'

21

I slammed the door of the cheap rental car behind me, shaken to my very core. Arrogance, indeed. How dare he. What a nerve he had.

Who was he to talk of arrogance? The witches were the most arrogant people I'd ever met. Dad, Sasha, Cate... even Hugh himself. They were all overbearingly confident, looking down their noses at my half-blood and Normals as if they owned the world.

And I too, was powerful, despite not being a full witch. This wasn't arrogance, I was just finally acknowledging my own power. And they could never take this away from me. I would fight to the death before I allowed that to happen.

I slammed the back door behind me too even though Hugh was long gone by then. The house was quiet. The lights of the parlour were still burning down the hallway, Edna and Mark deep into the pre-Christmas cheer no doubt. I stomped up the back staircase to let them know I'd returned, then stomped back down again to grab Hugh's stupid text books so I could at least pretend to be working my way through them. He'd probably go behind my back and check with Edna.

Psychology, Algebra, Religions of the world... even Philosophy 101. Arms laden down by the books, I nudged open my door. What did all these have to do with real magic? I could feel the power flowing through me, and there was nothing that smacked of the mystical in this pile of books. I didn't need this nonsense.

I tossed them in a heap on my bed and clicked my fingers. The bedside lamp turned on and I smiled, for I'd taught myself that trick, no help needed from Hugh for that simple feat.

Maybe I didn't even need him and his stupid, judgemental elders. I was doing pretty okay by myself.

··········

I was still majorly pissed off at Hugh the next morning so I didn't bother going to classes. Instead, I gathered my papers and laptop and hiked downtown to hang out at a coffee bar and work on the Lord of Misrule paper. Coffee Comfort was the perfect little hole in the wall to help me think. It had the best view of the Narrows and the wide ocean beyond, if you managed to grab the single window seat, and the place was sort of scuzzy so it wasn't very popular. The coffee was crap too which didn't help their sales, but it was good enough for me. The whole operation may have been a front for a drug op because a lot of streels hung out there later in the day, and it was popular with the bikers in the early evening. First thing in the morning though, it was empty.

The Lord of Misrule. I stared at the blank page before me, pen in hand as I waited for inspiration. Last week I had thought I knew where I was going with this, but now I wasn't so sure. Perhaps I could write the introduction after the body had taken form, then I would at least know what to write.

Also known as the Abbot of Unreason, this title was given to a nonentity, a dunce or the most unlikely leader of a community, and he was given full rein for that week while everyone else went mad with booze and illegal doings.

I googled the topic on my phone to remind me of what I'd wanted to write. Misrule was largely a British custom, but one that stemmed from the Roman practice of Saturnalia where the so-called king was sacrificed at the end of the week. Ugh. It was also, according to a guy called Asterius, responsible for the birth of capitalism in that children would wrap fruit in foil and exchange their gifts for things of more worth.

Forget it. As I leaned on my elbow and watched the sun dance on the waters of the harbour below, I let myself get into a daydream, nearly but not quite allowing Alt to come upon me. I could almost see the otherworld, overlain like a pencil drawing over the real time. Instead of the War Memorial, across the cobbled road in Alt was the back of the old wooden Customs building, a grand affair with much bustling around it. Leaning against this self-important building was a tall and cadaverously thin figure in top hat and ragged long coat, and then our eyes met.

It was the ghostly figure I'd seen not so long ago when walking up Duckworth Street before the craft fair, the very same, and he could see me, his face pleaded as he reached out his hand in my direction. I gave such a start that Alt dropped from my vision at once and I sat stock still in my plastic chair.

Dear God, I had to watch what I was doing, or Hugh and his elders might have a case.

I set my attention back to my study of Misrule.

Willem called himself The Lord of Misrule but that was just a conceit. No one had elected him to be king, he was just a failed sorcerer flogging his pathetic crafts in a city at the outer edge of the Americas. A pretentious little man trying to be important among a group of wanna-be witches.

Those Christmas figures he'd made sure were life-like though. Amazing how he did that with just paper and flour and unspun sheep's wool, the hours he must have put in to create those horrid little creatures, all representing a nasty aspect of Christmas traditions.

I remembered again my short visit to his booth, lit only by single spotlights on each of the Christmas creatures, and how they had appeared to be living and breathing with their eyes following my every move. Creepy things. Then I remembered also the feeling of dread and gloom that had come upon the house after Mark had brought the troll home and hidden it up in the attic. And how the paper bag which held it had rattled and shaken as if it was trying to escape.

Christ. What was Willem planning? Those creatures of his were full of magic and his evil intent. I watched as a huge supply boat filled my view of the harbour, loaded up with crates on the way out to the oilfields of the Grand Banks.

Misrule was afoot, there was no doubt about it.

We would go to Zeta's this evening, me and Alice, and I would get my medallion from him somehow even if I had to steal it. Yes, I was already thinking of it as mine, for I knew it was meant to be in my hands not his, for it had been held by my mother.

And while I was there I would find out what evil he was planning with those creatures. Perhaps Hugh had been wrong to dismiss the failed sorcerer out of hand. I did not have a good feeling about this.

22

I rode down to Alice's after supper, and then we walked our bikes over the footbridge to the old train station. I explained to her what I needed.

'I don't know about this, Dara,' she said as she slowly pushed her bike ahead of me.

'There's nothing to it,' I said. 'It's just a bunch of pretend for these people.'

'But you said he's a sorcerer,' she objected. 'Not that I believe in any of that stuff. But I don't want him, like, turning me into a toad or something.'

I hooted with laughter. 'Alice, he's going to be so entranced with you he'll just be slobbering at your feet,' I said. 'He'll be trying to get in your pants. All you have to do is look at him and act like you believe every word he says, and that'll free me to look through his stuff and get my medallion.'

'I dunno,' she said again. 'Seems rather deceitful. You want to steal from him, this guy Willem.'

Alice was the most honest person I knew, she hated deceit, unlawfulness and anything that wasn't strictly above board. She was the polar opposite of her brother Benjy. Loving the straight and narrow path as she did, I could never figure out why she couldn't see how bad he really was.

I would never, ever tell her that I only passed high school math by cheating off her, by getting myself into her head as she wrote the answers to the tests.

'No,' I replied. 'Nothing wrong with this. I'm just taking back what belonged to my mother.'

We reached the end of the bridge and she paused till I drew level to her. 'What else is there?'

'That's it, honest.'

'No, I know you, and there's something you're not saying.' She wasn't moving until I told her all of it, or at least enough to satisfy her.

'Okay,' I said. 'The thing is, Willem really is a sorcerer. That is, he does have some magic power, and... and do you remember those creatures of his at the craft fair?'

She nodded.

'I think he's planning something really bad with them, but I don't know what it is,' I confessed.

'How do you mean?'

'He's enchanted them, infused them with magic or something,' I said.

'Magic and the supernatural doesn't exist, Dara,' she said with a sigh. 'It's all in your weird little mind. I think you spent too much time alone as a child and read too many books.'

She got back on her bike and started heading toward the old train yard.

I bit my lip and followed her. How could she be so blind, even when she had the evidence right there in her own home?

'What about Nan Hoskins, then, Alice? You saying her ghost doesn't live in your parlour and make you watch Corrie Street with her? I guess that's not magical, is it?' I called after her.

That made her stop fast, her tires skidding on the gravel.

'It's not the same thing, not at all,' she said. 'Ghosts are natural, Dara. Nan Hoskins was a very strong character in life, and of course she couldn't go to her rest that easy. It was just her body that gave up, not her soul.'

'And the fairies up on the Southside Hills? The ones that took Benjy and spit him out again?' I was just taunting her now, taking out my frustration in spite. 'Your brother thought they were real enough, didn't he?'

'Sure and he spent a month at the Mental drying out afterwards,' she retorted, finally turning to face me. 'That was the drugs his friends gave him, he couldn't handle all that shit. There are no such things as fairies, Dara Martin. Grow up!'

She made me so mad, being in such denial, that I did something I really, really shouldn't have done.

'Okay, then, you're so smart and know everything,' I said. 'I'm going to show you something that will make you believe me. Come over here.'

'What? You're going to put a spell on me?' She made a rude sound with her mouth. 'Well, maybe my so-called elf blood will cancel your magic out. Isn't that how it works with your gaming friends?'

I threw my bike down on the ground and stalked over to her. Placing my arms around her, I hugged her tight. I didn't know if this was going to work or not, for I'd never brought another person over to Alt with me before, but we were going to find out now. If Willem could do it, well, so could I. She wanted proof, she was going to get it in spades.

Alice hated being touched, that was the elf in her, and she tried to squirm away from me but I held fast. I took a deep breath, and squeezed my eyes shut and made the mental flip into Alt.

....

When I opened my eyes again, darkness surrounded us, but I still held Alice in my arms. Success, of a sort.

She stood absolutely still, petrified in my arms, too terrified to even move or to shake off my touch.

'You okay?' I whispered to her.

'What's going on, Dara? What happened to the streetlights?' she asked. 'Did you make them go out?'

She was quivering like a songbird in the clutches of old Hal the tomcat. I let her go, but kept my hand on her shoulder, just in case.

I looked around, trying to make something out of the pitch black which surrounded us. I'd never flipped into this section of Alt before, because the west end of Water Street was creepy enough in real time. I could smell coal smoke and sewers and the peculiar odor of train tracks, but it was fresh creosote, not the lingering wispy leftover smell of the abandoned train yard that we had left.

I did a fast calculation in my mind. Were there trains in Alt? In my limited experience, Alt town was sort of like a Gothic punk version of real time, with gaslights and the women in long dresses and the men in top hats, some of them. There were rarely electric lights, as if Alt town was a fin de siècle version of real time, left over from the late Victorian era but with supernatural inhabitants.

Had the curtain between Alt and my time been thinner at some point in the past, and what had caused the divergence? This was no time to ponder the finer points of Alt existence, for I knew I had probably broken several of Hugh's major rules in this single act. I had shifted into Alt without prior knowledge of where I was going, and even Lack of Prior Due Diligence alone would have earned me a fail from his elders. Taking Alice with me had undoubtedly doubled the tally of lawlessness, so we couldn't stay here long.

But yes, there were definitely railways here, and as I turned I recognized the outline of a large iron steam engine right by us, a faint glow coming from behind it. The heat still rising told me it had only recently reached its destination.

'What the hell?' Alice whispered as she turned with me, her eyes huge. Her almost blonde hair glimmered in the gaslight, the ponytail hanging down her shoulder from under her toque. 'What's going on?'

'You wanted proof of the supernatural,' I told her. 'This is it. This is Alt town, like I told you about.'

'I thought that was in a book you read,' she said, moving toward the steam engine. It was filthy and real and hard beneath her hand. I moved with her, remaining in touch as I didn't know what would happen if we parted. 'I didn't think you were serious.'

She peeked out around the steam engine's cow-catcher grill and gasped. 'Look over there,' she hissed. 'Is this for real?'

I looked around with her and saw the old stone station as it used to be. In the light of two gas sconces, a man in a dark uniform was just entering through the wooden door leading from the platform. His strangely set ears prevented his hat from sitting properly. I drew her back quickly.

'Yes, it is, as real as Alt is anyway,' I said. 'Do you believe me now?'

'We have to get out of here, Dara, now! This place isn't right, it's not natural,' she said to me urgently.

We felt a rumble coming from the ground. I looked down at the iron rails by our feet. 'Another train is coming,' I said and I grasped her shoulder again, preparing to bring us back to the safety of the run down and isolated old station of real time, but just like that, she was gone, evading my grasp and running towards the lights.

'Move away from the tracks!' she said as she ran directly toward the light of the station. 'Run, Dara!'

'Get back here,' I hissed at her, but too late. 'Jesus, Alice, not that way, don't do that, you don't know...'

The station door opened just as she reached the platform, jumping up the whole three feet in a single bound.

'You, boy!' The uniformed guard yelled. And to my horror he reached out and grabbed her by the same shoulder I had held so tightly for her safety. I saw his hand in the light, hairy and misshapen like a paw with dirty big claws where his fingers ended. He whirled her around and shook her so hard I feared he might snap her delicate long neck.

I had to create a diversion even though it meant going deeper into Alt, so I ran and jumped up behind him, kicking him in the butt and then taking off into the station itself.

It worked, he dropped Alice and came tearing after me, blowing his shrill whistle all the time like a Keystone Cop. My plan was to run through the station then back around the other side, grab my friend, and switch back to real time.

It didn't work out that way though, for I had not taken into account Alice.

She ran after me, right through the old station, past the two ladies in their long dresses waiting for their carriage and the porter having a smoke by the entrance.

I was half way through the door before I realized she'd caught up to me. I tried to grab her arm but she raced ahead of me, she was a fast one that Alice.

'Wait for me!' I called out to her, but she didn't listen, she was like a hare with a fox on her tail as she turned east on the old cobble stones of Water Street. It was a dreary and scary place here, all the old wooden buildings huddled together, black with the smoke from the nearby railways, the odd candle in uncurtained windows of the bawdy houses and tenements. Jesus I couldn't afford to lose her in Alt of all places.

In real time, this whole area is taken up with the arterial highway with its ramps and empty concrete spaces and iron fences and shipping containers. It's a lonely uninhabited space, but in Alt it was still a long unlit neighborhood of slums and narrow alleys all backing onto the shipyard.

Disreputable forms slithered out of our way as we slipped along the stones and the reeking gutters. My friend was fast, yet I was fueled by terror because I had an inkling of what lurked behind those doors. I was gaining on her, but then I saw a door open suddenly. A skinny, stretched out black figure in a tall silk hat darted out to intercept her.

'Alice!' I screamed and forced my unfit body to push harder, harder and I was almost touching her when the door began to close. 'No!'

My foot stepped over the rotted threshold and I prepared to throw myself bodily in but to my surprise that same long arm grabbed me and with incredible strength and gentleness picked me up as if I was a kitten. The door slammed behind me and I heard the clunk of wooden bolts falling into place.

The stranger stepped back. The three of us stared at each other, consternation on all our faces.

We found ourselves in a rough room, bare floorboards and wallpaper peeling off the plank walls. A stone fireplace and chimney took up all of one wall and a rickety set of stairs led up to a dark second story. Two tallow candles burned greasily in the lanterns atop the rough table.

He was incredibly tall and thin, dressed in a long black frock coat that had seen better days. His silk top hat was equally battered and sat on his head at an angle over dirty blondish hair. A pointy ear poked out of the mass of his messy hair. And this strange being was familiar to me.

'You really shouldn't be out there by yourselves,' he said in a soft musical voice. 'Don't you know it's not safe?'

I collected myself. We needed to get out of here, and fast. I jumped over to Alice, grabbing her in both hands and shut my eyes to flick back into real time.

Nothing happened.

I opened my eyes again to see the stranger sadly shaking his head.

'It won't work, not till you get back to the spot you came from,' he said sadly. His voice was gentle and non-threatening. 'I don't know why that is, but it is. Like many things, no rhyme nor reason to them.'

I stepped in front of Alice, to shield her if there was to be any magic happening here.

'Who are you, and what do you want from us?'

'I could hear you coming, and I could hear old Barker yelling,' he said. 'And anyone running from him is a friend of mine.'

'You need to let us go,' I said to him viciously, trying my best to intimidate.

'It's okay, Dara,' I heard Alice speak behind me, then she stepped out. 'I don't think he means us any harm.'

She walked up to the stranger. 'Do you?'

It clicked then, seeing them both stand next to each other, both tall and slight with barely coloured hair, they looked more like brother and sister than she and Benjy did.

The stranger was an elf, but not like any elf I'd seen in my brief excursions to Alt over the years. That breed was usually so haughty and proud, dressed impeccably in their silk clothing and much cleaner than this specimen. Elves were cold and mean and arrogant, for the most part, but this one had a broken and vulnerable air about him.

Elves usually kept to themselves in their high eyries or distant valleys for they found other species quite distasteful. None of the elves I knew would ever find themselves in this humble home.

He smiled. 'You're safe here,' he said.

And weirdly enough, I found myself believing him.

23

'Please, take a seat,' he said. 'Be comfortable.' He indicated the single wooden chair by the fireplace to Alice. I took a three-legged stool, while he folded himself onto the rough bench by the table. He removed his hat and ruffled his hair with his fingers.

He told us his name, but the closest I could get to pronouncing it was Brin. He laughed softly and told us it was a Celtic name after all, so unfamiliar to our Germanic-based tongue, and so we shouldn't feel embarrassed or lacking at all.

'You're an elf,' I said, after he had poured some kind of tea for us both in cracked fine china cups that looked like they'd been rescued from a rubbish heap.

Brin nodded. 'I am.'

'But...' I looked around the humble room. It was clean, but oh so rough and homespun. How could I find the words to ask my question without risking offense? Elves were notorious for finding insults in innocent conversation, almost as bad as the fairies. Anything which didn't fit into the narrow elven view of themselves was quickly rejected.

Not Brin though. He smiled beatifically as if he understood my dilemma. Alice was still staring at him, which might be considered rude under some circumstances but it didn't seem to bother him at all.

'Why am I in such surroundings?' He looked around at the clean yet humble home.

It was my turn to nod. Exactly.

'I'm not like most elves,' he said simply. It was the understatement of the year, but he didn't offer any further information. 'You're from... Beyond, aren't you?' There was a note of longing in his voice.

'I've seen you before.' That tall thinness was unmistakable. This was the ghostly figure I'd seen out of the corner of my eye, lurking around the corner of the War Memorial. It had been this elf Brin, not a ghost after all. Just an elf who couldn't quite make it over from Alt.

'You could see me? I almost crossed the veil, I almost did, but it's too thick,' he said sadly. 'I can see the other place like a dream, but I can't quite reach it. I can't find a portal.'

'But why do you want to go there?'

'I want to be human,' he said.

'But you're Elf,' I replied. 'You can't be what you're not.'

'I'm not like the others,' he said again. 'All this being cold and aloof, living far away in secluded valleys and being better than everyone else... it doesn't fit me. I want to live, but not in this horrible old place. I want to live in your world, be modern, and fly in the air, and all the other stuff I've heard whispers about.' His pale grey eyes shone in the tallow light.

'I don't know if you can do that, not to live,' I said, my voice full of doubt. 'I mean, when I switch over to Alt, it takes a toll. You might have the same reaction, just in an opposite way.'

He said nothing, just glanced up at Alice. 'I think I'm ready to take the chance,' he said softly.

'Oh, God,' I said under my breath. Great, Alice had made another instantaneous conquest. I swallowed the rest of the tea-like stuff he'd given us and stood up. 'We need to get on the go. I'm sorry Brin, we have stuff to do. I can't take you with me right now, but maybe we can come back and try, another time.'

'I'd rather stay here a while,' Alice said. 'You go ahead without me.'

'Alice, we can't be here for any length of time, it's not healthy,' I told her. I could already feel a slight tingle at the tip of my big toes. Alt was weird - it had a peculiar effect on the human body if one stayed here for too long, although I must be getting used to it. Perhaps one could build up a tolerance to Alt, but I still had to worry about Alice. 'We've got to get back behind the station.'

'Take me with you,' Brin said softly. 'I can't stay here a moment longer, I can't bear it. This place is so... barbaric.'

'Yes, Brin should come with us,' she said.

'I don't think that's a good idea,' I said to them both. 'You don't belong over there, Brin.'

After a pause, he nodded slowly and stood with us. 'I understand,' he said sadly. 'Let me at least help you get back to your portal. I know of a path which leads behind the houses to the rail lines which will be safer for you. Follow me.'

He unbolted the door and peeked outside to the pitch dark. The railway lamps glowed in the distance.

'Come,' he said. Brin took us down a tiny alley which opened up to a no-man's land of weeds and alders between the ship yard and the run-down cottages, his long legs exaggeratedly tiptoeing through the underbrush. We walked along in single file till we reached the start of the rail line and the iron steam engine. We met not another soul, living or dead.

'Thanks,' I said awkwardly. 'We'll take it from here.'

I went to take Alice in my arms in preparation to flipping back to real time. She allowed me to do this, but her eyes remained on Brin with a small smile.

I took a deep breath and squeezed my eyes shut but felt Alice's arm move at the last moment, like she was reaching out and then I felt another's touch on me just as I flipped.

When I opened my eyes in the gravel of the old railway yard, there were three of us in real time.

24

'**B**rin, no!' I was honestly concerned for his health and wellbeing, for I had no idea of the effects of real time on one of the elven persuasion. Also, I had a strong suspicion that Hugh really, really would not approve of this, and that this sort of action was exactly what his elders were complaining about.

'Let me stay, just for a small while!' Brin breathed in deeply and dramatically. 'Oh, the promised land! Smell the freshness of freedom!'

Now, the diesel and salt was wafting up from the harbour and mixing with the whiff of creosote from the old railway tracks, while a dog had done his business somewhere recently amid the wasteland, but yes, compared to his neighbourhood in Alt with its overbearing coal smoke and the raw sewage running in the gutters, the air was comparatively fresher. But still.

'You have to go back,' I told the elf. But Alice was holding on to his arm and beaming. They made a cute couple, and I'd never seen my friend want the company of another being so much. Too bad it was an ill-fated match, a collision between two worlds. It was never meant to be.

'Just a little while,' she echoed him.

We were running late now, for time in Alt passed much as it did here. I needed to meet with Willem this evening.

Although... Perhaps Brin could help. I eyed him critically in the dim light. He had full elven power, look at the way he had lifted me lightly up off the street and into his house. Two magicks were always better than one.

'Okay, you can come to Zeta's with us,' I told him with a nod. 'But lose the hat, okay? That'll just draw attention to you over here. No one dresses like that anymore except at Hallowe'en. And... and try to tone down the elfness, if you can.'

He swept the hat off his head. 'I am so thrilled,' he began. 'This is the greatest adventure. Why, I will compose a song for you, for Dara who lifted the veil between my world and this heaven, for ...'

'No!' I interrupted him. 'Christ, no elf songs, please. We have to go.'

Alice and I rode our bikes up to Duckworth Street, with Brin easily loping beside us and keeping pace. My mind was working quickly with the problem of how to use the elf. By the look of her, Alice was too gaga over Brin to be of any help to me, she wouldn't remember to try to knock Willem over with her allure. But at least now she had to believe me about Alt and magic and things. There was no way she could deny what had happened this evening, not when we had living proof of a full-blood elf with us.

I tried to quickly give Brin the gist of what we had planned for the evening. He caught on quickly, although he quivered at the thought of tricking a sorcerer. The elf was about to shake his head but then he glanced at Alice's long fair hair again and visibly melted. He nodded. He was on board.

We drew near to Zeta's, and we locked the bikes to a parking meter down the road a bit. Looking at the pair of them together, I had to go back on my previous decision. Alice was supposed to entrance Willem, but there was no way she could do that with the elf taking all her attention. The two of them were radiant – in fact, I could see a glimmer forming all around Brin, an eerie elven glow.

'Brin, maybe it's better if you don't come in with us,' I said. 'I really need Alice to concentrate on what she's doing to help. I need you to stay outside, because well, Willem will see right off the bat that you're an elf. And that will mess everything up.'

'I will be like a shadow,' he promised solemnly, holding his hat before his heart, perhaps a little relieved. 'I will remain out of sight and hearing, deep into the depths of the darkness.'

'Right,' I said. 'You do that. Come on Alice, they're still in there. Remember, I need you to distract Willem any way you can while I look for that medallion.'

'I got your back,' she said, and I knew she meant it. She gave a last lingering smile to Brin.

The plate glass window and the door of the shop had been covered with heavy damask drapes, just a few small cracks of light showing that Willem and his group were still within. I pulled open the door and we entered.

Screens had been erected in the small store, and all the shelving pushed to one side to make room for the circle of women gathered around Willem. He totally ignored us. I could tell by the burning candles and the incense in the air that they had just finished some kind of circle.

'I totally felt the magic,' Carrie murmured as she looked down on him, her face ecstatic.

'The power is immense,' another said, sliding her eyes across at the sorcerer.

Oh my God. Willem was standing in the midst of the group, touching each woman on the forehead in turn as if handing out benedictions to his faithful disciples. I counted ten women in the space, of whom Carrie was the youngest. All the others ranged in age from their thirties to their fifties, and all were dressed expensively, and all turned adoring eyes on the small man.

'Go now, my precious ladies, my coven,' Willem said softly to them. 'Till we meet again.'

He looked up at me with a flash of anger in his eyes.

'We're finishing up here,' he said to me. 'Where were you?'

'Unavoidably delayed,' I said. I felt the resentful eyes of Carrie and Zeta and a few other women on us but I ignored them all.

He turned his back on us and spoke in a low voice to his groupies. 'You know what to do, my dear ladies. Now I send you off with my blessings. Remember, time is of the essence! And Carrie, you have your special job.'

She preened while the others regarded her jealously.

'Now ladies,' Willem added. 'If you can prove yourselves in this small task, you too might earn your place in the inner, inner circle.'

Damn, we'd missed the chance to find out what the sorcerer's dark intentions were, but no matter. It was probably all just an exercise to build his overinflated ego and fill his wallet.

At least they were leaving now, so Alice would be free to grab his undivided attention while I searched for the medallion.

'Willem,' I said after the women had all left the store, even Zeta had been dismissed form her own space. 'This is Alice. She's interested in joining your group.'

'You are a seeker of knowledge?' His lashless eyes sized her up. He must have sensed her elf blood, for a look of greed came on his face.

I closed my eyes momentarily to try to sense the location of the medallion. I could feel its presence, but only faintly. He didn't have it on him anymore – no, it was downstairs in the cellar, I was almost sure.

'I'd love to hear about your group,' Alice said in a breathless voice as she fixed her enormous grey eyes on his face. 'I'm so sorry we didn't make it to the meeting. Why don't you tell me what I've missed?'

In that moment, I no longer existed for Willem, but I was used to that after hanging out with Alice for all those years. I slowly edged my way over to the stairs leading to the basement, and Alice too moved, Willem following her closely until his back was to me.

The beaded curtain – that was going to make a noise, no way around it. I pointed to it, and she nodded.

She took a deep breath and we timed it exactly.

'Owww!' she screamed out, and bent to hold her calf in her hand.

Good old Alice. I was through the curtain in a flash and down the dark staircase with hardly a ripple of the beads.

'Charley horse!' I heard her explain to Willem. 'Oh, that's better. Thank you. How'd you do that? You really have a good touch.'

She'd let him touch her leg? I was impressed with her acting abilities. I left them murmuring together as I switched on the flashlight app from my phone. Nothing had changed down here since my last visit, except that the stone cellar was noticeably colder.

In the blue light, I could see that the piles of smoky junk from Zeta's store hadn't been moved at all and the air still tasted of ashes and ancient dust. I took a deep breath and sent out feelers for a hint of the medallion. Yes, I could sense its presence somewhere here, but it was still elusive and I could not get a grasp on its location.

These sensors of mine were pretty reliable, I knew. I could always find Edna's keys and other lost items by standing still, thinking about them and somehow thus locating them in space and time. I never told my aunt I was using witch power for this though, she always commented on my terrific memory.

It's hard to explain just how it worked. The sense acted like another nose, if you can picture invisible octopus tentacles but with sniffers at the end, sort of like that. The mental feelers I sent out were looking to match the feeling of the object in my mind.

I moved deeper into the space and the feeling of the medallion grew stronger, but the space itself was now empty save for the ancient wooden door at the end, the one which led under Duckworth Street.

It loomed at the end of the tunnel-like space. The medallion could only be hidden behind it, yet when I examined the rusty padlock, I could tell by the layers of dust and grime on it that it hadn't been disturbed for decades, except when I lightly touched it the other night. No one had handled that lock since then.

Yet it was inside that inner cellar, it was unmistakable now, that's where my sensors were locating it, faint though the impression still was. I set down my knapsack onto the dirt floor. I was still carrying around the tools I had collected from my house, those old-fashioned iron keys which I might be able to use to jerry-rig the padlock. If not, I had an assortment of hatpins and screwdrivers too that would help me get past this barrier.

I'd studied lock picking the summer I was twelve, after binge reading a bunch of British children's books - *The Famous Five, The Secret Seven* – all stories of intrepid children who led amazingly free and rich upper middleclass childhoods during the Second World War. They were leftovers from my grandfather's upbringing which were still lying around the family library. I was confident this lock would not get the better of me.

If I had only stopped to ask how the medallion could get behind the door without Willem having touched the padlock, I might have saved myself a bunch of grief, but I guess I just wasn't on top speed that night.

The lock wasn't budging, anyway, no matter how hard I picked at it, and the sound of raised voices from above caused me to pause as I tried to hear what was going on up there. There were three voices. Willem, Alice. My heart sank as I recognized the third. Brin, and he sounded very agitated.

I grabbed my bag and stuffed everything inside it including my phone, and stumbled through the dark to the old wooden stairs. When I reached the top I quickly took in the scene before me, Brin gesticulating, his shadow like a dancing spider in the candle light. Alice had transferred her adoring gaze onto the elf, and I could tell she wasn't acting anymore.

Willem merely stood stock still, flabbergasted and furious and speechless at this rude interruption of his imagined seduction of my friend. His eyes darted over to me as I burst through the curtain and a look of understanding and triumph replaced his anger as he realized what I had been up to.

He laughed casually and turned away from Brin.

'Didn't find what you're after, did you?' he said, sneering as he did so. His malicious eye caught mine. 'I've hidden it well.'

He turned back to the elf faction and dismissed them. 'Leave,' he commanded them. 'Dara and I have business.'

'No,' I said. 'We're all going. Come on, guys.'

Willem laughed again. 'No matter. You have my number,' he said. 'I'll expect a call. After all, that's the only way you will ever get your hands on your little treasure, is it not?'

'What is it to you, Willem?' I asked, tired now. 'What good is it to you?'

He paused before answering as if savouring the moment. 'You're right, I have no use for the object itself,' he said, then continued. 'There's magic in that medallion, but it's magic gone wrong.'

He saw the effect his words had on me, and pushed on. 'So it's no good to me whatsoever except that you want it so badly. I can use your assistance with some... work. You know how to find me. I'll expect a call before the end of the week.'

··········

He had me over the proverbial barrel. I did want that medallion he had secreted away, for it was the first hint of my mother I'd had since her disappearance. It was my only clue as to what had happened to her. And I knew it had been meaningful to her.

But he said *magic gone wrong*. I shivered. What did he mean by that?

We rode our bikes slowly back down to Water Street and to the old station, Brin keeping pace.

Along the way, the elf tried to explain, offering excuses as to why he had gone against my orders. He knew he had pissed me off.

'I could see through a crack of the curtain,' he said. 'And that creature, that sorcerer, was mesmerizing this precious gift and I could see he meant harm, he wanted to use her for his nasty ends. I could not allow it! As an Elf and a gentleman, I could not let that happen!'

'Alice was fine,' I told him. 'It was an act. Wasn't it, Al?'

'It was very brave of you, Brin,' she said. Out of the corner of my eye I could see her smile at him as he strode alongside us.

'Come on,' I said roughly as we turned into the yard, giving a small spurt to the bike. 'Let's get you back where you belong.'

I found the spot where we had landed back in real time, the grasses all trampled by our feet. Alice came to join me.

'Not you,' I instructed her, motioning her away with my arm. 'Just him. I need to flip into Alt and drop him back.'

I watched as they approached each other to say their farewells. All this back and forth to Alt had exhausted me, to say nothing of the debacle in Zeta's store, and I just wanted the evening to end. I needed to go home and curl up on my bed and think.

Alice left off their embrace and looked to be leaving the scene, heading back towards the footbridge, but she stopped midway and called out to me. 'Why can't Brin stay?'

'He doesn't belong here,' I said, turning to her with a sigh. 'It may be dangerous for him.'

'It's dangerous for him in Alt,' she said softly. 'All the elves, his own people, have rejected him because he's different, and everyone else there hates him because he's an elf. He should stay. He wants this, desperately.'

Alice, who had been in total denial of the supernatural at the start of this evening, had become a true believer.

'It doesn't work that way,' I told her gently. 'Now come on, Brin, let's go.'

I turned back to him but he wasn't there. In the faint light from the distant streetlamps I could see a long shadow running through the grasses toward the shrubs and trees growing along the river's edge. With his long lean frame and elf powers, I knew he could easily leap the river or at least wade through it before I could catch him and haul him back to the world he was desperate to leave.

'No!' I cried as I watched him disappear into the shadows. He was gone.

'Sorry,' Alice whispered to me from the bridge. 'But Brin needs to stay here.'

How could I explain to Alice that this action of his might cost me my future career, all my dreams of witch school and being taught to do the one thing I was good at? If Hugh's elders got so much as a whiff of this I would be banished before I even arrived in Scotland, my magic would be bound and my life in total tatters. Even my pseudo trust fund from Dad would dry up, I knew, for he wouldn't have to pay me to keep my powers leashed. The elders would take care of that for him.

25

My life was now officially and irrevocably a bust. The only saving grace was the fact that Hugh was thousands of miles away, safely across the wide North Atlantic Ocean in Paris and could have no inkling of the damage I'd done. For that I was truly grateful.

How would I ever convince Brin to go back to his own dimension? This world held hidden dangers for him, used as he was to the realities of Alt. Even a simple act like crossing the road would be a hazard for the elf, not being familiar with modern vehicular traffic and the speeds reached by cars even on city streets. He would be like a child here.

And where would he live? How would he eat? He had no birth certificate, so was a non-person in the eyes of the law and could not even legally hold a job. Brin was now an illegal immigrant, but a case which would surely confound the system.

This was foolishness, I would have to somehow deport the elf myself. I stormed and cussed at Brin in my mind, not admitting my own fault in this at bringing Alice over to Alt in the first place just to prove a petty point.

And Willem, God, what price was he planning to exact for that medallion? I couldn't even imagine what he wanted from me, but whatever it was, I would have to do it just to get my hands on it.

And on top of all that, I still had to do that paper, that stupid paper for Folklore. I played with the idea of just not bothering, and mentally calculated what the lack of a term paper would cost my final grade. Nope. It had to be done or I would flunk the semester and Hugh would use it as an excuse to cancel my education on his Scottish island.

My life sucked so bad I turned up the volume on the boom box to eight. Might as well spread the misery around, and I totally ignored Maundy's wailings from the next room.

Of course, there was no way I could even think of working on my paper, not when my life was so shit. For lack of anything better to do, I grabbed the more interesting of Hugh's pile of books, the Encyclopedic Knowledge of How Everything Works. It had been written before World War II, that's how ancient and out of date it was, but at least it had pictures and diagrams in it, so I flicked through and learned all about steam engines. Then locks from the medieval era, then early filmography. Like, how this crap was ever going to be helpful, I couldn't see. Hugh was just out to punish me, give me a hard time in order that I could prove my dedication and jump through all his hoops. Really?

··········

Before going to bed for the night, I checked my phone. I'd been so miserable and wrapped up in my own troubles I had totally forgotten about it.

Jack.

Crazy busy on this end with Mom's events & the band. How're things with you?

Our date the other night had sort of fizzled out. My head had been too full with my new dilemma of finding myself falling for a normal guy just when I was on the brink of reaching my true magic potential – a guy who couldn't even sense ghosts, for God's sake! That couldn't end well - look at what had happened with my parents. Not that I was tied up with all the traditional Witch Kin rules like Dad was, but I still couldn't let Jack distract me.

Yet we had kissed as we parted, and damn! I liked him.

Same old, same old. Well, I certainly couldn't tell him the truth, could I? Couldn't tell him how I'd gotten mixed up with an evil (yes, I'm sure he was evil) sorcerer and brought an elf over in to this world.

I didn't think there was anyone who could understand my dilemma and help me out of it, at least no one who would act with sympathy. Hugh, Dad – they would both be furious.

Unless... perhaps Sasha? I sat up straight on the bed and considered this latest idea very carefully, looking at it from all angles in terms of possible negative fallout on me and my future plans.

My half-sister, the legitimate offspring of Dad, owed me big time for last September. At least, she did morally, in a way that maybe only sisters would understand.

Once, we had been fast friends until life and the actions of grownups had gotten in the way. As teenagers, she and her friends had terrorized me in high school, she acting out of fear and her friends acting because they were asshole Witch Kin kids who looked down on half-bloods like myself. Things had come to a head this fall when her ill-chosen boyfriend tried to kill Alice, and we had sort of made up our differences and called a truce. Sort of.

But now it was time for payback. She owed me and I planned to collect on the debt.

26

We met in the basement cafe in the Sciences Building at the university, far from her usual gathering space at the top of the Arts Building, that glorious airy coffee house that the Witch Kin kids had claimed for their own hang out. Sasha, in her thigh high suede boots and tightly fitted dress from a Montreal designer looked out of place amongst the denim and flannel clad Biology students and the IT nerds who occupied the rest of the tables in this dingy old space.

'No,' she said, her sleek black hair moving like a waterfall against her shoulders as she shook her head. 'I'm not having any part of this.'

I hadn't even gotten to the bit about Willem, just told her of the Brin dilemma.

'And what are you doing flipping into Alt?' she asked in a scandalized tone, leaning closer over the table to me. 'How the hell do you even know about that place?'

Hugh had explained to me that only the topnotch witch students were allowed to take the course on Alt, and that was only after courses of study in which the rules were explained to them. Not like me, who had found the place on my own. I was still sort of smug about all that.

'I've always known about Alt,' I told her, letting a note of scorn enter my voice. 'I mean, it's all around us isn't it?'

That made her go quiet, and I rejoiced in that small victory. But only for a moment.

'You're going to be in so much trouble for this,' she said, a tiny smile forming on her lips. 'When Dad and Hugh find out.'

'Sassy,' I said, purposely calling her by her old childhood nickname, the one only I had used. We had been so close, once upon a time. 'Don't. Please. You know I have to go to Scotland after Christmas, and if this gets out I don't stand a chance. I need to contain the damage before it goes any further.'

She shrugged. 'And what do you want me to do about it?' My sister stared across the table at me, her expression unreadable now. 'I'm not getting involved in your mess.'

'I thought... I thought maybe you could talk to the elf and convince him to go back, tell him why he needs to return to Alt...' Even as I said the words, I realized how weak it sounded. Brin had made his choice and now that he had his so-called freedom, nothing would dissuade him, even a de Teilhard Witch would hold no sway on this wayward elf.

'Of course, you could always try to magic him back to where he belongs,' she said casually. 'Seeing as how you're such a powerful witch.' She raised a finely manicured eyebrow at me.

Well, that was something I couldn't do actually and I had no idea if she knew that or not. Hugh had helped me learn some things about using my power, but only as it related to me, to things I could do like sending my mind flying out over the city, or learning how to camouflage myself so that I blended into the background. I'd never been able to touch another being with my magic, and Hugh had expressly said that spells were, quite frankly, bullshit. But Sasha seemed to think otherwise and she set off a flare of hope deep within me.

'Can you help me with that?' I asked her quietly. 'I haven't gotten that far with my education.'

'No, little sister, I cannot be of assistance there,' she said, standing up and preparing to leave. 'I have to go for a fitting for my ball gown. You know, the big do that the Witch Kin have every year to kick off the Yule season? Oh, you obviously don't. It's invitation only.'

She leaned down to speak closely in my ear, away from the gob-struck nerds who sat around us, awed at her presence. 'And only *witches* get the invitations. So what does that make you?'

My half-sister straightened up again, but continued in a low voice. 'You're either a witch or you're not. If you're stupid enough to go messing about with things you shouldn't, with things that are beyond your control, then perhaps you need to learn a lesson. Perhaps despite that innate power you claim to have, you're not fit to be a witch if you don't have the wisdom to figure out the consequences of your actions before you act.' She leaned closer to hiss into my ear. 'Perhaps this is why half-bloods are not welcomed into the Kin.'

She gave a smirk and with a toss of her beautiful hair, sashayed out of the cafeteria, leaving me to sit and stew in thoughts of revenge - sweet, unattainable revenge. We were sisters, yes, but would never be equal for Sasha would always be the oldest and the full blood witch, while I would always be the castoff half blood.

But there was also truth deep within her words, and that's what hurt the most.

....

That being said, she had put an idea inside my head, one that buzzed around like a bee and wouldn't quit.

If I could only get my hands on a book of spells, surely I could work some magic and get Brin to go back into Alt before he caused me grief. I had no training in spells, true, but how hard could it be?

The only real problem was, I didn't know where I could lay my hands on said book. The libraries in town were useless, even the one at the university, for I had already scoured them all for anything magical. Perhaps I could sneak into Dad's house, there was probably something in his office...

And I laughed at myself. There probably was a lot of good stuff in his house which would help me if I was to be so foolhardy. Even if I could let myself in, Cate would smell my presence and have me brought before the Witch Kin so fast my head would spin. Worse, all my support would be cut off and I'd have to go to trade school, be a plumber or something.

Out of the question.

The only other person I knew who worked in magic was Willem. He wasn't involved in the Kin, in fact like myself, he was shunned by them. He was a creepy guy, yes, but this was my future at stake. I couldn't take the chance that Brin would behave here in real time because, well, because he was an elf and they were notorious for their self-absorption - he simply wouldn't realize he was misbehaving. If any hint of my inadvertent actions came to Dad's ears, then my future was finished.

The only catch was I might have to explain to the sorcerer the whole situation in order to request his help. Unless... unless I maneuvered all my ducks in a row.

I walked over to the student center deep in thought. Willem would have no love for the elf, for I'd seen the desire in the sorcerer's eyes, the longing kindled by Alice. Brin had stymied his attempt at the seduction. Willem would be on board with sending the elf back to where he belonged.

After climbing the stairs to the center where I planned to buy myself a slice of pizza, a buzz of laughter interrupted my thoughts. Looking up, I saw a gathering of students, all clustered around a table but keeping their distance, and there in the center of the crowd bobbed a tattered black silk hat. I stretched my neck to see around their backs, and my heart sank.

Jesus, that frigging elf was here at the university and making a spectacle of himself. He had a sub sandwich before him, and was picking out the bits which looked distasteful and laying them to the side. This wasn't so bad, but he was singing loudly to himself as he did so, a long and monotonous elven song which must have caught people's attention. He looked like a madman, with his spindly long legs and arms and the hat set askew on his head. The pointy ears were painfully visible through his untidy long hair.

'Brin,' I called, pushing my way through the crowd. I put my hand over someone's phone held out to record the spectacle and gave them the dirtiest look I could. The elf greeted me with a delighted smile.

'Dara! Come join me and help me figure out the elements of this meal,' he said as if he had no clue how pissed off I was at him, then he licked the pastel orange sauce off his fingers.

He looked like he had slept rough, there was animal fur all over his long wool coat - he'd probably spent the night in Alice's shed with the feral cats that she had adopted over the years. He certainly smelled like it. Elves were supposed to be such fastidious creatures, I could see why the rest of his clan had disowned him.

'What are you doing here?' I asked in a low voice as I slipped into the chair beside him. I shot menacing looks at the cluster of students all around to tell them the show was over, and the crowd slowly drifted away.

'Waiting for my dear Alice,' he said. 'I have strict instructions to stay in this very spot. She gave me coinage to purchase this repast, but it is so strange. Look! All the elements of a meal, surely, but put together in layers. It is quite awful, I think.'

'Yeah, it's a sub sandwich,' I told him. 'It's supposed to be like that.' Then I had an idea. If I kept him close, he wouldn't be able to get into any mischief, and I could somehow persuade him to go to Zeta's store with me and give Willem an opportunity to show his stuff. 'Look, why don't you come with me? I'm going home. I'll fix you a real meal.'

'To your home?' His eyes widened as he thought about this. 'But Alice...'

'I'll fix it with her,' I said, and took out my phone. 'I'll just text her, let her know where you are.'

And I did.

He stared with fascination at the phone. 'What is this magic plate?'

I held it out of his reach. 'Later,' I said as I stood up. 'Let's go catch the bus.'

Brin followed me quite happily once I told him Alice was okay with it all. I was going to ask him to take off the top hat again so as to be less noticeable, but I realized with his rangy height he stood out in the crowd anyway so what was the point? He folded himself onto the narrow bus bench, his face plastered to the window, entranced by the passing scenery.

I had to do something about his wardrobe, even if his stay in real time would not be long. Brin just didn't fit into the twenty-first century dressed as he was and he looked like he was freezing in the December winds. It might be raining out, but the wind chill was way below zero Celsius so we made a pit stop into the Sally Ann's downtown. Due to his height and thinness he was hard to fit, but the volunteer workers eventually found a shirt and a pair of jeans that worked well enough despite being baggy and too short, and fitted out in a pair of men's runners and thick socks underneath along with a bulky parka to keep him warm, he could just about pass for human. A knitted watch cap covered his ears.

He kept his old clothes in the plastic bag provided, and proudly wore his new togs as we made our way up the west end of Water Street and then to my home. Brin chattered all the way.

'It is so different from my own realm, this Other-land,' he said. "Look, my poor home no longer exists, can this be the same place? How can it be?' He looked at the wasteland of concrete with sadness in his eyes.

'Your time. Or land, or Alt,' I began, trying to explain to him what little I knew. 'I think the two split at some point in the past, some time when magic wasn't accepted anymore by Normals, or those you would call 'Nonsupernaturals'.'

'What caused this split?'

'I think,' I said. 'I think maybe it was because Nons just stopped believing in all of it, magic and elves and fairies and things. It's like with the coming of the modern age they became blinded and perhaps their nonbelief might have thickened the veil between the two.'

I thought about luring him over to the patch of weeds by the bridge and forcing him back to Alt there and then, but he was keeping a watchful and wary eye on me as we passed the train station.

When we started up the long drive way to Richmond Cottage, he paused among the weeds and looked up at the house. From this vantage point, with the late afternoon sun shining on the long French windows, it looked almost pristine. It was only when you got closer that you could notice the paint peeling from the clapboard and the moss growing on the roof.

'I know this house!' Brin clapped his hand to his cheek. 'This grand estate. Are we to enter its hallowed halls?'

'It's my home,' I said shortly. 'We have extra bedrooms, so you can stay here tonight.'

Edna's old jeep was in the back driveway, so I pulled him aside before we approached the door.

'Remember how I said the Normals here don't believe in magic and things?'

He nodded.

'My family are Normals,' I said. 'You cannot tell them you're an elf, or from Alt, okay?'

He nodded again as he looked down at me, the stupid smile still plastered in his face. 'Pretend to be human, you mean?'

'Exactly,' I said. 'We'll tell Edna that you're a cousin of Alice's or something, that they haven't got room for you to stay in their house. I think she'll fall for that.'

And she did. My aunt was a little puzzled with this strange person in her house, especially since I hardly ever brought friends home with me, but she accepted him all the same. She sized up his height with delight.

'You'll come in handy when we're putting up the Christmas tree,' she said decisively and with distinct approval. She'd been charmed by the elf's open smile. 'Brin can stay in the pink room, I guess.'

'That's Maundy's room, Edna,' I reminded her. 'That might not go down so well. How about the green striped room?'

Edna knew about Maundy, our resident ghost, though I don't think they'd ever met, and I don't know if she really believed.

'Fine, the green striped wallpaper room,' Edna said. I could feel her rolling her eyes from where I stood.

Brin of course was ecstatic about his bedroom, despite the fact that the 'forties era wallpaper was peeling in places and the window sill showed distinct signs of dry rot. It was a far better lodging than he'd had in Alt. He placed his bag carefully by the side of the bed and whirled around.

'A real bed!' he said. 'And all for myself?'

'All yours, Brin,' I told him. 'I'm just down the hall here, so I'll let you get settled in.'

His would not be a long stay, but I didn't tell him that. Instead I snuck off to make a call to Willem.

27

Mark was not nearly so welcoming of my strange new friend. But he'd been a cop for thirty years, after all, and being suspicious was ingrained into his psyche by now.

'A Hoskins cousin, eh?' he said as we all sat down at the kitchen table. We were having a plain meal of soup and salad fortunately, food that Brin could understand. 'You a cohort of Benjy?'

'No,' I jumped in. 'He's closer to Alice. Much closer. Doesn't hang with Benge at all. Not into all that shit.'

'Language, Dara,' Edna said, and smiled sweetly at Brin as if she'd never let a cuss word pass her lips in her life.

'Sorry,' I said to her.

I'd arranged to meet Willem after supper, but hadn't told him what it was about. Just that it would be to his advantage. Alice, I'd fobbed off with a couple of texts and she said she would meet us after eight as she had a late lab that night. I dreaded to see her face when I broke the news that Brin had decided to go back to Alt, but it couldn't be helped.

The Rocket Cafe was the best place for Brin to wait for me. I sat him down at a little table in the back room where he could remain out of sight and not freak out too many people, with strict instructions to keep the watch cap on over his ears and not to move till I came back. He would be happy enough with his hot chocolate and croissant while I slipped around the corner to meet Willem at the Grog Shop underneath Zeta's store. The sorcerer had demanded we meet there, although I was uncomfortable with the venue after the last time I'd been there, when he'd dragged me into Alt against my will.

But thinking back on that incident gave me confidence that Willem could help me with the elf problem. If he could force me into Alt without even touching me, then surely he could do the same with an elf.

He wasn't there when I arrived, so I chose a seat by the bar and ordered a coke. Looking around the meager space, I saw there were few patrons this early in the evening, just a couple of the usual drunks and some guys setting up their sound system.

Damn! Jack was playing here again tonight, it had totally slipped my mind that we'd agreed to meet. He wasn't here yet, so I took my drink down to the corner and hoped I could escape his gaze when he came in. Jack wasn't expecting me this early, for I'd told him I'd drop in later towards the end of his set. I had a lot to do before then. Dump an elf off in Alt and grab my mother's medallion back from Willem. Then meet Alice and Jack as if nothing had happened. I could pull it off.

'Perhaps we could step into a quieter space.'

The sorcerer had taken me unawares, appearing like that. Dressed in his affectation of a long black robe, Willem nodded his head towards the fake brick wall of the bar, behind which lay the ancient door to Zeta's cellar in Alt, not in real time. Which meant I would have to flip.

'You're the one who wanted to meet here, not me,' I grumbled. I really didn't want to go into Alt again, especially not with Willem for I didn't trust him a bit. I could feel he had something up his sleeve, yet I had to play along with him, reminding myself that I held cards too, that he wanted something from me that I could only give willingly. 'Fine, but we're flipping back to real time as soon as we get into next door.'

'As you wish,' he replied with a gracious smile on his face. 'After you?' He gave a small bow and indicated the wall again.

A thought struck me. 'How are we going to flip back again if we're not in the same spot?'

He laughed. 'You have so much to learn. It's not a problem if you know what you're doing. I can flip us.'

I had to trust him, so I shut my eyes and flipped with Willem directly on my heels.

It looked like the patrons of the Alt Grog hadn't moved from their spots since the last time I'd been there, or maybe they were all of a sort, the women in their tight, tawdry ragged dresses, the men in the various uniforms of international sailors and labourers.

As I looked at these people, I began to wonder. Were they all supernaturals? Why let themselves be in such a state of poverty and addiction if they were? None of them were paying us any mind this time, caught up as they were in pouring the demon rum down their throats as soon as possible to numb their pain.

'There are Normals in Alt, too,' Willem whispered in my ear. 'When the Witch Kin created the veil between the two dimensions and allowed it to thicken, the ancestors of these poor unfortunates were left behind. Caught up in the pain and miseries of their lives, they were unable to keep up with the real time. Instead, they listened to the whispering of a magic they could never hold, and remained behind here in Alt, thinking that just one more whiskey, one more drop of laudanum would help them reach their paradise.'

His breath was too hot on my neck.

'Can they be helped?' I asked.

He laughed nastily and shook his head. 'It is what it is,' he said. 'They and their misbegotten offspring will remain on this side of the curtain forever, subject to the whims of those supernaturals amongst them. Look at them – they are uneducated superstitious fools, no better than cattle. Fodder for the vampires, unable to break away from the lives they have.'

I turned away from them, uncomfortable at the thought of the misery of these masses of lives. Willem removed a key from his robes and unlocked the old oak door, allowing me to enter first. I ducked through the narrow portal and he shut the door tight behind us.

The medallion was here somewhere, I could feel it like a force field and I realized that bastard sorcerer had hidden it inside this cellar - but in Alt. I looked toward the end of the tunnel-like room, up to that other small door under the road. I knew it was there, could almost taste it and I was confident I would get it on my own time. I just needed to play along with Willem until he sent the elf back to Alt. That was my priority tonight.

True to his word, he grasped my elbow and we immediately flipped back to real time in Zeta's cellar with its piles of smoky junk still untouched. The bare bulb shone over the space.

'Take a seat,' he said, indicating a couple of wooden crates. 'Sit down, and talk to me.'

We stared at each other across the shadows.

'So what is it you need from me?' I stuck my chin in the air, letting him know he wasn't going to get what he wanted, not easily.

He spread his hands out before him as if to show he had nothing up his sleeve. 'I want your help,' he replied simply. 'And I want to be perfectly honest with you, for you deserve no less. We are equals, Dara, you and me.'

'What do you need my help with?' I was right to be suspicious of him.

'The witch circle,' he said. 'My coven.'

'Witch circle? You mean Carrie and Zeta and those other foolish women who can't see through you?'

A delighted chuckle emerged from his throat. 'Yes, I was right Dara, we are truly equals,' he said. 'Yes. I need your continued presence there, to help add legitimacy to the group.'

Willem leaned closer, his eyes shadowed by the dim light. 'You see, these women are extremely bored with their lives. They want more. They want to be powerful, to be special. They want to possess magic.'

'No one can *give* magic powers to someone else, surely,' I said. 'You're either born with it or you're not.'

'Indeed, you are correct,' he replied. 'But we could give them... hmmm, the illusion of holding magic powers, the belief that they are part of something bigger.'

'And,' he continued, holding up his hand to stem my reaction. 'They have the means to pay for it.'

'So let me get this straight,' I said to him. 'You want me to help you... what, con money from Carrie and other women like her?'

'No, not con, nothing illicit about this,' he said, shaking his head as if with horror at the thought. 'Perish the thought. We merely, through the coven, give their lives meaning, make them feel important and powerful, belonging to a sisterhood...'

'Where do I come into this? Surely you can do that on your own?'

'Ah, but you will join my coven, and be the example of the heights they could reach if they only work harder, pay more money....' he said. 'The other night was just the beginning. You see where I'm going with this? My prize student.'

I saw plenty, and was totally repulsed by his petty scheme. But what could one expect from a failed sorcerer? He needed to pass me off as his fraudulent prize student in order to trick the women out of their money. I didn't know who to feel sorrier for, Willem with his pathetic con game or the women he was fooling and I scornfully told him exactly what was on my mind.

'Fraudulent?' He drew himself up and stared me in disbelief. 'You saw the magic you held in your grasp. Whose power was that – who called it up? Certainly not you with your untutored powers. Could you do that without my assistance?' He placed his hands on his hips and waited for my reply.

I opened my mouth to rebuke him and closed it just as quickly. Apart from the times I would play magic games with Sasha as children – no, I couldn't get up a stream of magic like I'd held the other night. I could feel my outrage and self-righteousness collapsing inward.

'You will of course get a portion of the proceeds,' he added quickly, in a gentler voice. 'I'll make it worth your while.'

I shook my head. 'I don't want your money,' I said slowly. 'But I do need assistance in other ways.'

He nodded slowly, his eyes narrowed. 'I thought so,' he said. 'And the medallion you seek, I can give it to you, in exchange for becoming part of my coven.'

'And more,' I said. 'I don't just want that. I need you to help me clear up a small... problem.'

Willem leaned back on his crate, his eyebrow risen in question.

'I inadvertently brought that elf into real time,' I confessed. 'I need your help in sending him back to Alt.'

'He won't go back himself?' Willem asked. 'Why on earth would one of the elven persuasion want to be here?'

'Brin isn't like other elves,' I told him. Although I suspected my friend Alice was part elf, I'd only ever seen real elves in passing on one of my forays into Alt. Haughty, aloof, they left a cold draught in their path like the north wind. 'I mean, he is a full blood elf, but he doesn't think like the rest of them, and so he's been shunned. He's a mutant.... he's... nice.'

'Oh,' Willem said, as he thought about it. 'How unfortunate. That I really cannot picture, although he is a shoddy specimen. But if he's been rejected by his own kind over there, why not let him stay?'

'Because if the Witch Kin find out what I've done, they'll probably bind my magic,' I told him in a rush. It felt good to get it off my chest, to explain to someone who understood my dilemma. Having known the scorn of rejection from the Sorcerers' College, he could surely sympathize. We were unlikely accomplices, true, but as he had pointed out, we had some things in common.

'Hmm,' Willem leaned his back against the stone wall as he thought, his narrow eyes on me all the time. 'That's the elf who accosted me the other night. Send him back where he belongs, yes, that's a good idea. Serve him right.'

I nodded.

'Alright,' he said decisively as he stuck out his hand to seal the deal. His eyes glinted out of the shadows. 'We are partners.'

As our hands touched I stuffed down the frisson of dread that crept up my spine, submerged it right down there with the knowledge I might be making a pact with a devil. Arrogant as I was, I had no doubt whatsoever that I could prevail over Willem. He was, after all, merely a failed sorcerer, while I was a young witch on the brink of her mature powers. After I got what I wanted I could simply break the agreement at any time.

I would playact with him for his so-called coven, and I found I had no sympathy for the women who were being bilked out of their money - even if Carrie was an acquaintance of mine, maybe even a friend in a former life. They wanted what they could not have, and would be delighted with a mere illusion. Foolish women.

Whereas I, on the other hand, I was a powerful witch who needed a clean record in order to be allowed to study. Willem would send Brin back to where he belonged, and I would be able to act as if the whole incident never happened.

Even more, I would get the medallion which would lead me on the trail to my mother.

'Can you do it tonight?'

'Brin?'

'Yes, of course,' I said with a touch of impatience. 'He's right around the corner at the Rocket. What do we need to do?'

'Where did he come over?'

I sighed. 'Over by the old railway station,' I said. 'But he won't go back there, because he knows that's the only place I can make him return.'

'It won't be easy, what you ask,' he said, thinking hard. 'In fact, I couldn't possibly do it tonight. I need to gather some supplies....'

He paused, then spoke again. 'You know, Brin could be quite helpful to us. In our venture.'

'No!' It burst out of me before I could catch myself. I needed that elf gone, and now. No time for this flimflam and hedging. 'Can you do it or not? I need to see that you can really help before I get mixed up in your schemes.'

'Of course I can do it,' he snapped at me. 'But it's not that easy, okay? You'll need to get me some of his hair, and I'll want a blood candle. Zeta doesn't carry any real ingredients like that in her store.'

'A blood candle?'

'What, are you stupid? Never heard of one of the most basic necessities for the dark sorcery arts?' he asked, the sneer in his voice magnified by his Dutch accent. 'What kind of halfbaked witch are you?'

I said nothing for a moment. I was a natural witch, one quite 'unread' as Hugh put it, having had no formal education in the craft of witchery. However, Hugh had also poo-poo'ed the idea of spells and such, for as he put it, true magic came from the mind and the power of the witch. All that stuff, eye of newt and hair of toad and incantations, that was all just fluff and smoke and meaningless to a true witch. So Hugh said.

'Where are we going to find a blood candle, then?' I was beginning to feel like I was wasting my time here.

'Oh, I'm sure I can rustle something up,' he said dismissing my worries. 'But it's not going to happen tonight obviously.'

'When then?' I needed to pin this guy down, he was being far too slippery.

'I don't know,' he snapped. 'Give me time to think.'

Which he did, for a moment, then turned to me with a smile quite unsuited to his face.

'Tomorrow – yes, that timing is right. You will help me with my next project,' he said. 'Maybe this little witchling will go to the ball after all, hmmm? All of my friends, we shall attend the grand soiree *en masse*.'

He stood, to let me pass through the door. 'Bring the elf's hair first,' he hissed, too close to my ear. 'Upstairs. Tomorrow evening.'

I paused before leaving, my eyes on him uncertainly. What did the Witch Kin ball have to do with all this? I had no desire to crash their party – my aim was to remain totally under their radar until the elf was safely brought back to where he belonged. Willem started to laugh from deep within his belly when he saw the hesitation in my eyes.

All my senses were screaming not to trust him, but by this time I had no choice. I let him bring me back into Alt.

··············

I went through the door into the Alt Grog and flipped back to real time immediately. Willem didn't follow me, but I could hear the echoes of his evil laughter ringing against the stone walls.

'Hey, where did you appear from?' Jack was staring at me with disbelief. We were standing together at the bar.

'Oh, you know me,' I said weakly, giving no answer at all.

He shot me a weird look, but then reached over with his arm around me and gave me a peck on the cheek. 'Thanks for coming,' he said in my ear. 'It means a lot to me.'

It was a comforting place to be, within that embrace, but I couldn't stay.

'I have to go out again, but I'll be right back,' I said, and smiled apologetically over my shoulder as I left to find Brin.

The elf was still sitting exactly where I'd left him, thank God, a ring of chocolate and cream around his mouth and a cascade of croissant flakes down his front. He was seat-dancing to the jazz playing overhead, unmindful of the strange stares he was getting from the other patrons. I brushed him down and wiped his face, and he was good to go.

'Will Alice be there?' he asked as we left the bakery.

'Yeah, she'll be coming along soon,' I told him.

At the Grog Shop, the band had started their first set. I elbowed my way through the crowd, towing Brin in my wake. The coke I'd left on the bar was still there, the ice long melted, but I ordered a couple of bottles of water for us both, not knowing how much sugar an elf could take in his system. And I wouldn't take a chance on giving Brin alcohol.

And then Alice came in. Suddenly it was as if Brin had his own private spotlight, the glow coming from him was so strong. He clung to her, and she let him.

Jack's band weren't topnotch, I had to admit, being a little rough around the edges but it suited their grunge sound, and they had something good happening. Brin seemed to love them. He became so engrossed in the music that he even forgot Alice after a while, so entranced was he by the guitar and its electronic sound. After the first set ended, Brin bounced over to Jack and the guys.

I used this space of time to let Alice know about Brin's new sleeping arrangements.

'Thanks, Dara,' she said, a little sheepishly. 'We don't have the space in my house. Guess we didn't really think that one out, but...'

And I didn't tell her off, I didn't point out how their actions could be costing me my future. The elf wasn't long for this world, after all, for Willem would be sending him back to Alt tomorrow night, and I would let them enjoy what time they had together.

Besides, after my course in Scotland, then I could afford to return to Alt and re-unite the pair. At least that's what I told myself.

When the next set began, Brin still hadn't rejoined us, and to my horror I saw he'd now gotten up on the tiny bandstand with the guys. To stop his head from banging on the low ceiling, he hunched his back and kept his head low, all knees and elbows sticking out, but with a beatific smile on his face.

'I know that guy,' I overheard someone at the bar say. 'He was up at the Student Center today.'

'Crazy looking dude,' his friend added.

And then the elf began to sing, it was an elven ballad by the sounds of it, but he jazzed it up to go with the music provided by the band, and though his voice was as beautiful as a gentle rain in summer, to my ears the whole effect was truly awful.

'Oh, pale lady of the waterfall,' he crooned, smiling over at Alice the whole time.

Yet almost everyone else in the room became caught up in his spell, and the crowd yelled out for more. It might be a long night, for elves were well known for going on and on with their endless songs, even without encouragement from a drunken crowd.

Jack was the only person in the room who wasn't entranced. He hid it well, his lean body stoic and barely moving as he played bass, but I could tell by the way his eyes shifted to the elf and then to his band mates that he was puzzled that they allowed this interloper to interrupt their set. Jack did not feel the magic Brin had spread across the room.

I considered darting back into Alt in order to grab the medallion hidden in the cellar, but I didn't know if Willem was still over there or not, and didn't want to take the chance.

28

When we finally got home that evening, I convinced Brin to let Edna give him a haircut. I told him it was so he'd look good for Alice, and he didn't see me place the sweepings in the zip lock bag afterward.

He actually did look much better all cleaned up. With his hair soft and gleaming and neatened up on the edges, and the layer of coal dust scrubbed off his face so you could see his natural skin tone and his eyes all shiny with his new-found happiness, Brin could even be called beautiful.

The elf spent the next day helping Edna with the decorating, his height allowing him to easily put the star on the tree and affix the old-fashioned paper accordion streamers from the corners of the room. These were getting sadly tattered over the years but my aunt refused to toss them, claiming that they were irreplaceable and a necessary part of Christmas.

She was delighted by Brin, needless to say, and he'd even charmed Mark eventually after the cop saw there was absolutely no evil intent in my new friend's mind. The elf's soul was as clean as the driven snow, which made me feel even shittier for what I had to do.

While on the bus back from university, I received a text from Willem.

Do you have the elf's hair?

Yes. I texted back reluctantly. Even I had to admit Brin was really growing on me, and if it wasn't for the fact that his presence in real time had the potential to totally screw up my future plans, I would have let him stay on. Even Maundy was okay with him, and she could usually only tolerate family.

Good. Leave the elf in the bar while you meet me in Zeta's.

What are you going to do?

He didn't reply.

I let Alice know to meet us in the bar again later on, and I would have to steel myself to tell her the bad news. My heart broke for her, it really did. She finally found the one person she might be able to have a deep meaningful relationship with, and I had to send him back to his own dimension. I comforted myself with the idea that his return to Alt was in fact only temporary, and I would stress to her the need for her to devote her time at her studies. Alice had her heart set on a PhD eventually, so spending all her spare hours in bars watching her boyfriend sing in a band wasn't going to help her on her path, was it?

Brin was having the time of his life over here. As we made our way downtown, he skipped in circles all around me with his long legs. The passing cars slowed to gawp at this strange sight but I didn't hold him back as I figured he wasn't going to be this happy again for a long, long time.

I dropped him off in the bar where the guys were just setting up again. The rest of the band was happy enough to welcome Brin back, so I don't know if they had any recollection of his music the previous night - the enchantment of the elf spell may have wiped their memories. However, I caught Jack giving us an odd look.

'Who is this guy anyway?' he asked me in an aside.

'A friend of Alice's,' I said. 'A cousin or something. He's only visiting for a short while.'

'Oh,' Jack said, not meeting my eye.

'Why?'

'It's just that he's... weird,' he said.

'Tell me about it,' I said. It came out pretty vehemently. 'To make matters worse, he's staying with me.'

I wished I could tell him the whole story, but Jack didn't even know about my witch blood yet so the whole 'Elf from Alt' business had to stay under wraps for now.

'Oh, God,' he groaned. 'I know it's going to sound like I'm jealous or something, but I'm not! Not at all. I love jamming with all kinds of folk up on the stage. And I know everyone likes his music.'

'But?'

'Well... he's not actually very good,' Jack said, his clear eyes finally meeting mine. 'Is he?'

Brin had the power to take all eyes upon himself when he sang on the stage, and his voice was like an angel's as he wove the spell up and down and in through people's hearts with the threads of his elven song. But Jack was right, he really didn't fit the grunge vibe, and he sang to the beat of a different drummer. He wasn't a great fit for Jack's band.

And Jack was unenchantable.

'Not for a band where he has to play with other people,' I said. 'You're right. But can I ask a favour? Let him play with you guys for a bit again tonight. Please? I have to go off, but I'll be back really soon, and I can't have him wander off.'

He sighed and looked away. 'He's a little simple, isn't he, this guy Brin?'

'Simple is a good word for him.' Not that the elf was simple in the usual way the term was applied, but it worked for now.

'So you want me to babysit him.'

'Yeah,' I replied, then turned my most beseeching look on him. 'Please? I'll only be a couple of minutes, I promise, and Alice will probably be here before then.'

I left the bar to take the concrete steps up to Zeta's shop. As I huffed up those stairs, I thought about Jack being totally immune to the spell of the elf's song and wondered how it bode for our future relationship, if we ever got so far as to have one. I wouldn't be able to pull any shit over him, no confusing him with mind games or witchery. It was a comforting thought.

The heavy drapes were over the store's windows again. I let myself in. The room was fairly dark, lit only by a couple of candles on the counter.

'You have the hair?' Willem was on top of me the moment I walked into Zeta's. There was no one else around, just me and the sorcerer. He was looking almost feverish with excitement with high colour in his cheeks and eyes bright, but as he spoke his glance darted all around the room as if he searched for shadows within the shadows.

'Calm down,' I said, and handed him the plastic bag. 'Where's the coven?'

'We don't need them,' he replied absently. 'You and me, we are enough.'

'What do you mean?'

'Those women – useless. Now that I have you on board.' Willem turned to me finally and forced himself to smile. He let out a laugh that held no humour, and patted the pocket of his black robe. 'Their homage has been liquidated into gold and jewels. Interdimensional coinage, you might say.'

Discomfort was spreading through me at being alone with him here, with his frenzied manner. The small room was crowding in.

'Okay, so you and me together, we can send Brin back?'

He shrugged, but I could see the tension in his whole body as he turned back to the counter.

'We're sending Brin back to Alt, right?' I pushed again, determined to get a straight answer from this slippery sorcerer.

'Why do you care so much about the elf? He is a minor player!' He exploded and whirled to look at me. His pale eyes looked a little crazed. 'In the face of... '

He paused and his gaze turned suspicious. 'In the face of all that has happened today.'

'What's going on?'

'You don't know?'

I shook my head, and his face remained doubting. He stared at me as if looking past my face, trying to see my very aura for signs of deception.

Finally Willem breathed. 'I received my deportation orders. From your beloved father, no less.' His forehead was lined with stress, and he stared at me accusingly.

I stepped back, my hands raised in defence. 'It had nothing to do with me,' I said. 'We're not on speaking terms, me and Dad.'

His eyes narrowed in distrust as he sized up my words.

'They're sending you out of the country?' The Kin had the power to do that, I had no doubt, mixed up as they were with every government in power.

He let out a puff of air and flicked his hand as if brushing away a noisome fly. 'Some trifling trouble in Australia. All trumped up charges. Why they would bother with occurrences in that far away backwater, I don't know.'

He was right, they wouldn't exert themselves over problems in a country they didn't control. The Kin must fear something from him here and now, so the sooner my whole business with this sorcerer was finished, the better.

'So you did not betray me? Did not tell them what I plan?'

'I'm the one who *wants* you to toss the elf back into Alt! My life is on the line here, why the hell would I tell them anything?'

His face said he remained unconvinced.

'Why would I – you're the only one who can help me...' The conviction and the pleading in my voice must have satisfied him that I was telling the truth.

'Witch Kin,' he mumbled as he turned back to his task, his shoulders still fraught with tension. 'They think they rule the world, they believe they are the only power. I will show them they cannot trifle with me.'

He looked up again with his particularly nasty grin. '*We* will show them, eh, Dara? You and me together, we will show them.'

I started in alarm. Involving the Kin was not, and had never been, part of my plan. I needed the opposite, in fact, I needed to not draw their attention to me, and I told him that.

He brushed my objections aside. 'We will pay them back for all the hurt, all the rejection over the years,' he said. 'Do you not have a desire to see them fail, to see them fall flat on their beautiful faces? To watch them helpless in our hands?'

His eyes were lit by an eerie glow, and his face almost beautiful in the candlelight which lent a warmth to his features.

'I... I understand how you feel,' I said. My mind was racing, tripping up in itself as I tried to reach an argument to stop him. I didn't know what he had planned, but my heart knew instinctively there would be trouble in it for me. 'But do you really think this is the appropriate time to do anything drastic? Besides, your coven – you can still milk them for loads more money, some of them are uber-rich...'

I faltered as he shook his head.

'This is bigger,' he said. 'Far bigger.' He looked up at me. 'You're going to love what I have planned. All your dreams will come true, Dara – even the ones you haven't yet dreamed.'

The sorcerer was really creeping me out here. His eyes burned into mine as if he knew me, while a small smile danced at the edges of his mouth.

He held the clear bag up to the candlelight, his eyes shining with anticipation, then he opened the bag and sniffed deeply. 'Oh, yes. Let's do this thing.'

'Here,' he said in a normal voice again as he handed me an open bottle. 'Drink this down, you need hydration for the ceremony. It can really take the good out of you.'

Willem twisted the cap off another and downed the whole bottle in one pass.

'What exactly are you doing?' I asked after I'd taken a couple of swallows. It was raspberry flavoured vitamin water, horrible stuff. My eyes were adjusting to the dark. I forced myself to lean on the counter in a relaxed manner, chin in hand, watching him measure up things into a bowl. He was referring to a very large, thick old book with leather bindings.

He looked up at me sharply. 'I said, drink it all. Believe me, you will thank me.'

'Do you have any unflavoured water? This stuff is gross.'

He shook his head. 'You need the electrolytes. Down the hatch!'

I could feel his eyes on me as I took another mouthful, then he turned back to his preparations and I spit it silently back into the bottle.

'I've never done this one before,' he said almost under his breath. 'It will be interesting to see how it turns out.'

'You're not experimenting with Brin!' I said, shocked. 'I thought you knew what you were doing.'

29

He tch'ed at me, dismissing my fears. I sat back on the stool and watched him more closely. Willem had power, some. Although the potions offered at the fair lacked magic, and it had taken no unearthly power to hook the women in his coven, just flattery and bullshit, I knew from firsthand experience those horrible creatures of his held entrancement deep within them. And look at the way he had whisked me into Alt that time, and how we had together harnessed that blue magic in the coven.

'So, what are you doing?' I asked him again.

Willem looked up at the wall in front of him with his back still turned to me and spoke in a very patient and nasty voice. 'I'm creating a spell for the elf, what do you think I do? You asked me to do something about him.'

'I thought... well, I just thought you'd be able to make him go back to Alt,' I said. My voice sounded slow and all of a sudden I didn't feel like I was firing on all cylinders, like I was missing a beat in my thought processes. I shook my head to clear it. 'Convince him, like. I didn't think you'd need to create some hocus pocus spell.'

'Perhaps you don't know much about magic at all,' he sneered. 'Now shut it, I need to concentrate.'

When he'd finished what he was doing, he turned back to me.

'Bring over that candle,' he commanded. 'Place it on the shelf.'

I did as he bade then joined him at the center of the room where he had arranged a small table. He held a small glass beaker in his hand, the sort we used to use in Chem lab.

'I need you to put your fingertips on this, lightly, as if you are using a Ouija board.' he said, laying it on the surface before him. The liquid in the glass was murky grey with things floating in it. I could see bits of Brin's hair but couldn't identify the black lumpy blobs. 'It is of the utmost importance that you fully concentrate on this.'

Resting the tips of my fingers on the smooth surface, I found I couldn't avoid touching his hands even at the base of the beaker; the small digits thin and cold like a snake's skin. I forced down the bile that was gathering at the back of my throat and allowed his fingers to rest next to mine.

'That's it,' he said with a new soothing tone in his voice. 'Just like that, good girl. This is what we need.'

It was not too late to turn back and just walk out on this, cancel the whole thing. I was already feeling so tired of it all and losing the urgency of my feelings of even just an hour before. So what if Brin stayed? I could let the elf be, let him try to forge his own path in this new world and confess my wrongdoings to Hugh, and maybe I would have if I had thought Willem's potion was going to have the least little effect. But Hugh had promised me that true magic didn't rely on outside glamour and shimsham, it came from inside or it came not at all. That's what Hugh had told me last September, and I still believed it.

'I need you to focus your mind now,' Willem said. 'Close your eyes and think.... of nothing, nothing at all, focus on that place deep inside you.'

His voice had a hypnotic effect and I found myself going along with him, relaxing and growing heavy in body. The beaker was warming beneath my fingertips, and even his hands were losing their repugnance. We sat comfortably in our touch.

'Now Dara, I'm going to enter your mind,' he said softly. 'Has anyone ever done that before?

I thought for a moment, reaching through my memory as I tried to grasp the concept. I shook my head. Hugh had read my mind before, yes, but I'd never felt him inside me. Willem had no power over me, he could not enter the head of this witch.

'Good,' he said. 'An untouched mind. Your mind is pure, clean. Relax, and let me show you.'

He was filling my mind's eye and then I felt him enter, a cold small hand reaching in. I flinched slightly and felt him withdraw, yet still he hovered close.

Then like the softest breath, like the morning mist barely there, Willem came back. 'Hush, now,' he said. 'Hush, it's okay.'

My body was growing ever heavier, and then the feather-weight of his being gradually entered through my defences. I tensed only for a moment, but it was as if he was stroking me from the inside, smoothing down the quills in my mind, taking care of everything, and all of a sudden my distaste for the man had dissipated, I felt myself wanting more of that soothing touch within. Hungering for more of the peace his strange light touch was spreading through me.

'Yes, Dara, yes, good girl. Let me fill your mind, let my presence enter, take down the barriers,' he droned on.

And I did. I felt his presence filling in my head and didn't even fight it. He wasn't doing anything, just lingering around inside there and his voice was monotone and I didn't have to think. I found myself drifting off in a warm fuzzy haze of relief, and even my body was responding to him, growing warm yet excited, all my defenses down as his fingers found the hidden private places in my mind and he inexorably drove deeper and deeper, imprinting himself within.

I couldn't even pick out his words anymore, was he speaking Latin? Perhaps I should have made a start on the little grammar book Hugh had left for me but none of that seemed important right at that moment. I silently stepped aside, made room for Willem in my mind, allowed him to settle there and let his loving touch brush over the places that had never been touched before. It was strangely comforting, having another inside my head, for I could give up the fight, let him make the decisions, direct me. He nestled in, burrowing in, creating a place in me that was his alone and I could let my mind just drift.

And while drifting, it dawned on me that Hugh was wrong. This, this moment was right, with the sorcerer's presence deep inside me, this was true unity, the comfort of another with me. I didn't have to make all the decisions anymore, I could just be.

Hugh and all the Witch Kin. Hugh and his James Dean looks, the lean darkness of him. Hugh flying with me, that safe presence behind me, bolstering me up. Hugh talking about Willem, telling me something...

I had no sooner settled into my comfort zone than I was jolted out of it as a flash of lightning cracked through my brain, that same feeling of falling when you're on the brink of sleep, and I physically jumped.

'What just happened?' I opened my eyes to see the sorcerer triumphant across the space, his eyes ablaze with power. Our hands still touched, I quickly withdrew from the beaker. My voice was slurred. 'What the frig, Willem? What the hell are you doing?'

'I think we have it,' he said, his eyes now on the glass.

In the short space of time I had closed my eyes, the liquid in the container had changed texture, it was now frothy, creamy and thick. It almost looked good enough to drink if I didn't know its origins.

'How'd you do that?' I felt dazed and discombobulated, trying to shake off the feeling of his touch within me.

'We did it, Dara,' he said triumphantly. 'Well, I did it, with your assistance. We will go far, my dear.'

'I don't... understand...'

He interrupted me. 'No, you'll feel dizzy for a short while still,' he said. 'Quick, now. You need to get the elf here. Immediately.'

'You're not going to make him drink that, are you?' I asked.

'It won't harm him, merely give him thoughts about his childhood home,' Willem looked at me and smiled. 'Do you think I'd allow your friend to be hurt? After what we just shared?'

30

I didn't want to think about what had just happened, the bile was rising in my throat again even at the sight of his tiny fingers. But he was right, I did still feel dizzy from whatever had happened back there. I stumbled down the outside steps and into the bar, and beckoned to Brin. He was just about to get up on stage with the guys.

'I want to sing,' he said.

I shook my head. 'Never mind that right now,' I told him, leaning against the doorway of the bar and trying hard not to think of Willem inside my head and how good it had felt and how I wanted to throw up. 'Lots of time for that later. I need you to come with me.'

He only pouted a little before coming outside with me.

'Alice is not here yet,' he pointed out. 'Will you use your black box to tell her where we are?'

'Yeah, I'll text her,' I said. The stairs loomed steep above my head, and I had to stop for another moment. I entered the message into the phone as I tried to collect myself. Still my stomach heaved and I couldn't help it, I had to let loose into the corner of the steps.

'What's wrong, Dara?' Brin asked as he hovered over me, his wide mouth drawn down in consternation. 'You're sick and you don't seem yourself. Were you imbibing?'

I shook my head as I wiped my mouth. 'No, I'm okay, I just feel a little funny. I'll be alright.'

I flashed him a weakly reassuring smile and led him up to Zeta's where Willem awaited.

'Ah, my friend,' the sorcerer said, welcoming Brin onto the shop. 'Come in, let's let bygones be bygones, and we'll all have a drink of hot chocolate. How jolly it will be.'

Brin stopped on the threshold of the store, his ears beginning to quiver. He shook his head vehemently and braced his arms on the door jambs of the entrance, for all the world like a cat being told to get in his carrier for a trip to the vet.

'Dara?' he asked me, his voice trembling just a little. 'I cannot come in here. Evil awaits.'

'It's alright, Brin,' I said gently. 'Willem wants to be friends. He's not going to hurt you.'

I took his arm and patiently nudged him inside. He stood there shivering for a moment longer, then allowed himself to be brought in to the store, his eyes on mine the whole time. The warm smell of chocolate diffused through the store, mixing with herbs of cardamom and cinnamon that were Zeta's magic stock in trade.

I knew I was betraying the elf's trust, but I told myself it was for his own good, brushing aside his fears in my need to get this awkward problem solved. I could feel Willem's approval at my actions and a part of me deep inside longed to drink from that well. But that wasn't why I was encouraging

Brin to follow me, I told myself. Brin needed to be sent back from whence he'd come.

A pulse was beginning to throb inside my head, thudding and banging till it was like a hammer and I was feeling a terrible thirst. Willem had been right, whatever it was we'd done had made me dehydrated. I could hardly make it to the chairs Willem had laid out in a circle.

'See?' The sorcerer was holding up a tray with three mugs of steaming chocolate with whipped cream and sprinkles on top. He lifted his upper lip into a smile, displaying an even row of chiclet teeth. The elf had followed me reluctantly inside the store, warily keeping his distance from Willem. He moved his chair closer to mine as if for safety.

I took the mug handed to me automatically, but hesitated before I brought it to my lips. The strange feeling I had, could Willem have drugged my bottle of water? I sniffed the hot chocolate, and even sent sensors into it, looking for something that wasn't the basic milk, cream, chocolate and sugar.

It wasn't drugged. My eyes met Brin's. His drink had the potion that Willem assured me wouldn't cause harm. I took a careful sip and the sugar rushed to my brain, clearing my head a little.

Brin saw the effect on me, nodded and lifted the oversized mug to his lips. But he had no sooner taken one swallow than his face crumpled and he let out a loud howl. The vessel fell to the floor, smashed, the contents splashed everywhere.

'Christ, Willem!' I said as I forced myself to rise and stand over the elf. 'What the hell did you do? Brin, are you okay?'

'There's no physical harm done,' the sorcerer replied calmly as he hefted Brin's lanky body back into his chair. 'It's all in his mind.'

The elf's eyes stared unseeing into the distance, his face contorted into a silent scream.

'No harm?' I stared at the elf in horror. What had I done, what doors to hell had I opened for him? Beautiful, gentle, fun loving Brin. 'Look at him! He's in pain.'

'Hmm,' Willem rubbed his chin. 'I may have been heavy handed on the worm wort, but it will not be long lasting. He only drank a little bit, after all.'

He stood up calmly. 'Get away from him, Dara.'

I refused to leave the side of my friend, but Willem strode over and roughly manhandled me away. The small man had surprising strength in his grasp. He shoved me against the nearest shelving with the books and jars and baskets of stuffed unicorns and turned his back on me and immediately started his loud incantations in Latin again.

Picking myself off the floor I turned in time to see faint wisps of haze surrounding Brin, and then they were gone as if they'd never been. I dashed back over to be with him only to find myself smashing against an invisible, unyielding wall.

After a moment I recovered from the blow, and tried again this time hitting out with my fist. It bounced back as if I had hit a Plexiglas window. The sorcerer stood by with his arms crossed and a superior smile on his face.

Brin sat there unmoving in the chair as if he didn't even hear me shouting and railing against Willem.

'I don't know why you're complaining so much,' Willem sneered. 'You led the elf into the pentacle yourself.' He held the candle aloft to shine onto the floor.

For the first time, I saw a design on the inlaid wooden floor. Scuffed through years of hard use as it was, the soft glow of the candle now showed the dark woods against the light, mahogany and oak and chestnut and elm, all pieced together to create an intricate pentacle like a Celtic knot.

And Brin's chair was in the middle of it. Slightly off center, true, for he had moved closer to me when he sat down, but still inexorably and uncontestably within the wooden marking.

'I thought we were going to send him back to Alt,' I said. 'But he's still here.'

'It does not suit me to send him off yet,' Willem replied. 'I still need your cooperation, and you won't give me that if you have everything you need, will you? Even though I have branded myself onto your virgin mind, and you can't ever escape that. I still need to ensure your obedience.'

My stomach lurched up again at his words. Was it true? Surely I could control my own mind if nothing else in my life, there was no way his threats could be true.

'You cast a spell on him,' I said slowly as I sank into the nearest chair. 'What did you do? You said the potion wouldn't hurt him.'

'You asked me for assistance for something you can't do,' Willem said slowly, turning to look at me. 'I'm a sorcerer, of course I'm going to cast a spell. That's what sorcerers do.'

'I didn't think you knew any real magic though,' I blurted out. My head was still pounding.

'Then you underestimated me, didn't you?' he said, a vicious grin coming across his face. 'Like all your kind do. Witch Kin.'

'But you failed Sorcerer's College,' I said to him. I rallied my head together. 'How powerful can you really be?'

Even as I spoke I heard Hugh's words again. Not failed, not at all, but thrown out for cheating. There was a huge difference between the two.

He looked at Brin and laughed again. 'Powerful enough, don't you think? Although your assistance was invaluable. No, I couldn't do it without you letting me access your mind's power.'

'You... drugged me, in the bottle of water, you added something,' I said. 'But it wasn't magic, I would have sensed it.'

'No, just a few of Zeta's benzo's,' he admitted. 'Probably just as well you didn't drink the whole thing. It did the trick of relaxing you enough.'

'And the potion you gave him?'

"I told you it would make him think of his homeland,' Willem replied, oh so smugly. 'Unfortunately, it had a tinge of grief added to the mix, which has exacerbated his own painful memories. Interesting, isn't it?'

'You need to undo it. Now. Please. I'll.... I'll do whatever you need. Just let him go.'

'I don't think so,' Willem said, shaking his head. 'It suits my purpose to keep him right where he is in order to convince you to give me your wholehearted assistance. You se e...'

With that he spun around and faced me, the candle lighting his face from below. He loomed over me as I sat.

'Do you know how difficult it is to kill an elf?'

I shook my head numbly. I had largely skipped over the elf bits in Lord of the Rings. As I said before, the songs bored me tremendously.

'They can be wounded if pierced through the heart, in battle,' he said. 'Or, they can die of grief.'

The meaning of his words slowly sank in.

'But, you sent him into a grief spin, remembering his sad childhood,' I whispered. 'You mean he could die of this?

Willem nodded briskly. 'Yes, so time is of the essence.' He laughed, a horrible sneering laugh, and sounded quite pleased with himself.

'But why, Willem? Why are you doing this to Brin?'

'I'm not doing it *to* Brin, dear Dara,' he said. 'Brin is inconsequential to me. I don't care if he goes back home, stays here, or cries himself to death.'

He smiled at me. 'It was the easiest way to ensure your cooperation.'

Willem pulled up the chair next to me. 'Now, I'll just tell you what I need from you,' he said briskly. 'And then maybe we can dislodge this spell from your friend.'

I listened numbly to what he told me, my heart sinking further and further with every word. Finally I nodded.

'Do you promise on your word, for what it's worth, to let Brin go?'

'Oh yes,' he said, as if surprised. 'I told you, I have no need for him.

'And,' he added as he patted my knee. 'You shouldn't worry about the whole 'dying of grief' thing. I'm sure that won't really happen. Besides, he only drank a swallow or two. He'll be recovering from his woes soon enough.'

He got up and stretched as if working out a particularly hard knot from his shoulders. 'Of course,' he said. 'He can't move from this spot till I allow him to. This has upped the stakes quite a bit, wouldn't you say?'

31

Willem told me his plans for the following night, plans in which I figured largely, if unwillingly.

The Witch Kin Ball, that exclusive display of the wealth and privilege of the witches, this year it was to be held at the old Colonial Building. Recently renovated to a finer state than it had been for decades, this once-forgotten stone symbol of British Colonialism had been left to rot after the province joined forces with Canada and the first premier created his own phallic monument of brick standing high over the city. The original seat of government was used to house the archives of the province and forgotten art works and other things of little importance in the dawning age of oil found in the Grand Banks offshore.

The building had been rescued at the last moment, however, and returned to a standard of perfection it hadn't seen for years, even the paintings on the ceilings had been cleaned and retouched, and it was all freshly glowing and ready to be opened to the public.

But, not quite yet, for the Witch Kin had claimed the right to hold the inaugural event here, and it was to be the exclusive do which kicked off the Christmas season for those in power. Of course it was an invitation only event. Even the catering staff and musicians had to be rigorously vetted before they were allowed in.

Willem had a chip on his shoulder about the Witch Kin, a boulder in fact as big as Signal Hill. I had seen his reaction to Cate at the craft fair, the loathing in his tense shoulders, and the deportation order from my father must have been the last straw which pushed him to the brink of madness. It was with great glee that he told me he would be interrupting the ball and ruining their night.

'You can't get in there,' I told him, still stunned with the realization of how I had let him ensnare Brin. 'The security at that place, they won't let you get past the door.'

'I don't need to get inside,' he said. 'Not for what I'm planning. In fact, nobody will be crossing that gate while I'm wreaking my havoc.'

'And how can *I* help you? Why do you insist you need me?'

'It's nothing you've not already done,' he replied, a greasy smile breaking over his face. 'Just like this evening, you will allow me access to your power.'

'I don't understand,' I said as I clamped down on the shiver that threatened to take over. 'What's the point of all this that you're doing? How are you gaining here? I can understand the coven – you want their money – their gold and silver and jewels. But why bother with the Kin? You'll only piss them off and they'll still run you out of town, if not worse.'

'No one will be running me out of town,' he replied haughtily. 'I'll leave under my own volition. The point of it all is that they will know my name then, and they will not be laughing.

The Kin think I'm nothing but a failed sorcerer... and they will see their mistake. *I will undo their own work!* They will know the extent of my power, and that, my dearest sweet Dara, that is my sole purpose.'

What could this one small man possibly do, outside the Ball, to harm and bother the Kin? The Colonial Building would be packed to the rafters with powerful witches. He was a single sorcerer who never graduated, who needed even my untutored skills in magic to help him cast his spells.

But if he was able to do serious damage.... I realized the implications of his plans. Christ. My little forays into Alt and inadvertently bringing an elf back were nothing in comparison to this. He was going to actively cause havoc at the Witch Kin Ball, and only because he was so pissed at them for not allowing him to join, for rejecting him. It was an act of pure spiteful insanity. Worse, if my part in this was found out, even though I could argue I had been forced to help him, I would lose all my dreams for the future so quickly I probably wouldn't even remember that I was ever magic.

I had a choice of course. I could simply say no, and in doing so lose any chance of getting the medallion which was the only clue to my Mom's disappearance. Brin would be left in God only knew what hell hole Willem had forced him into, and Alice would never again know her true happiness.

But that deep place within me where he'd left his mark like an infected bite, that dark little corner of my mind where he'd left his foul touch, it wanted more, it wanted nothing more than to peel off the scab and see the pus ooze, probe it deeper and relieve the itch.

I told myself my actions were done out of nobility, out of a desire to see my friends' happiness.

....

Hugh had accused me of arrogance. Maybe he was right, maybe I was more arrogant than an unread half-blood witch had any right to be, but that arrogance helped me quickly work through my despair so that all I was conscious of was a deep and thorough anger.

And now I should tell Alice that Brin had returned to Alt. It wouldn't be a lie, for in his head he had returned home, or so Willem said. And the elf would be going soon enough, right after I helped with the final plans tomorrow night. Willem would get his revenge on my father and his Kin, this harmless prank he was playing. Then he'd send the elf back where he belonged, I'd get my medallion and pack my bags for Scotland. I could only pray that my part in Willem's doings would not come to light.

On the other hand, Alice could help me, and would, if she knew the truth. Oh sure, she'd be plenty pissed at me for allowing Willem to enchant the new found love of her life, so much so that our friendship might never recover. We went back a long way, me and Alice, right from grade school when we were both two little weirdos no one else wanted to play with. She had never cared about the stuff the other kids thought was so important, like money and who your folks were. Hey, she was the great-granddaughter of Nan Hoskins, the terror of Southside Road, so she had no room to be snobby, did she?

But if I didn't tell her the truth, well what kind of friendship was that? I would always know what I had done, and not being able to tell her would place a barrier between us.

The band was still on their second set - how little time had passed since I'd brought Brin up to the store. It felt as if a day and a night had passed, but it couldn't have been more than an hour.

She was waiting by the bar, all hunched over on her stool like she wasn't enjoying the music and couldn't wait to leave. Her eyes brightened when she saw me, but strayed to the door behind me.

'Where's Brin?' she asked immediately.

'He's...,' I didn't get to tell her because the band finished their set and the room was full of loud clapping and cheering and then Jack was at our side, all perspiring and happy and pumped with his group's success. He gave me a hug and greeted my friend.

I introduced the two of them, not mentioning the elf.

Jack couldn't wait to tell us his news.

'We're going to be playing at the Mummer's Parade tomorrow night! At the bandstand in Bannerman Park, where it all wraps up,' he said. 'How cool is that, right? The guys who were booked had to drop out, so it's pretty last minute, but whatever!'

The Mummer's Parade. That glorious celebration of make believe for Normals, where they dressed up in costumes and pretended to be mean and scary, but meanwhile everyone knew it was just for fun. And no one would suspect that any real wrong doing was to occur.

I didn't know exactly what was going to happen, but deep within me I knew it couldn't just be a harmless display of the sorcerer's power to the witches, despite Willem's assurances.

'Where's Brin?' Alice interrupted Jack and was almost beside herself now as she shook my shoulder. I had to look her in the face, and she knew me well enough to see the truth there.

'What did you do with him?' she shouted over the noise of the crowd. 'Dara, is he in danger? Did you trick him into going back to that place?'

I sent an apologetic look at Jack and dragged Alice out of the bar.

She was almost in hysterics by this time. 'I know something's wrong with him, I can feel it,' she said to me furiously.

This might be the first time she ever admitted to having intuition or anything that wasn't, in fact, based on scientific origin.

'Okay, 'I said to her at last. 'Just calm down. He *is* in trouble, and it is my fault.'

'I knew it! What did you do to him?'

I glanced up above our heads to where Brin was sitting in the middle of the inlaid pentagram inside Zeta's store. The side window was blank and covered with the heavy damask curtain still, with no hint of the evil it was hiding from prying eyes.

'Is he up there?' She made to run up the concrete stairs, but I grabbed her arm.

'You can't get in there,' I said. 'And yes, he is there and can't get out. But he's safe enough where he's to.' I hoped that Willem was telling the truth about the grief potion wearing off before it could stop the elf's heart, before he simply pined away in anguish.

Her eyes filled with tears. 'He's very sad, isn't he?'

'Alice,' I said. 'There's nothing we can physically do for him at the moment. Like I said, he's safe enough, and nothing can touch him. But...'

'Yeah?'

'Maybe you can send him love,' I said wretchedly. I was really grasping at straws here. 'Love and hope and knowing that the two of you have found each other, and you can be happy again in the future.'

Hope. That might be the only thing that would save the elf's life. If she could somehow convey that to him and keep him strong, well, that was one less thing I had to worry about. And I knew for certain at that moment that I wouldn't be sending Brin back to Alt, back to that cold and loveless land where he'd been rejected all his life.

She stood on the stairway and stared up at the window, and began humming a tune. I recognized it as one of Brin's own that he had cast for the crowd last night.

I felt a movement out of the corner of my eye, and turned to find Jack standing in the doorway staring at us, his arms crossed and an unreadable expression on his face.

'What's going on?' His voice was quiet against the buzz of the crowd inside.

I left Alice and walked over to him. 'I don't know where to begin,' I said, keeping my voice low. 'And I don't think you'd understand.'

A look of accusation had crept into his eye. He had just watched me devastate my best friend in the world. While he didn't understand what was going on, still he had every right to be suspicious of me and not want anything to do with me.

'Whatever, Dara,' he replied. He made to turn away, but hesitated, giving me one last chance. 'You going to the parade tomorrow night?'

The parade. Oh, yes I would be there, an unwilling accomplice to Willem, but yes, I would be there. I nodded.

I could see a reluctant hope flare in his eyes again. 'Catch you later, then.'

There was one thing I could have done for Alice, and that was to unlock the door to Zeta's store to allow her in to sit vigil with Brin. That lock was an easy one, for Zeta had no magic to cast on it and Willem had never bothered. I also knew Willem would have come up with some excuse for Zeta not to enter her own store, and that she would go along with him, lovesick fool that she was.

But I couldn't do it, couldn't allow her to sit with him overnight, for it would only torture her more. Instead, she called up her brother Benjy to come pick her up, and she left without a word, not even offering me a lift home.

32

When I went back in the bar to pick up my bag, Jack was nowhere to be seen. I didn't bother trying to get him through phone or text; instead, I made my slow way up the west end of Water Street by myself, past the stumbling drunks on their way to George Street, past the homeless drifters looking for a bed to stay at the hostels and decrepit boarding houses in the neighbourhood.

I paused under the overpass, looking across the road to where Brin's humble cottage was located in that other realm, Alt, now just a sea of concrete and iron link fences, and the reality of my situation burst upon me. As I headed up the long dark driveway to my home the tears ran cold down my cheeks, almost freezing in the north wind.

Edna and Mark were still up, and the kitchen was alight with their laughter. I brushed aside the wet from under my eyes before coming through the back porch to join them.

'Mummer's Parade tomorrow night!' Edna sang as she saw me. 'Are you excited?'

She held up a baggy pair of woolen trousers from the last century. An ancient steamer trunk lay open before her.

'Mark lugged this down from the attic for me,' she said. 'I'd forgotten about all of Dad's old clothes. Perfect for costumes! Whadda'ya say, think these'll fit me with a pillow stuffed down the front? I even have the matching suspenders.'

Mark just sat at the table with his coffee mug in front of him, grinning like a fool at her childlike anticipation of the seasonal celebrations.

'And look, Aunt Sadie's house dresses!' Edna was truly in her glee. 'She was a big woman, Mark. I think I've found what you're going to wear!'

'Oh, no,' he laughed. 'Sorry to burst your bubble, but I won't be dressing up tomorrow night.'

She turned a mock frown towards him, blue eyes peering from behind her brown curls.

'I'm on duty,' he explained. 'I'll be at the parade, but not in costume. We've been seconded to the RNC for the night.'

'Why the big police presence?' she asked. 'Sure, it's only a bit of fun, the Mummer's Parade.'

'Technically, mummering is still illegal, at least in some parts of the island,' he noted. 'But there's also a big gala happening at the same time in the old Archives Building. A costume ball for the high and mighties of town.'

'A masquerade?' Edna slowly lowered the tatty old trousers in her hands, her eyes softening. 'You mean, like with fancy-dress and feathered masks?'

'Yeah,' he agreed. 'They're celebrating the opening of the building, all the renovations finally finished done and over with, even the little glass tower atop which hadn't made it into the original building because of budget over-runs. It'll be a slap-up affair.'

'Can anyone go?' She dropped the pants and rooted through the trunk, finally pulling out an old silk ball gown of her mother's. It was the colour of autumn leaves, the golden satin all shimmery and shot with russets and ochre. Edna shook it out and stood with the dress held against her body, her face shining. 'This would be perfect.'

'Sorry,' Mark said, shaking his head. 'Invitation only, I'm afraid. We won't even be inside, just on the periphery outside, to ensure it remains private.'

He harrumphed, and continued. 'I don't necessarily agree with using publicly funded police resources on a private function, but then again I'm not in charge, am I?'

I remained silent throughout their discussion, my heart rising with hope at Mark's news. If the police were going to have such a large presence at Bannerman Park and its environs tomorrow night, then surely Willem wouldn't be able to get up to much mischief, would he?

Would he?

'Well, I don't want to go to their stupid hoighty-toighty ball anyway,' Edna said as the silk fell back into the trunk with a rustle. 'I'll stay with the proletariat on the sidelines, and we'll make our own fun, won't we, Dara?'

I wouldn't call my plans fun, but I smiled at her weakly anyway.

'Oh Dara, I almost forgot,' Edna said. 'Speaking of the upper classes, Hugh is trying to reach you. He phoned twice tonight on the landline.'

'He didn't try my cell?'

'Said he did, but it was cutting right into voice mail,' she said, fishing out the pants and suspenders out of the trunk again. 'Not like you not to have your phone on.'

I shrugged, but she didn't see it. 'Did he say what he wanted? Or was he just sending me a long-distance nagging to remind me to get on to the books he wants me to read?'

'He said something about wanting to see you tomorrow,' she replied as she closed the trunk and stood up.

'But he's in Paris!' I blurted out, aghast. Surely to God he was still in Europe. He wasn't due to come back here at all before Christmas, and I would be meeting him in Scotland in the New Year. At least, that was my hope and understanding.

'Maybe he wants you to call him tomorrow, perhaps that's what he said.' Edna shrugged. 'He kept interrupting my writing hours, so perhaps I wasn't really concentrating on what he actually said. Something about tomorrow, anyway.'

'I'll call him in the morning then,' I said, much relieved.

That would be just what I needed, Hugh showing up in the middle of all this mess.

....

The snow started the next day, falling softly, making everything outside my window a monochromatic landscape, all shades of white and silver and the palest grey, no sun to create shadows, just a luminousness, a brighter white, where the sky used to be. It was the kind of snowfall you'd rather have on Christmas Eve, a blanket settling down on the town and shutting the place up in a cozy Yule duvet.

Unfortunately, it wasn't Christmas yet and life went on.

It was still just December 10th and the Prof was expecting my paper to be emailed in today by noon, the last possible deadline. Any later and he wouldn't have a chance to mark it.

I reread his last email to me and the other errant students in the Folklore class. He was pretty cool, really, just a young PhD student from the mainland, desperately looking for tenure at a university like ours. It dawned on me that he couldn't afford to have too many fails in his class, not in his precarious position. His missive to us even had a note of pleading within it.

A 3000 word paper showing you have done the necessary research to garner a deeper understanding of the chosen topic. I don't care what form it takes – come on, guys, this is Folklore! Write me a short story if you want, just as long as it meets the minimum word count and you show its relevance to today.

Easy enough for him to say, but what was he really looking for?

I sat on my bed under the patchwork quilt and sipped my coffee, the results of my research spread out all around.

Willem proclaimed himself to his followers as the Lord of Misrule, yet the proper season for it didn't begin until after the official holidays on Twelfth Night, or January 6 according to the modern calendar. A bit of artistic license on his part, no doubt, or maybe just ignorance which he didn't bother to correct.

The whole tradition was little more than blowing off steam at the unfairness of life, really. Back in the medieval years, a person's life path was pretty much seen as written before they were born. Once a peasant, always a peasant. A member of the royal family, however, would always live a life of privilege, even if they had to sponge off their richer relatives to do so. Back then, you were what you were, and there was no moving beyond it.

So to reverse the roles even if only for a couple of days, perhaps it gave people a chance to pretend, to mock their betters, to wreak a little revenge while they were at it.

Was this all Willem wanted? To ruin the ball, make a mockery of all those wielders of magic who considered themselves superior to him and had closed ranks against him? That's the gist of what he had said to me, but I had my doubts. There was so much repressed fury in the man.

My papers were long forgotten by now as my thoughts took me further along this road, remembering those poor lost souls in Alt - human, yes, but because of an accident of birth stuck forever in the pain and misery of being unmagical creatures in a magical land, unable to imagine a better life and finding solace only in their gin.

Even myself, born from a Witch and a Normal without a foothold in either world. With the disappearance of Mom, I had been stuck in a no-man's-land of being magical but not being allowed to exercise this power or learn to use it properly. Until Hugh had arrived and recognized me for what I was.

Hugh. Call Hugh back.

Shoot, I'd left my phone in my knapsack downstairs. Still if he really wanted to talk with me, he'd phone the landline again.

I brushed that aside and tried to focus on the paper again, and that's when it hit me. I could write the story of Willem. It would take the form of 'fiction' of course, but be set in our modern times, and would definitely show that I understood the concept of the Lord of Misrule.

Laughing to myself, I set about writing on my laptop. I was going to ace this one after all, why had I even been worried?

33

I finished the short story just half an hour after its deadline and smiled to myself as I closed down my laptop. Apologies for the lateness had been sent with my work, but I was pretty sure he would enjoy it. Might even decide it was well worth the lateness, and give me accolades for my cleverness and originality.

My foot had fallen asleep for Hal the cat had cuddled on top of it, and he was no lightweight. I dislodged him as I got off the bed and stretched. He moaned for a moment as if mortally wounded, but soon rolled over and the groan morphed back into a snore.

Bouncing down the stairs, I was feeling the buzz of accomplishment and decided to finally phone Hugh back. My call went straight to voice mail, and he hadn't called me either.

In fact, nobody had contacted me, not even on FaceBook. A little disgruntled and wanting to spread my good feelings around, I tried Alice, but she wasn't picking up. Jack hadn't answered my text.

The fridge had food in it anyway thanks to Mark, so I ate a small lunch and then looked at the steamer trunk still on the kitchen floor. It was the solid kind, created from wood and leather and made to withstand the rigours of a trans-Atlantic steamship journey.

The silk dress still lay on top where Edna had dropped it when Mark told her she couldn't attend the ball. I fingered the soft satin with velvet detail on the tiny cap sleeves and at the waist. Normally, I've always been a hoody and jeans kind of girl, but something in the fabric spoke to me. I laid it against my body as Edna had done last night, and let myself imagine actually wearing an outfit like this 'Fifties confection, the large skirt with the stiff petticoats floating out all around, and I twirled as if in a dance.

Could I ever be the kind of person who wore this dress?

Maybe, after I finished my course in Scotland and found my place in the world, maybe then I could discard this tomboy self and be a full-fledged witch, maybe work with Hugh with his witchy Interpol even, and be sophisticated enough to be invited to the Witch Kin balls.

With my free hand I took my hair and piled it on top of my head, the way Sasha did sometimes and I danced on my tiptoes as if I wore her Manolo Blahniks. For that moment in time, I floated on dreams of my bright future.

My graceful turn around the kitchen brought me smack up against the window and the sight of the unshovelled driveway outside. The snow was letting up a bit, I could even see patches of blue sky trying desperately to break through the heavy clouds. That could only mean the wind was rising.

'Edna?' I called out. 'Edna, you think the parade is still going ahead with this snow?'

I held my breath. If the parade was cancelled, then the ball probably would be too, and I would be under no obligation to the sorcerer tonight. I would have time to sneak downtown and pick open the lock on Zeta's store and rescue the medallion and try to figure out what to do about Brin. I swallowed, and shoved the dress back into the trunk, feeling just a little guilty for not making him my top priority that morning.

'Yeah,' I heard her shout from inside her office, deep within the house. 'It's turning to rain, the radio says, so you better shovel now while you can. The snow'll get too heavy to move soon.'

'Maybe Mark'll want to do it,' I called out to her as I eyed the four inches of snow covering everything on the ground. Guys liked doing that stuff, it made them feel manly, didn't it?

'Just shovel the god damn driveway!' she barked back at me. 'Don't leave it for Mark. And then figure out what you're wearing for a costume!'

With a heavy sigh, I took all my cold weather gear from the closet in the hallway where they'd been stored for the past six months. Boots. Parka. Hat, scarf and the felted mitts that Edna knit. I'd been putting this off as long as I could, like I did every year. But the fact of the turning of the seasons was inexorable, especially here in Newfoundland, and we'd be lucky just to have four months of this weather.

Mark had already left for work in Edna's jeep, I could see the tracks through the snow, He was such a gentleman, he wanted her to drive his SUV because it was more sturdy on the snow covered roads and hills.

My mind worked as I began to uncover the gravelled driveway beneath the mantle of snow. A full one third of our lives were spent in the harsh grasp of winter here, a fact easily forgotten when the summer sun beamed its glorious rays on us and the world was green. How much we took the good weather for granted, how short our memories were.

What the hell were we thinking, all of us Newfoundlanders? Hadn't anyone done this math before? I grumbled till I'd shovelled the grouch right out of my system and found myself at the road just as the rain was starting. I hadn't realized the wind was getting warmer, working furiously as I'd done. I threw the shovel into the snowbank I'd created at the side of the house and ran to the porch. With the heavy cloud cover, it was already dusk, and still only three o'clock in the afternoon.

A quick check of my phone showed me that no one had contacted me. Not even Willem. I bit my lip. I had agreed to meet Willem in Zeta's store before the parade began.

He'd promised he was only going to raise a little hell and havoc and embarrass the Witch Kin, though why he needed my help for that I couldn't conceive.

....

'That's what you're wearing?' Edna stood before me. 'Just a pillowcase over your head? That's not very imaginative.'

'Edna, it's cold and wet out there,' I said. 'I'm going to wear this stupid dress over my coat, alright? Just not yet, I have to do something before the parade begins. I promise I'll put in on afterwards.'

I picked up Great Aunt Sadie's flowery house dress as proof, then held it against me and smiled up at Edna.

She caught her breath and looked at me, a horrified recollection on her face. 'Marian wore that one year... Oh God, I forget sometimes how much you look like her.'

I clutched the dress to me, and now I remembered too, the last time this dress had been worn. Mom, one summer evening, coming out to the lawn from the French doors, giggling and laughing as she twirled around in Aunt Sadie's voluminous dress and little else, not even sandals on her bare, tanned feet.

Dad laughing with her, getting up to dance with her to the music which poured out the windows from the old stereo, it may have been the Beach Boys.

That was back before the fighting had started, before the anger.

I shook the memory from me. 'Well, it's time this dress went out and had fun again, don't you think?'

Edna herself wore her full regalia of men's rubber boots (with thick hand knit socks inside), the oversize pants with suspenders, a couple of sweaters and a windbreaker underneath the checked flannel shirt. She held a large straw sunhat in her hand – it would go over the filmy scarf meant to cover her face and hair.

'Okay then,' she said. 'Let's go – I want to leave the SUV up by the park, so we'll walk down to City Hall.'

The Mummer's Parade traditionally started at City Hall, with speeches and everything from the Mayor before it wound its way up through Duckworth Street and Cochrane then in front of the Lieutenant Governor's mansion and on to Bannerman Park.

The sidewalks along the route were cleared at least, and she took the last parking spot outside the ice cream store, still open even in this weather. She made me take the keys, seeing as I had deep pockets in my coat. From there we headed down Queen's Road toward City Hall but as we reached the short lane that led steeply to Duckworth, I mumbled my apologies and told her I'd catch up to her later. Before she could say a word, I darted down the hill to Zeta's store.

I flung open the curtained door and there was Willem waiting for me, his cheeks flushed in his usually colourless face, in a state of high excitement. Black candles were lit in strategic spots, and the air itself was thick with the smell of burning incense.

He shot me a look which sparked right into that tiny corner of my mind, that dark space I had been trying to ignore that leapt to meet him. His pale eyes were almost luminescent from the shadows.

'Come here, my dear,' he said in a soft voice. 'Our hour of glory is upon us.'

I found myself drawn to his hand before I could fight that horrid fascination and tear my eyes from his.

'Where's Brin?' There was no sign of the elf, the center of the shop was cleared of everything, including the chairs. I looked around wildly searching as if I might see my friend tucked away under a shelf. Dear Jesus, had Willem sent him back to Alt already?

'Your elf?' Willem laughed. 'I've moved him down to the cellar. We need the pentagram for more important things.'

'I thought he was stuck in the circle,' I said as I approached the center. I slowly moved my hand through the air over where Brin had sat just yesterday. Nothing stopped me this time. 'Is he okay? I need to see him, to make sure.'

I didn't trust the sorcerer.

'Oh, ye of little faith,' Willem said, shaking his head. He wore a clean black robe today, I noticed, and his short hair was freshly cut. 'We are partners, are we not? I gave you my word. But if you insist, go ahead. He's just down there.'

He flicked his thumb at the curtain leading to the basement stairs; beyond the strings of hanging beads, the darkness stretched before me.

'I need light,' I said, and moved to take one of his candles with me.

'No, don't disturb that one,' he squawked. 'Don't you know anything?' With a huff, he handed me a tiny pocket flashlight, the kind you get at the dollar store.

I flicked it on. At least it worked, although the light was dim, and I made my way down the stairs.

There was Brin, in the same chair as yesterday, sitting inside a pentagram roughly scratched out of the packed dirt floor. He looked like he hadn't moved a muscle since I'd seen him last.

'Brin?' I called softly as I stepped onto the last tread. But he either couldn't hear me, or if he did he couldn't move. I tried but couldn't get through Willem's magic circle to touch him; like yesterday, it was as if the elf was sitting in a dome of glass.

I shone the light on his face and saw how pale the elf had grown, how drawn his face was as if his life force was slowly trickling away in his grief-stricken dreams. Through the despair that was emanating from him, I could also catch the hint of the medallion somewhere, the thing that had started all this.

'Oh Brin,' I whispered. 'I'm so sorry. I'll get you out of this, I promise, real soon. Just hold on till then, okay?'

He gave no indication of having heard me. There was nothing more I could do for him, not at that moment so I turned my back and rejoined Willem in the shop.

'What exactly are you planning to do tonight?' I asked him.

'I told you,' he said, his eyes hooded by the candlelight. 'Create havoc and mischief, let the Witch Kin know they're not the only ones who hold power in this town.'

'But how?' I pressed. 'Does it have anything to do with those horrible creatures you created?'

'Oh you are the clever one, aren't you?' he said. He stopped what he was doing and stared at me. 'Those creatures, my creations, are as you have probably guessed, so much more than simple papier mache. Tonight they will come alive in their true forms. Tonight I will show the Witch Kin they don't hold the monopoly on power in this town after all.'

34

A shiver ran through me at those words.

'How do you mean? I thought you were just going to crash the ball.'

'I don't want to go to their stupid ball! They think they are so almighty, so ... needed, in keeping the veil between Alt and now firmly closed,' he said, then he laughed. 'You remember those poor souls down there, in the Grog Shop, don't you?'

I nodded.

He leaned closer to me. 'You asked if there was any hope for them, if they were doomed to live their lives of pain, finding solace only in the bottle and in their opiates,' he continued, his voice growing soft. His eyes were focused on mine, I couldn't lift my gaze from him. 'It is the Witch Kin who keep them there, stuck in a dimension so wretched that they have no hope for escape.'

'I don't understand.'

'It was the Kin who brought the veil down and have kept it in its place for all these years, do you not see this? It is they who decided to place all supernaturals on that side of the veil, and all who could not escape, those considered sub-human, they left them there without a lifeline out of it. The Witch Kin thought they knew what was best for everyone else.

'But you and I, Dara, my own sweet Dara, we will give those forlorn souls hope tonight. Together, we will rip apart the veil of Alt and free them, allow them to take their rightful place in human society.'

'Lift the veil?' I whispered in horror, a cold chill freezing my spine as I realized the scope of his plans. 'But... but the others in Alt?' The vampires and the dwarves and the fairies and trolls and God alone knew what other dark creatures who lurked there in Alt, the ones that the Witch Kin had barred from real time. Was he saying he would also free them to come amongst the modern world? This was awful. 'How about them?'

'Too long have the Witch Kin imposed their rule on the worlds!' he thundered, bringing his fist down on the counter top. 'You and I will be known in both lands for bringing free-dom, for toppling those arrogant worms who believe they are at the top of the heap.'

That was all the answer he was going to give me. He lifted a glass beaker in triumph.

'No more. It is time for us to begin.'

'Where are the others? Zeta and Carrie and everyone?' I asked suddenly, desperately grasping at the only straw I could find. Yes, I wanted to free Brin, and I wanted the medallion, but at what cost? The world as I knew it was threatening to shatter.

If the sorcerer succeeded in his plan, and even if he didn't, my education would never come about, not when the Witch

Kin elders found out about my participation in this night's work. 'Your coven? Don't you need them here to help you with the spell? Surely, with more involved in your spell, it will make for more power. More guarantee of success.'

He dismissed the ten women out of hand. 'Yes, they insist on playing their part, but that is later. If they had any magic or power in them, they would be useful,' he said. 'But not for this. You on the other hand, you have power.'

'But Alice – she could help,' I said. 'She's part elf, I know she has power. And she would do anything to free Brin.'

He thought for half a moment, then shook his head. 'No time for that. Come.' He snapped his fingers at me.

'It's not a problem, look,' I said and I brandished my phone. I started typing in a text to her. 'She'll come right over. She's fast, like an elf, even if she has to run here.'

'Leave it!' he said as he strode over to where I stood and knocked the phone from my hand. It went spinning along the floor towards the shelves, and I had no idea if the send worked.

He took a deep breath, shut his eyes and let it out again. When he re-opened his eyes, they were calm again.

Outside the shop, there was the sound of movement and voices and music. The parade had begun, and the mummers were walking by right at that moment. The cheerful cries and catcalls were made in merry ignorance of the events about to happen not twenty feet away from them in this very room. They didn't know of the horrors which were about to descend upon them.

'Now, you need do nothing,' he said, ignoring the hubbub outside. 'Merely come into the circle and hold my hand.'

I couldn't do it. Not for fame or fortune, not for Brin, not for Alice. Not for all the misbegotten souls in Alt. Not even for Mom. I couldn't allow this sorcerer to wreak havoc on my world, so I stood my ground, blocked my mind from him and refused to move closer.

Where was Hugh when I most needed him?

Willem saw my resolve written on my face, and he lost his cool again so suddenly that I doubt he had regained it to begin with. 'You will do this!' he screamed.

Suddenly he was upon me, striking out with his closed fist against my temple. I began to feel myself falling to the floor but he took my arm in a firm grasp and yanked me over to his pentagram and started chanting, both his hands on my shoulders like an iron vise. I fought and I squirmed through the dizziness but he had the advantage of madness in his body which lent him unnatural strength.

As he held me and looked deep into my eyes he began the chant again, the same as last night. My brain scrambled from the blow, I struggled weakly in his arms but couldn't break free. His pale eyes pinned me again and spoke right into that fouled corner of my mind as he whispered the words, the merest hint of a smile on his face as he watched my internal struggle, the triumph spreading over his visage just as my will broke and I allowed, I had no choice, I let the darkness swell over me and I found myself looking at him with hunger, with lust, willing him to enter me again and use me. I felt my lips part and I reached to him, but he kept me at arms' length, his voice running over and through me and the dark corner of my mind jumped up to lick the flames.

I felt it happen, the magic, like a burst of electric blue light through my head. I might have been able to prevent it if not for the blow to my head which had scrambled my senses, but I had no desire to stem its flow. It ran through me like a lightning streak, leaving me gasping and weak. Willem let me fall with a thud as he raised his arms in triumph.

He left me lying shivering on the wooden floor as he turned the overhead lights back on and snuffed the candles.

I felt used, raped. I had no strength left in my body. Still trying to catch my breath, I managed to push myself up with the arm he had not grasped so hard. The other was paining me mightily.

'Now,' I gasped out. 'You've got what you wanted. Free Brin.'

'Your elf?' He laughed casually and clicked his fingers. 'There you go, and good luck with him. Why don't you come with me to see the show, see what wonders you have wrought?'

'You're serious?' I said with a sinking heart. 'You've re-moved the veil?'

'We, my dear Dara, we together have begun the process of raising the curtain between the two worlds,' he said. 'Did you not feel the bliss? Now we should go and claim our success and adulation from those whom we have freed.'

'What comes next?' Slowly I helped myself to a standing position, nursing my sore arm. I leaned against the counter. 'What other evil have you unleashed?' I refused to take any credit for the night's doing.

'How well you know me,' he said thoughtfully as he looked at me again. 'You understand that the veil was not my only goal. Come with me. Watch the fall of the Witch Kin at their grand ball. Watch as those they have subjugated for so long revolt in fury against them. I am the conductor of the grand orchestra of destruction.'

My heart fell into the pit of my stomach. 'Haven't you done enough already?'

'No, my dearest Dara, the night has only just begun,' he said softly. 'Come watch as I lead my minions through the fall of the Witch Kin. Come and be by my side as I am crowned the Lord of Misrule. You shall be my consort.'

He extended a hand towards me, and when I didn't move, he merely laughed and placed his sorcerer's hat upon his head. Willem turned off the overhead lights and stood silhouetted in the opened door. 'I will not forget, you know,' he said in a terrifyingly gentle voice. 'Thank you for your help, it will not go unrewarded. Your medallion can be claimed whenever you desire.'

My help? I spit on the ground in disgust, feeling the path of magic through every vein in my body. His words were as appropriate as a date rapist thanking his victim for such a lovely time.

'And should you change your mind, well, the ship sails tonight. If you hesitate, you may be lost.' He paused before shutting the door. 'The witches... if they survive tonight, they will see your imprint on the magic along with mine. You would do well to hope for the worst for them.'

He hoisted two large duffel bags onto his thin shoulders. Whatever was inside was stirring.

'We must depart, my creatures and I,' he said. 'They are awakening. The veil dissipates.' The door shut quietly behind him.

I became aware of faint music, the song of Isindor sounding through the shop. The ringtone I had allocated to Alice. The phone had skittered away in the darkness, and I felt beneath the shelves.

I found it too late to answer her call, but then she burst through the door, out of breath and her phone still in her hand.

'Where is he?'

'Downstairs,' I said. 'The spell should be lifted.'

I hoped desperately that Willem had told the truth.

She ran directly over to the curtain and down the stairs in the dark, her flashlight app already turned on. I was right behind her, and switched on the overhead bare bulb on the string.

Brin still sat in his chair, but this time we were able to reach him. She took his tall form awkwardly in her arms and crooned his tune again, the song he had sung to entrance the crowd. He stirred a bit, then looked up at her.

'My Alice,' he said weakly.

'He needs food,' she said briskly, meeting my eyes. 'What do you have?'

I ran back upstairs to rifle through my bag and found a half-eaten chocolate bar. When I presented it to her, she looked at it with disgust, and took it between two fingers. With her other hand, she distastefully picked off the accumulated lint and then broke off a piece to place in his mouth.

The effect was immediate. Brin brightened and was able to stand with her help, banging his head off the rafter.

'My hat?'

I found the watch cap tossed into the corner on top of Zeta's junk piles and dusted it off for him. We made it back up the stairs and he placed it on his head.

'Help me bring him round the corner to the Rocket,' Alice demanded, her eyes hard on me as she supported the elf. 'He needs real food too.'

'I can't,' I told her. I glanced out the window. The parade had long passed, the street was empty. 'I need to go after Willem.'

'It's the least you can do,' she scolded me. Her eyes were furious. 'After getting him into this mess.'

'Look, I don't know what Willem has got planned, but I have to go warn Dad,' I said vehemently. I bit my lip. 'Brin is okay in your hands now, and I'm afraid...'

'Fine,' she said in that tone which meant it was not fine at all. Alice turned her back to me and began to lead the elf to the door. 'Go after your stupid witches. Never mind you almost got him killed.'

I almost went to help her, but knew this was a far more important thing than even our friendship. Yet even as the door slammed behind them, my thoughts went also to the medallion which waited, hidden, down in the cellar in Alt. I could nip down there now and flip into the other dimension, quick as a flash, and try to unwork the spell Willem had undoubtedly placed over the lock and finally get my hands on this only clue to my mother's life.

But as I'd told Alice, this was way more important, and Willem'd had a head start on me. I had to go after the sorcerer and stop his awful machinations, or at least warn my father of the havoc the sorcerer planned to wreak.

I quickly put on my parka and hat, then the dress and the flowered pillowcase over my outside clothes, for I needed to hide from the sorcerer. The flimsy costume wasn't much, but it was all I had.

35

The night air was crisp and cool even through the fabric of the pillowcase and I adjusted the cut out eyeholes so I could see. I retraced my steps up the hill towards Queen's Road, the most direct route to the park and the Witch Kin's ball, for the parade was taking the long way, down Duckworth and on past King's Road till they reached Cochrane Street. I hoped I wasn't too late.

Was there something different in the air? I sniffed deeply, but smelled only the laundry scents of bleach and fresh air-dried cotton covering my face, and the wood smoke on the breeze, all odours of real time. But wait! Was that a faint undertone of the gutters of Alt, or was it merely the sour smell of my own parched mouth being breathed back in? I pulled the case away from my face and drew in another breath. I could have sworn that the moldering scents of the Boreal forests and winter fields were closer tonight, but it could have been my imagination.

Was the veil lifted or not? I couldn't tell, not right yet, but I caught slithering wet black shadows out of the corner of my eye and I could sense loose unanchored magic in the air.

What would be unleashed with the lifting of the veil? Vampires would be free to feast on the Normals to their cold hearts' content, the humans here would literally be fresh blood for them. Fairies and trolls would emerge from under their rocks and make up for lost time, and all sorts of unmentionable ancient gods could throw off the mantle of their hibernation and battle for their lost crowns. And I could kiss my future education goodbye – if the veil was lifted here in Newfoundland, one of the last true strongholds for the Witch Kin, it would quickly spread all over the earth and civilization as we knew it.

And if Willem's plan didn't work? Well, my world was still lost, for the Kin would smell my touch on the magic he had wreaked.

The roads were clear and slippery by now, but they were easier to travel than the sidewalks which had long since hardened to ice. I ran as best I could, but I've never been in the shape that Alice was and found myself huffing and short of breath by the time I crested the hill towards Rawlin's Cross.

The frozen slush crunched underfoot as I hurried across the roundabout encircling the buildings. I could hear music from a distance, and at last I saw the swinging lights from the lanterns at the head of the parade begin to come round the curve of Military Road past the Lieutenant Governor's estate.

Crowds of people lined both sidewalks to watch the spectacle. These inhabitants of the real time world were unaware of what was about to be set loose upon their lives. Little children clapped mittened hands, led by their older siblings as they skipped along the route. Those not in costumes kept time to the music, dancing their ways up the road and accompanying the mummers on to the big party planned at the park.

The merrymakers were now drawing level to the old Colonial Building and as a body, they paused to take in the wonder of all the windows glowing from the light of the chandeliers, a sight not seen here for more than fifty years. The soft light sparkled on the untrodden snow outside, secure within the iron fences designed to keep the populace in their place. Music streamed lightly from the open door, classical waltzes from composers long dead, and the silken gowns of the women flashed brightly through the space. As I drew closer, I could even see the glittering face masks of the masquerade. That red glow passing by, surely that was Sasha, my sister, in her signature colour.

And by her side - that tall figure in a black tuxedo, could that be Hugh? No, he had no business being here, unless Sasha was his business. 'Christ,' I swore. 'Don't let that be Hugh. Don't let him be in town.'

Those indoors did not spare a thought for the crowds outside now silently watching. The mummers' accordions and fiddles and bodrans and tin whistles had stilled at the display of luxury within the stone walls, the evidence of the old order alive and well. The commoners in their ragged and patched clothing, coverings made of old flour sacks and threadbare pillow cases and moth eaten scarves, they all looked upon the magnificence through the grills of the newly erected iron fence, the gate now tightly locked against invasion of the less fortunate of birth.

It was a momentary pause only, the contrast forgotten in a heartbeat as the rough music picked up again outside, the fingers of the musicians having to play on lest they freeze on the strings, and all were eager to press onward to the bandstand where mulled wine and hot drinks awaited.

I cast my eye over the crowd, looking desperately for Willem but caught no sight of him. I did see some odd costumes among the heaving throng of people though, as if the simple traditional attire of mummers had not been enough to satisfy their urges for the fantastic and the terrible. A pointed but crooked hat rose up, and next to it a broom stick. One figure towered over the crowd, horns on his head and a devilish mask hiding his identity. They were good, these costumes, yet familiar at the same time.

And I realized then that they weren't costumes, for these were Willem's creations come to full sized life in all their terrible glory. Grylla the Christmas witch cast her eye about at the closest children, the mini-mummers all bundled in their snowsuits and scarves, forgotten for the moment by their parents in this gathering of neighbours.

And there, standing too close to my aunt were the Icelandic trolls, their long limbed bodies hungry for the blood of sinners and thieves and the petty miscreants of human life.

All of the anti-Santas had come out to play, brought to life by their creator. I looked on in abject horror, yet that tiny dark space inside me rejoiced at his success. At *our* success.

The solid wall of figures poured through the gates of Bannerman Park where the band stand and skating rink waited, all brightly lit and welcoming. The smaller gazebo also had its share of lights on, a band beginning to play there, the Celtic tinged grunge striking a familiar note as it pushed through the noise of the crowd.

Jack's band, their last minute gig. I wondered if he were still speaking to me, if he had seen me for who I truly was and wanted nothing more to do with me. I brushed aside that worry for the moment, for I had to concentrate on saving the world as I knew it.

Wildly turning my head, trying to pick out individual figures in the forest of the crowd, Military Road was almost empty before I spotted Willem. His black-robed arms were lifted high in the air as if he really was a conductor of an unseen orchestra. He lingered almost alone on the gates of the iron fence of the Colonial Building, just a little distance from a group of women. Zeta, Carrie and the others. His erstwhile coven.

They were waving their hands in the air in time to his chanting, believing themselves caught up in a greater cause than their own small lives, unaware that they were contributing to anything other than Willem's overarching ego. And maybe to his mind that was contribution enough, giving him more reason to believe himself justified in his work. Confidence was everything in matters of magic, that I knew. If you didn't believe you had the power, then you didn't and never would have. It was that simple.

The door to the Colonial Building slammed shut, seemingly on its own.

What could I do? I should run over and… and what? Knock Willem to the ground? I had no doubt that Carrie and the others, whipped into a frenzy by now, would make short work of me. They'd tear into me like harpies on a hapless rabbit. No, there had to be another way…

'Did you get lost, little mummer?' The voice seemed to come out of nowhere. I turned around and there was Mark right behind me, his plains clothes not disguising the fact of his copness, never in a million years.

'Great Aunt Sadie's dress is unmistakeable,' he added with a smile.

I whipped off the pillowcase. "Mark, oh Mark thank God!"

He frowned at my obvious terror.

'Jesus, Dara,' he said. 'What the hell's going on with you?'

But then screams erupted from the crowd inside the park, and I could see slithering black creatures creeping from the shadows, those who were emboldened by the smell of the fear of the humans and attracted like magnets to the terror.

The veil was disintegrating before my very eyes.

36

And just that quickly Mark was gone from my side, throwing himself into the disorder, not even thinking of his own safety as he sought to bring order to the melee.

'No, Mark...' I whispered. He had no idea what he was getting in to. His solid normality would be no match against the magical creatures in the crowd.

I could see beyond the iron gates that the Witch Kin had been alerted to something happening beyond their noses. The bright dresses crowded to the windows, the witches jostling amongst themselves for a view of what was happening outside to the rabble in the park.

'Come out and stop it! What's wrong with you all?' I screamed at them, but they couldn't hear. They didn't move from their windows, although I could see by their agitated silhouettes that they were worrying.

Willem remained at the gate, a blue electric power beginning to grow and leap between his hands as his coven crowded around and swayed and chanted. A sudden wind tore through the treetops, high above all our heads, not touching anyone or stopping, an impotent gust.

I could hear Jack's electronic band falter, their joyous Celtic grunge failing into minor notes amid the growing mayhem all around them. And still the Witch Kin did nothing, did not exit their stronghold to aid the crowd outside, whose screams of terror showed that the Alt world had fully burst upon them. What was going on with them, why didn't the Kin stream out and put a stop to this evil, repair the veil between the worlds?

And Willem continued. I saw something glitter in his hand, a glass beaker. I recognized it as he pulled out the cork stopper with his teeth, it held my power inside it, that which he had bottled those nights previously – it seemed like another century ago. Back when I was still arrogant enough to believe I could get the better of him. The blue light it held within was now pouring out and growing as it hit the open air, mixing with that lightning bolt which jumped from his hand, small billowing clouds of brilliant vapour all colours of the rainbow and it was spreading to the iron gate where it landed and clung, wrapping tendrils all around each post until that too was glowing as if electrified. Soon the entire gate was aglow, each cross post, the curlicues on top, even the lock which held the gate shut.

Iron was not impermeable to magic then, at least not to the sorcerer's power. I realized then that the gate was now unopen-able - it mattered not if the Witch Kin escaped their stone prison for they would never be able to get out of the enclosed yard, not while Willem held the gate closed with his spell. Using my magic.

The screams from the crowd hardly even touched me now, for my ears could only hear the roaring of his chants like

243

the lure of the ocean waves as they pounded the shore, un-
ceasing and insistent. I found my feet moving slowly towards him now as if they belonged to someone else, like they
weren't mine at all.

That part of me which he had branded deep within was
responding to the call of my own magic which he had unloosed, as if I was to reclaim it and share with him this triumph. I needed to go over and help Willem, to join with him
and let him subjugate my will for this gloriousness. I'd never
wanted anything so much in my life – the lure of education,
Alice, Jack, all that was nothing besides the enchantment
promised by Willem.

The bloodcurdling yells may have been coming from vic-
tims or the creatures of Alt in their newfound freedom of
blood lust, I couldn't tear my eyes away to look. Everywhere
around me there was blood and pain but my eyes only saw
the glowing gate that held my magic, *my* power, a physical
manifestation that showed the Witch Kin that I mattered,
me a half-blood long since dismissed by my sister, my father
and his wife.

Then Willem lifted his arms for the last time and chuck-
ling now, met my eyes through the empty space. An unseen
wind whipped all around the stone building, lifting the snow
in a flurry to blind those within and further mark their defeat
at his hands. He turned away, leaving his coven still chanting
and entranced with their own imaginings. I watched as he
slipped away down the tiny lane between houses which led
to the back of the elementary school in real time, a dark
shadow among the depths. Alt had taken a firm grip on this
neighbourhood by now, and the respectable houses I knew
had become shanties and lean-tos in a maze of alleys, and
Willem strode into the deep shadows.

'Wait,' I whispered at his disappearing back, for he was taking a part of me with him.

But then finally the Kin burst open the grand doors of the ballroom and poured down the stairs, but far too late to stem the damage. The veil was almost fully lifted between the two worlds here at the epicenter of the sorcerer's spells, and they could only stare at the wreckage of their work. The iron gates still blazed blue-white like daylight, and the Kin were locked inside the prison of their own arrogance. Even my father stood helpless in front of the gate, unmindful of the snow whipping his tuxedo.

My father. Helpless as he watched the terror unleased by Willem and myself. Jon de Teilhard, the most powerful man I knew, he could do nothing. I should have felt triumph over him for all the slights dealt to me by him and his family over the years. Instead, I felt empty.

But he was not helpless for long. Dad pulled himself together, calling out to his wife and the others. He had seen beyond the gate, and understood immediately that the veil between worlds had been torn asunder. I couldn't see what they did to work against the carnage, for this magic of witches was invisible, their attempt to rip apart the worlds again, but the wind rose again with a terrible moan and I could almost feel a shift in the air. Almost, but not quite.

In the midst of this, his eyes lifted and caught sight of me in the light of the gas lit streetlamps of Alt, and I knew I would never forget that look on his face as he saw, not his shunned daughter Dara in that ridiculous flowered dress of Aunt Sadie's, but my mother as she had worn it all those years ago, on that long gone summer day.

That split second lasted an hour, I watched as his face registered joy, then realization of what was gone and finally recognition of myself. The terrible love still rested in his eyes as he looked at me through the fence.

And in that moment I knew right then that he had had nothing to do with her disappearance ten years previous, that his heart had surely been broken as hard as mine when she left us.

This knowledge ended the spell I'd been under as surely as a splash of water in my face on a freezing winter's night – it loosened the hold that Willem had on my heart, cut the knot of hatred and confusion that the sorcerer had snagged on deep inside.

There wasn't much time. Willem was headed back to Zeta's store, I knew. I also knew this would be my last chance to retrieve Mom's coin. I had an advantage over him, for he was on foot, but I – I had Mark's SUV at my disposal.

I tore off up Military Road towards the vehicle, the keys already in my hand. I reached it before I remembered the automatic lock, unlike Edna's ancient jeep, this was a recent model. I clicked it twice impatiently, then threw myself into the driver's seat, turned the engine over and wrenched her into reverse.

We were almost fully into Alt now, so no need to obey the twenty-first century rules of the road with all the one way lanes and four stops and roundabouts. I needed to get to the store before Willem did and so took the most direct route.

That the vehicle even worked with so much Alt all around was a miracle, but I didn't have time to ponder the ins and outs of the dimensional interfaces. I tore off down Prescott, now a frozen lane of cobblestones and horse muck with wooden steps for sidewalks despite the grandeur of the towering houses on either side. I had to take a sharp right onto Gower, for as I approached the intersection a whole army of the poor and wretched from the rum shops of Alt were making their way up the hill. These were human beings, even if they didn't belong to my world, and I couldn't simply mow them down. I skidded round that corner, and then almost immediately down the last leg of Victoria Street, remembering only when it was too late that it ended in stairs.

Turning the wheel again, I heard a noise, but it was coming from inside the vehicle. My spine froze when I glanced into the rear view mirror.

There loomed a large head with horns on either side of its animalistic skull, its two eyes green and rheumy with snot.

Dear God. Mark had left the troll inside the vehicle instead of bringing it safely into the office at the RCMP headquarters, and it had come to life this night with its siblings. Unable to get out of the locked car, it had lain in wait for a victim on which to unleash its terror. It roared and lunged over the back seat at me.

I swerved the car again, to try to knock the creature from its perch, but to no avail, it kept coming at me. One eye on the road and the other on the troll, I dipped and swerved all over the hills of Gower Street, but still it kept on.

In Alt, the east gate to the Anglican Cathedral had never been closed, so I ran the truck up over the rotted wooden walkway and to the south side of that church, yet this was worse, for the ghosts of the thousands buried in the sloping boneyard were rising along with the resident ghouls, and they flocked to the vehicle, too stunned to know they couldn't get at me in my modern metal tank.

The tortured souls long dead, their lives cut short in this brutal climate from plagues and worse, all those in unpeaceful rest rose up with the lifting of the veil. I didn't have time to pity them.

From the crannies underneath the cathedral and from the old forgotten doors of the crypt slithered the nameless demons banished long ago, bound by the magic of the Christian church, and unloosed by Willem's actions. Like sightless moths to a flame they sensed my living blood and hungered for its warmth.

They all passed through my consciousness but I didn't have time to register them. I could hear the troll breathing heavily as it steadied itself in the back seat and rustled next to my ear, then felt its cold claw come over my face.

37

The vehicle was now headed down the short run of Cathedral Street, slipping in the muck as it slid sideways down the length. I could hardly see to steer past the hairy arm of the troll which was determined to choke the life out of me.

The snow had begun in earnest now and the wind was picking up speed so that there was nothing but a solid blanket of white in front of me. I flicked the windshield wipers faster to clear my vision.

I tried braking hard again and again as we slid down the hill, and finally succeeded in knocking the troll's horns so hard against the roof it lodged through, poking a hole in the metal. I could now see to steer, yet he fought back. The sturdy back of my seat protected me, but wouldn't hold out too much longer, not with the way the claws were ripping through the leather. Enraged and stymied, the troll was eating its way through the foam and polyester and steel frame in order to get to me.

I heard something heavy rattling around the foot of the passenger side and when we almost flipped onto Duckworth Street, I ducked down to retrieve it.

A lug wrench of heavy iron, the one Mark had looked out to attend to Edna's snow tires.

Finally out onto the cobbled stones of Alt Duckworth, the large tires spun for a moment before regaining their grip on the wet rock. The buildings, what I could see of them through the storm, were fading in and out of Alt and real time so they looked like organic breathing monsters lurching up above my head.

With a yell, I stepped full on to the accelerator and simultaneously swung the wrench over my head, connecting with solid bone behind me, a satisfying crunch which took the pressure off my throat.

I drew up to Zeta's in the middle of the road – more fully into Alt now, there was no other traffic and I locked the car door behind me. I had no idea if the troll was living or dead, and I didn't know either if the car would remain as Alt closed in.

This door to the shop in Alt had only a flimsy lock, easily smashed by the heel of my boot in one giant kick and I was in. I stared around me, catching my breath and the smell was horrific. Pushing aside the entrails and slabs of meat still on the counter, I grabbed a huge knife in case the troll found me again.

There was no light to help me make my careful way down the rough wooden staircase, holding my breath the whole while. When I reached the bottom, I felt around for the flint box that Willem had left by the rough iron sconce. It took me ten full tries to light the tallow candle, my fingers were shaking so much.

But finally, I had a small light. I ripped the candle from the wall and brandished it before me; the rounded arch of the ancient door was directly ahead.

And the medallion was inside, I could feel it so strongly my bones were aching with longing. In fact, here in the heart of Alt as I was I could see a dim glow through the cracks in the wooden door ahead, just like in that dream. So close I could almost touch it if it weren't for the immovable oak door.

The street door creaked alarmingly above my head and I could hear the wind whistling through and all around the store. Only a colder draft penetrated down below, but it pushed me to move. A few quick steps and I was there, but the old lock held solid. Not a padlock here in Alt, but the original medieval iron lock set fast within the oak. The hinges had rusted into the very grain of the wood, I would never work them out, and I had no time to run back upstairs to look for a bone cleaver to smash my way through.

The blue power. I could summon it and make it do my bidding, surely. I set the candle down into the dirt of the floor next to the carving knife and I closed my eyes in concentration.

What were the words of the incantation? My mind went blank, so instead I concentrated on the glow itself. I rubbed my hands and started over, and there! A spark came from my left hand, then one from my right.

But it was no use, I could get nothing but a weak glow – without Willem connecting with me, I didn't have the necessary words to summon this power.

I was a failed witch, useless. And by this time I knew I'd screwed up my future so irrevocably, so totally, the power that I did have was no good to me anyway. There would be no magic in my future, not once the Witch Kin found out who was responsible for lifting the veil between the worlds, and my part in it.

All was lost.

The beads of the curtains at the top of the stairs clattered lightly in the breeze, or maybe it was a stealthy hand drawing them apart. There was no hope now. The medallion was so close, but just out of my reach.

I shut my eyes and would have cried if I'd had the strength.

But it was then that a memory of Hugh's voice came upon me. 'All those spells, and incantations and magic dust,' he scoffed. 'They're nothing, only for second rate magicians to bedazzle with, the better to stroke their egos. The true power of a witch lies inside you.'

What did I have to lose? I could hear the rustle of a long gown and sensed the silent footsteps as my opponent made his slow way down the stairs behind me.

In my mind's eyes I examined the lock, that huge iron mechanism all rusted. It was medieval in origin, in its design, based on the earliest of lock mechanisms.

I recalled the only book I had really flipped through of the pile given to me by Hugh, the encyclopedic knowledge, the one that claimed to have all knowledge you needed to know. I'd dismissed it as a child's book at the time, thinking it an insult from Hugh, but it at least had had pictures in it. And one section had been about locks and their construction.

I sent one quiet tendril of my mind's sensor in, and felt the cold touch of the metal. I was inside the lock, and could see that it was a warded lock. Like the old locks on the doors in my house, the ones requiring the big ancient iron keys, this lock had slots to guide the right key into place.

I could feel the inner notches that the key would fit around, could almost see them before me as if I was peering into the innards of the lock itself. Now I had to find the inner lever to release the lock.

The quiet measured steps behind me didn't disturb me, were not allowed to disrupt my concentration. It was Willem, surely, for his troll would never have been so subtle. I could have allowed him to step forward and open the lock for me to retrieve my treasure, for he surely owed it to me as I had helped him achieve his ends of lowering the veil between worlds and proving to the Witch Kin his power as a force to be reckoned with and not for mockery.

But I had no reason to trust him to keep his word. I doubted that he'd had any intention of ever delivering up to me what was mine.

I could feel a cold breath of movement behind me, but still I pushed with my mind. And there – that was it, the slight small knob. If I were made of iron or sterner stuff I could click it and be done, but no, my soft mind muscle could not rely on strength but a constant pressure, upward, always upward, then I had it. The lightest touch, a nudge was all it needed, and the less I tried the better it worked.

The sweat was standing out on my forehead and my heart was racing, but I forced myself to breathe slowly and regularly, and let that one forgotten muscle of my brain do the work needed. I eased into it and then - success!

The moment I felt the click I reached out and took the handle of the door and swung it open.

But Willem was standing there before me in the archway. He had beaten me to it on his silent feet and reached behind him to take up the medallion. It glowed in his hand as he held it aloft, the magic sparkling in the dim light.

38

'Very clever, m'dear,' he said. 'I've taught you well.'

'You taught me nothing!' I was so mad I could spit, and I did. 'Your stupid magic didn't open this lock; I did it myself. Nothing you showed me helped.'

It was all Hugh and myself; it was the information in the books Hugh had demanded I read that had given me the knowledge of what needed to be done, and it had been Hugh's insistence on the source of my power that had shown me how it had to be done.

He raised his eyebrows calmly, unruffled.

'You're a fraud, Willem!'

'Did we not just lift the veil of Alt?' he asked. 'Together, me and you?'

I was silent for a moment as I watched the medallion dangle from his hand, then I shook my head.

'No, Willem,' I said. 'It wasn't us together, there was no team in that effort. You took from me what you wanted. I didn't give it willingly.

'You fucking raped my power to do what you did,' I whispered.

He laughed. 'You could have told me to stop any time,' he said. 'But you were hungry for it, I know you like I know myself, Dara.'

Willem let that sink in before speaking again in a low whisper. 'We're two of a kind, did you not recognize that yet? Frauds and cheats, the pair of us.'

'I'm not like you,' I said, but I think I was trying to convince myself, not him.

'I somehow don't think the Witch Kin will see it that way,' he said, shaking his head with a sad little smile on his face. 'You lied to your tutor before even beginning your course, you have deliberately gone behind his back in consorting with me.'

I could say nothing in reply. He reached over with his small cold fingers and lifted my chin so I had to look straight at him. His pale eyes appeared to soften in understanding.

'Don't forget, I've been where you are now,' he continued. 'I know what their rules are like, how stringently they enforce their laws, those stultifying strictures.'

I opened my mouth to take a breath and deny all he said, but his finger moved up to my lips to silence me.

'Your Witch elders have a nasty punishment for errant little half-bloods who meddle in mayhem, do they not?'

Binding. A lobotomy of the magic soul. I shivered.

'Seems to me like you have two choices, dear heart,' he said, a terrible kindness in his cold eyes. 'You surrender to them, now, and give up all your dreams of magic. Live the Normal life you would have had if not for the accident of your genes. It won't hurt, you know, or at least you won't remember the pain. You won't remember the magic either, they'll make sure of that. You won't feel any loss except that deep longing within for something, but you'll never know what it is, you'll just be conscious of that big hole inside of you that can't be filled with any amount of drugs or sex.'

The candle flickered at our feet.

'Or you can come with me.' His voice was hypnotizing. 'Keep your magic powers and everything that makes you Dara de Teilhard. We'll travel the world together, you and I.'

Willem held out the medallion, showing the inscriptions on it. 'I can teach you what these mean, and I can help you.' He slipped it deep into the folds off his robe. 'But no matter, you won't even remember it once the Kin are finished with you.'

The electric bulb overhead spluttered into life before quickly dying. We both glanced up.

'There's not much time,' he said tersely. 'We have to go, now, before they get the veil fully back into place.' He walked quickly down to the old oak door into the Grog Shop and laid his hand on the wood.

'Are you coming, or not? No matter to me either way, I'm just offering you your only salvation.'

The words he spoke were true, there was no other way open for me. I remembered how Hugh had made me get out into the fog and wind to relay this to me, as if he'd feared even speaking the words inside the car could have repercussions on him.

I picked up my bag and parka off the floor, still undecided in my mind, but my feet were following him out the door and into the bar.

The Grog Shop was empty and it was hard to tell if we were now in real time or Alt, the bar had changed so little over the centuries. Outside on George Street the wind was blowing the snow in a thick curtain. Weak gas lamps flickered in competition with their stronger more modern streetlights, but the cobblestones were slippery under foot.

'We have to get to the harbour before it's fixed back into place,' he shouted above the howling wind as he grasped my hand and pulled me along. 'Quickly! The ship is waiting.'

I shoved my coat on as he pulled up his own hood and our steps quickly took us to Water Street. Creatures still slithered about in the shadows and I didn't dare look at them or catch any eyes. As we hurried along, my heart cried at the thought of losing my newfound powers. Could they really do such a thing, strip me of the magic that made me myself? The magic given to me in my genes from my father? I shivered again to wonder at what such a drastic measure must entail, the ripping apart of the very genetic code.

There was shouting in the distance, muffled by the wind and the snow. Willem looked over his shoulder and urged me forward. I stumbled over a curb – a modern day curb in the street.

'Come on,' he screamed. 'The veil is slipping back into place. We can't get away if the harbour turns back to real time.'

We turned down Beck's Cove, the last small lane leading to the water, the buildings on either side of us tall and dark and looming, and spirits moaned on the wind. No lights lit the way as we pushed through the knee deep snow.

I heard my name as if from a distance, and shielding my face from the wind, turned toward the sound. A tall figure waved to me through the thick falling snow.

Could it be Hugh? My heart sank. I thought I had spied him at the ball, though I'd been sure he was still in Paris. I couldn't be caught by him, it would break his heart to see the hurt inflicted on me by his own Kin. I couldn't do that to him.

I turned back to Willem and found my feet running over rough wooden planks. We were still in Alt, on the rickety wharves behind the merchant houses. He stopped by a vessel, a boat whose sides were made of wood but which had a huge iron chimney puffing smoke out into the cruel blizzard all around us.

He reached for my hand to help me over the side, his long robe flapping in the wind but before I could get to the safety he promised I was physically accosted by long strong arms which held tightly to my shoulders.

Jack. He forced me to turn to him. 'What the fuck is going on here, Dara?' he screamed over the howling wind and the chugging of the vessel as it prepared to leave port.

His clear hazel eyes burned through me but as if from a distance. I stared at him. He could be my future, this wonderful upright man, this sensitive musician who brooked no bullshit. Without the magic, I could be happy with him, we could live around his bay by the ocean, I could... I could be a plumber for God's sake, or continue with my studies or anything I wanted to do as long as it belonged in his world and his ken.

Without my magic. And I wouldn't remember the pain.

He flickered out of view.

'Jack!' I screamed, but then he came back.

'I can't reach you,' he shouted. 'How did you get behind the iron fence?'

How much of Alt could he perceive? I looked all around me, and I still stood on the rickety wooden finger pier with Willem about to board his vessel. The sorcerer held the medallion deep within his robe. If I stayed with Jack, I would never hold it again, and would never find my mother. If it hadn't been my father who caused her disappearance, then I needed to find out who or what had done it. She needed justice and there was no one else who could find it for her but me. And I couldn't do that without my magic.

Jack was wavering in front of my eyes again. I had to make my decision right now, there was not a moment to lose.

'I'm sorry Jack,' I whispered as I let him go, and with him, let go of everything I held dear. Edna, my home, Alice. Maundy. The patchwork velvet Christmas stockings. I could hardly see through the tears which were freezing on my cheek. 'I'm so sorry...'

But before I could finish my goodbyes, I felt another whirlwind pass me by, a long black shadow racing by me toward the boat, sliding along the wood almost knocking me off the wharf in its haste.

I gasped and held onto Jack's outreached arm to right myself. The shape had launched itself onto Willem, wrestling him onto the body of the boat which tooted its mournful horn and prepared to turn away from the wharf.

'Brin! I shouted to him over the gale. I recognized the long legs as the two struggled. 'The boat is leaving, come back!'

The vessel was five feet off into the harbour before he stood up and, realizing what was going on, made a gigantic leap onto the wharf. His long feet in their clumsy modern boots slipped and slid on the icy edges of the wood, but I reached out and hauled him back to safety.

'Brin? What were you thinking?' I hugged the elf and refused to let him go no matter how much he squirmed.

'Too close, too close,' he muttered stiffly until I finally released him from my arms.

'He's gone,' he whispered over my head, and we watched the wooden ship steam out of view into the blizzard. I stared after the boat as it took my dreams, my magic and my future with it, I stared until I could see nothing but the static of the snow on my eyes, then I let go a deep sigh.

The decision had been made for me. I looked down at my feet, trying to hide the tears which threatened again, and found myself rubbing the pavement clear. I choked back a sob. We were in real time, the veil had been brought down again, and I would never again have the opportunity to visit that strange land of Alt, nor would I even remember it.

I gave a watery smile to Jack and Alice where they waited past the iron fence. The snow had stopped falling. The wind was picking up, blowing the clouds clear out of the sky.

'I rescued it,' Brin was jabbering, his long arms and legs dancing in the snow. 'I didn't let him take it from you.'

He held up a metal disc, reflecting the blue light of the streetlamps in its silvery glow, and he offered it to me with his smile.

'How did you know?' I whispered as I reached out my hand, almost afraid to touch it.

'I could hear everything,' he said. 'When he caught me in the grief-pain, I could still hear everything you spoke. And I smelled the coin on him, I couldn't let him take it. It's yours.'

'Oh, Brin,' I said, the tears in my eyes spilling over. After all I had done to him, the elf did not hold it against me.

'Thanks,' I told him, and took it into my hand finally. It still throbbed with magic, and if I held it to my ear I know it would speak with my mother's voice. I didn't, though. I considered sending it spinning into the harbour, to drift into the tides and maybe make it all the way to Ireland, or perhaps it would be swallowed by a fish or taken by the mermaids who lived just outside the Narrows. For all the good it would do me once I was stripped of my magic.

But I didn't do that either. It was too hard won. Instead, I pressed it back into the elf's hand.

'You take it,' I said softly. 'And maybe you can remind me some day after I've forgotten. Remind me of my mother.'

39

The iron fence surrounding the harbour apron wasn't so difficult for me to get over, not with Brin on one side heaving me up and Jack on the other to catch me as I fell. The elf, however, was forced to make an elaborate maneuver over the water at the fence's end in order to avoid being burned by the iron. The clear night was now bitterly cold, the moon and stars crackling above us, the fresh laid snow below untouched by footprints or tire tracks. The wind which had blown away the storm kept up its steady clip, and we all drew our coats close.

'How did you know where to find me?' I asked as we trudged back up to Water Street and the welcome electric street lamps and Christmas decorations all over. I stopped and breathed deeply of the fresh air despite the cold. The city was coming to life again, the cars travelling silently down the snow packed roads, people venturing out into the now safe public spaces.

'We were at the Rocket,' Alice said. "When everything began to go off kilter.' She looked around with a puzzled air. Jesus. She'd been in Alt and she was in love with an elf. How could her mind still deny the existence of the supernatural?

Brin and I shared a silent look of understanding. He wouldn't bring up Alt if I didn't.

'I knew you were in trouble,' the elf said, and left it at that.

'There *was* something weird happening tonight, wasn't there?' This was from Jack who had plowed on ahead of us, his hands shoved deep within his pockets. He paused and let us catch up. 'We were playing in the bandstand for the end of the Parade, then everything went to shit. The lights and power started to go, and people started screaming for no reason at all.'

'How did you end up downtown?' I asked him. 'Last I saw you were playing in the gazebo.' Yet he had somehow appeared at the water's edge in time to save me from running off into the Alt snowstorm with the failed sorcerer. I didn't know whether to be elated or to cry.

'The crowd went out of control,' he said, staring off at the memory. 'They overran us. They... Someone smashed my guitar.' He swallowed deeply. 'I had to get out of there. I was actually headed to the Grog Shop to drown my sorrows. But I saw you come out of there with...'

I gave a moment's silence out of respect for the loss of his instrument. 'Did you see anything... anything out of the ordinary?'

'There were some pretty weird costumes,' Jack said after a pause. 'Funny, you know, they reminded me of Willem's creatures, those papier mache dolls of his. Actually it was more like Hallowe'en than December, with the witches and trolls and vampires everywhere.'

We walked a little longer, and I felt the unspoken weight between us. Then he could hold back no longer and the question I was dreading came up.

'Did he... were you about to go off on a boat with Willem or something?' Jack stopped and stared at me with accusation. 'What the hell was that about?'

I didn't think his logical brain would allow him to remember what had really happened. Alt had that effect on the head. If a person had no reason to believe in magic, then they just wouldn't see it, and their mind would turn somersaults trying to squash a reasonable explanation to fit over the unexplainable. It was that simple.

'No, no,' I lied. 'I was just seeing him off. Getting something from him that belonged to me.'

'Hmm,' was all he said in reply.

We were now heading up Prescott Street, staying to the sides of the road to avoid the cars sliding down. My steps were growing slower with every yard, and it wasn't just because of the uphill gradient.

I had made my choice, or rather, it had been made for me, and now I was going to suffer the consequences. I may as well just hand myself over to Hugh with full *mea culpa* and on my knees begging for mercy than try to run away, for there weren't many places to hide from the Witch Kin, and I'd missed the boat out of Alt. My father and his compatriots would be out for blood now that the veil was fixed back in place, for Witch Kin hated to be embarrassed even if no one else knew about it. It was their job to keep the dimensions separated and Willem, by causing it to waver for even that short time had thumbed his nose at them and hurt their pride. They couldn't get their hands on the Dutchman now, but I was still here; technically, I had helped him and the mark of my magic would be all over it. I would be their scape-goat.

We didn't have to make it all the way to the Colonial Building. Hugh, Edna and Mark were waiting outside the ice cream store on King's Road.

'There she is, I told you she'd show up,' Edna said with relief in her voice as she enveloped me within the folds of her winter parka. Her costume had been discarded, except for her large rubber boots. 'And she'll have a perfectly reasonable explanation as to where your car is, Mark.'

'The SUV has been located down on Duckworth Street,' Mark said grimly as he ended the call on his phone. 'She couldn't have taken it, not with it in that condition. Must have been hoodlums taking advantage of the power outages. We'll catch up with them soon enough.'

He looked at Alice through narrowed eyes, as if she might have had something to do with it. Poor kid, it wasn't her fault she had Benjy for a brother; Mark really shouldn't hold it against her.

I was off the hook for the troll damage to Mark's vehicle, at least, which was morally satisfying because that one truly wasn't my fault. I had told him to bring the troll in his office, yet Mark had forgotten all about it and left it in the back of the SUV. Still there was other music I had to face, so I turned to Hugh.

He said nothing, just stared at me darkly. I swallowed a huge lump in my throat. This was it, this was when I said goodbye to any magic dreams I might hold. Well, at least Brin had gotten his wish to stay in real time for ever. I left the safety and security of Edna's arms and walked back to Jack.

'I have to go now,' I said, keeping my voice low. 'I'll call you. Okay?'

Jack looked at me, then over at Hugh who was waiting. He gave a short dip of his head before turning away.

Still in his fine tuxedo with a long wool coat to protect him from the elements, Hugh slowly placed the leather gloves on his hands.

His face was unreadable, and he merely nodded to my family and friends before leading me away, and there was no room for arguments. The ambulances flashed red and blue lights as they passed us, sirens echoing into the distance as they left the scene.

When we were at a safe distance away from the others, I began my apologies, not that I thought they would be of any use.

He cut me off, shaking his head.

'No,' he said. 'Just... just stop.'

We turned down Military Road toward the park grounds.

'I still can't believe that Willem lowered the veil as he did,' he said in a low voice as if thinking aloud.

We walked the rest of the way back to the scene of the crime in silence, down to Bannerman Park where the merry-making crowds had gathered in their harmless fun of mummering and dress-up to celebrate the season of peace.

It was hard to miss the aftermath as we walked through the trodden paths. In the circle of the streetlamps human blood lay all splattered around on the snow, purple in this light, or maybe it was just the strewn contents of the broken hot chocolate urns. Rags of costumes fluttered, caught on thorny bushes, while over at the gazebo the band's instruments lay wrecked, the drum kit rolled off into the snow and there was Jack's bass guitar, his one proud possession, cracked off at the neck with the strings barely lifting in the breeze. There looked to be blood on that, too, and I couldn't stop a gasp escaping my throat.

'Did anyone...?' I looked miserably at the carnage all around.

'Die? Not human, no,' Hugh said shortly. 'Many people were hurt, though, both by supernaturals and other humans.'

By this point I was more than ready to have my magic stripped from me, and I burned to tell him to just do it right there and then, perform the necessary dirty business and help me to forget it all. Forget all the pain and suffering I had caused to come about through my actions.

Yes, my participation in this particular episode that led to the wreckage had been unwilling, yet by going against Hugh's advice I had placed myself in a position where my magic could be used for destruction. I had thought I could beat Willem at his game.

Maybe the old me, the one before the veil had been lifted, maybe that Dara would have whined and pleaded for clemency from Hugh, pointing out that she hadn't meant to participate in Willem's anarchy, that she had been on a holy quest in search of her mother and things had gotten in her way. That she had played with fire and been burnt, and had now learnt her lesson and so deserved to be forgiven.

No. If nothing else, I guess I'd matured enough over the past few months to see how the real world worked. I had been arrogant, and Hugh's elder on that far off Scottish island was right.

I wasn't fit to hold the mantle of magic.

We continued our silent meandering path through the wreckage of the night, pausing at every drop of blood, every burn mark on the trees we passed as if to bring home more fully what I had done.

Finally our steps took us to the front of the Colonial Building. It at least was untouched, though I could see that the fine wrought iron gate, newly erected, had warped with the power Willem had used to keep the Witch Kin at bay, prisoners in their finery, helpless to stop him.

A ragged scarf flapped on the now cooled metal, the melted polyester turning to ice on the iron.

Hugh touched the worst of the fence's damage thoughtfully, bits of static jumping from his gloved hand as he stroked it, leftover magic burning in on itself.

'Just do it!' I burst out. I couldn't stand it anymore. 'Just do it now and get it over with, if you can. I forgive you in advance, alright?'

I held my breath and shut my eyes and waited.

But he only sighed, a small puff of breath into the frozen air.

'It's not that simple,' he said. 'And you don't get off that easily. There will be an Inquiry, of course.'

I opened my eyes. 'An inquisition, you mean,' I said bitterly.

'No,' he said, a tinge of impatience in his voice. 'I mean an Inquiry. We need to know how this breach was accomplished so it can never happen again. You will play a major role in this as you were the only one present, apart from Willem de Vriejz, of course.'

'He took off on a boat, a wooden steamship,' I said. 'In Alt, not real time. Do you think they'll catch him?'

'Oh, yes,' Hugh replied, nodding. 'Eventually. He'll want to come back to our time at some point, and the only place he can do that is at the point he went into Alt. So the Kin here will be keeping a close eye out for him.'

I didn't tell him that Willem wasn't bound by that ordinary rule of the veil, that I had seen for myself the sorcerer could flip back and forth without being in the same exact location. It would come out soon enough during the Inquiry. And I had no doubt the Kin would find him and exact their revenge.

Of course, I wouldn't be a part of that operation. This half-witch would be stripped of my magic long before Willem dared show his face in these parts or anywhere again. I wondered if I would even remember the sorcerer, after...

I sighed. It would be trades college after Christmas for me, and my future would hold nothing but pipes and drains. And perhaps Jack if I was really lucky, if I hadn't freaked him out too much this evening.

'Where and when will the Inquiry be?' I asked, scuffing through the slush at my feet. 'Will they at least let me have Christmas here?

He gave a rueful laugh. 'The wheels of bureaucracy don't turn as quickly as we'd like,' he said. 'They never do. Yes, you'll be spending the season here at home.'

'And after?'

It had started snowing again as we walked, the wind having blown itself out and the clouds settled back over the city. Large flakes were falling now as the temperature of the air rose imperceptibly.

Hugh shook his head, dislodging some of the snow from his unruly hair. 'The Inquiry will be held in Inverness,' he said, his green eyes unreadable in the mercury light of the streetlamp.

A lump had formed in my throat, and I was just then becoming aware of it. I pictured a row of Elders, powerful Witch Kin, all dressed in severest black and pointing accusing fingers at me. Then would come the binding...

'But perhaps they won't... Maybe if I explain what happened and tell them everything I know...'

My life was now in freefall as if I was teetering from a high clifftop, scrabbling at scree, weeds in the grass, anything to stop my inevitable plunge into my doom.

He paused and turned to stare at me.

'You *will* tell them everything you know,' he said firmly. 'That's a given. What happens after that, is their decision.'

He shook his head and set his lips. The look in his eye turned sorrowful.

There... there was my branch growing unexpectedly out of the rock face. I grasped it with all I had.

'You believe in me, don't you?' I said. 'You really truly believe I could be a witch to your high standards, even if I've messed up before?'

'I only know it would be a shame for the world to lose your talent,' he said, shoving his hands deep into the pockets of his overcoat. 'I have no say in the matter, though.'

We began to head back to the parking lot, our tour of the carnage completed.

'Is there... is there anything I can do to mitigate matters?' I asked. I would do it, whatever he asked. This was my life at stake. I took his arms in both my hands, trying to force him to stop and look at me straight on. 'Before the inquisition, I mean.'

He refused to meet my eye, staring instead at the trees beyond.

'If there were to be the slightest chance, and I mean the very slimmest, you would have to prove good intention to the Elders,' he began, his voice slow. 'You would need to show dedication and humility. And maturity.'

Hugh shook off my arms, but finally looked at me again. 'I want to help you, but you... you have to want to help yourself. You have to want this more than anything else you've ever wanted, and you have to want it for the right reasons, or else...'

He spread his hand out to indicate the park where the heavy snow was now filling in the footsteps and covering the shed blood, whitewashing the world clean again.

I nodded, unable to help the small smile forming on my face, even in the face of my despair. Maybe I still had time to save myself. And with time, there was always hope.

His phone buzzed. His face was pale in its light as he read the message, and when he looked back to me, there was little hope on his face. "Looks like you'll finally get your wish to travel. Unfortunately, it's to Scotland, to stand trial before the Kin Elders."

··········

Dara's story continues in An Errant Witch, Book 3 of The Witch Kin Chronicles!

ACKNOWLEDGMENTS

As with any book, a lot of people helped bring this story to life. The germ of the idea began with Karen, who is the very font of so many wonderful, creative things. Alison, thanks for your willingness to walk and explore in the rain. Janet and Kathryn, Amanda and Jean, thanks for your invaluable insights. Joanne, oh editor extraordinaire, can I ever stop thanking you enough? I learn so much from you. Every. Single. Time. As for those Book Gremlins – wow, I love you all.

And to all my readers, of course, you are very special. And you know what? You already have the magic inside you.

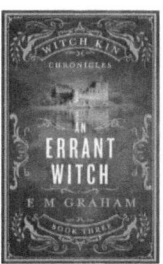

On a lonely Scottish island stands an impenetrable stone tower, which harbors a terrible secret deep within its center...

Dara Martin has been given a second chance to redeem herself in the eyes of the ruling Witch Kin. They will teach her how to wield her powerful natural magic and eventually, perhaps, to work with Hugh, on the condition she gives up her errant ways.

The tower's mystery inevitably draws her in, and while she has sworn to be open to the Kin, she must hold fast on to her own secrets or lose her only chance of freeing her mother.

And she doesn't mean to get caught up in an international rebellion against the Kin, but sometimes these things just happen.

ABOUT AUTHOR

E M Graham is the fantasy pen name of Liz Graham, who is a voracious reader of all genres. She writes out of her home in St. John's, Newfoundland which she shares with an ever changing menagerie.

She's a multi-genre writer, but all her books share the elements of mystery and sharp humor! Check out her shop for pop-up deals. For news and updates, follow Liz on BookBub and Face Book, or sign up to my newsletter!